I0660507

TOMORROW

THE MCBRIDE CHRONICLES
BOOK FOUR

VALERIE GREEN

Tomorrow

a novel

THE McBRIDE CHRONICLES
BOOK FOUR

Copyright © 2024 Valerie Green

Cataloguing data available from Library and Archives Canada
978-0-88839-784-3 [paperback]
978-0-88839-785-0 [epub]

FRONT/BACK COVER DESIGN: J. RADE

FRONT COVER ARTWORK: Shutterstock

PRODUCTION & DESIGN: J. Rade & M. Harrison

EDITOR: D. MARTENS

We acknowledge the support of the Government of Canada through the Canada Book Fund and the Canada Council for the Arts, and of the Province of British Columbia through the British Columbia Arts Council and the Book Publishing Tax Credit.

Hancock House gratefully acknowledges the Halkomelem Speaking Peoples whose unceded, shared and asserted traditional territories our offices reside upon.

Published simultaneously in Canada and the United States by
HANCOCK HOUSE PUBLISHERS LTD.
19313 Zero Avenue, Surrey, B.C. Canada V3Z 9R9
#104-4550 Birch Bay-Lynden Rd, Blaine, WA, U.S.A. 98230-9436
(800) 938-1114   Fax (800) 983-2262
www.hancockhouse.com   info@hancockhouse.com

"You cannot escape the responsibility of
Tomorrow *by evading it today."*

Abraham Lincoln
(1809-1865)

"You may give them your love,
but not your thoughts.
For they have their own thoughts.
You may house their bodies but
not their souls,
For their souls dwell in
The House of Tomorrow,
which you cannot visit,
Not even in your dreams."

"Of children" from *The Prophet* by Kahlil Gibran.
(1883-1931)

DEDICATIONS:

This book is for my dear friend Colleen and for
Chloe and Aubrey, my sweet Cotton girls.

Who were all cheated of their tomorrows.

With my eternal love.

AUTHOR'S NOTE

The final book in the McBride Chronicles brings the McBride family story full circle and into today's world—with some of life's present-day problems.

When I began my story of the fictional McBride family set in the 19th and 20th centuries, I wondered how someone decades later would deal with an inheritance from an unknown person who claimed to be a family ancestor.

For Victoria Blake, it was not just an inheritance; it was the discovery of something far greater— learning about her biological father and a family on the far side of the world about which she knew nothing.

In this fourth and final book in the series, I gave my protagonist a variety of emotions to deal with this—shock, anger, hurt and bewilderment— combined with an overpowering sense of adventure. She is overwhelmed by the size of her inheritance, but once she learns the whole story of how she is the missing piece in the McBride family mosaic, she becomes obsessed with her past and the house she now owns. This obsession comes at the risk of sacrificing her present and her future—through no fault of her own. Did she simply make some wrong decisions along the way? Or was that the way her great-grandmother, Jane Hopkins, intended—for Victoria to prove she had the absolute right to own Providence and truly appreciate its history so it could survive into the future?

In the first three books in the series—*Providence*, *Destiny*, and *Legacy*—I wrote about the problems people faced in those times—poverty, inequality of women, class distinction, childbirth, and two world wars. In *Tomorrow*, I have tackled some modern-day issues—mental illness, living with a narcissistic partner, sexuality, and suicide. In addition, in British Columbia as well as many places around the world, engaging in a process of truth and reconciliation with Indigenous Peoples. I hope I have dealt with all these issues with sensitivity and compassion.

Coming to terms with what life deals you, good or bad, is what Victoria must learn in this story as she embarks on her own life story, in a new country with a new family. As her children and grandchildren grow, she must find the strength to overcome her many misfortunes, just as her great-grandmother and grandmother found theirs.

But will her descendants understand the truth and find reconciliation with those who lived on the land before them? Can Providence survive as a result?

I hope you enjoy this book, and I thank all my readers for their ongoing support and interest in the McBride Chronicles.

Valerie Green, 2024

TABLE OF CONTENTS

THE McBRIDE FAMILY TREE

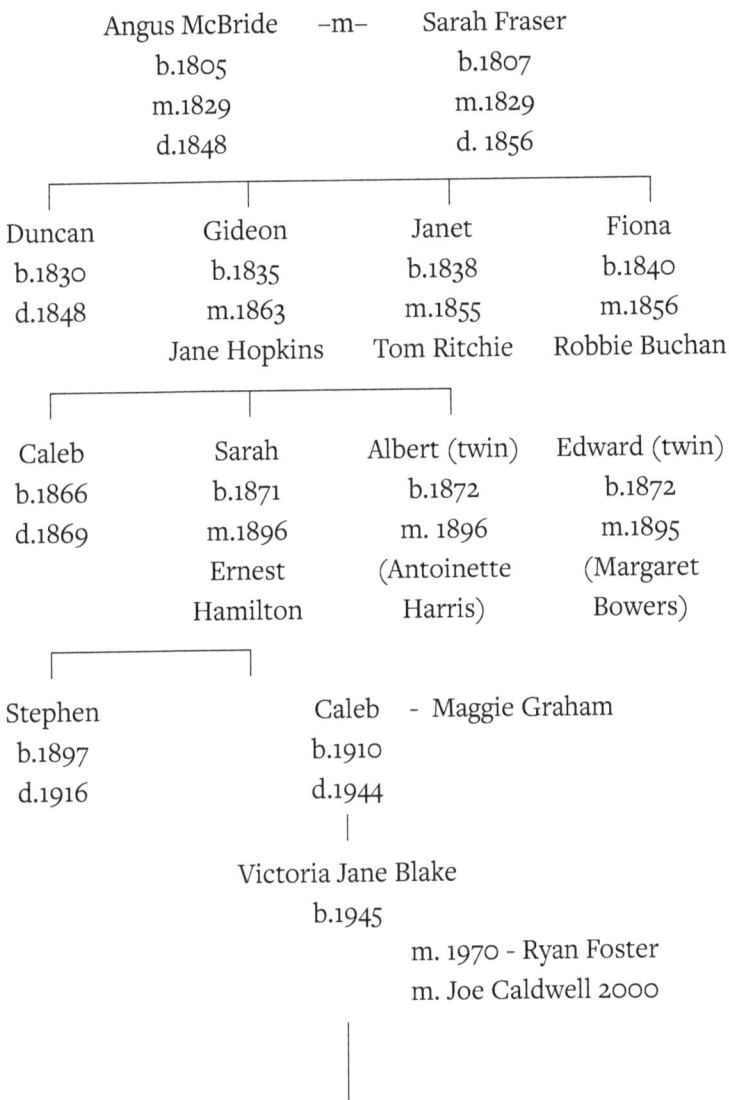

Angus McBride   –m–   Sarah Fraser
b.1805   b.1807
m.1829   m.1829
d.1848   d. 1856

Duncan   Gideon   Janet   Fiona
b.1830   b.1835   b.1838   b.1840
d.1848   m.1863   m.1855   m.1856
     Jane Hopkins   Tom Ritchie   Robbie Buchan

Caleb   Sarah   Albert (twin)   Edward (twin)
b.1866   b.1871   b.1872   b.1872
d.1869   m.1896   m. 1896   m.1895
     Ernest   (Antoinette   (Margaret
     Hamilton   Harris)   Bowers)

Stephen   Caleb   - Maggie Graham
b.1897   b.1910
d.1916   d.1944

Victoria Jane Blake
b.1945
m. 1970 - Ryan Foster
m. Joe Caldwell 2000

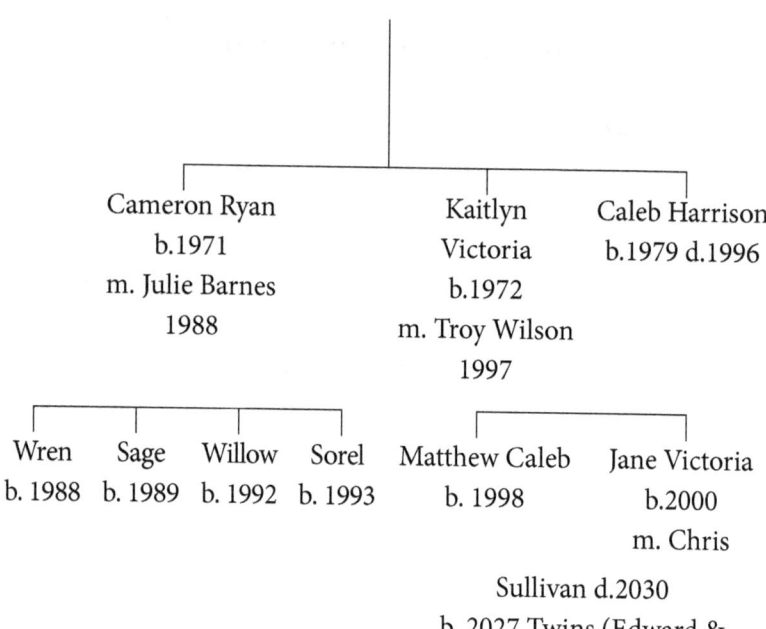

Cameron Ryan
b.1971
m. Julie Barnes
1988

Kaitlyn
Victoria
b.1972
m. Troy Wilson
1997

Caleb Harrison
b.1979 d.1996

Wren
b. 1988

Sage
b. 1989

Willow
b. 1992

Sorel
b. 1993

Matthew Caleb
b. 1998

Jane Victoria
b.2000
m. Chris

Sullivan d.2030
b. 2027 Twins (Edward &
Simon)

THE CALDWELL FAMILY TREE

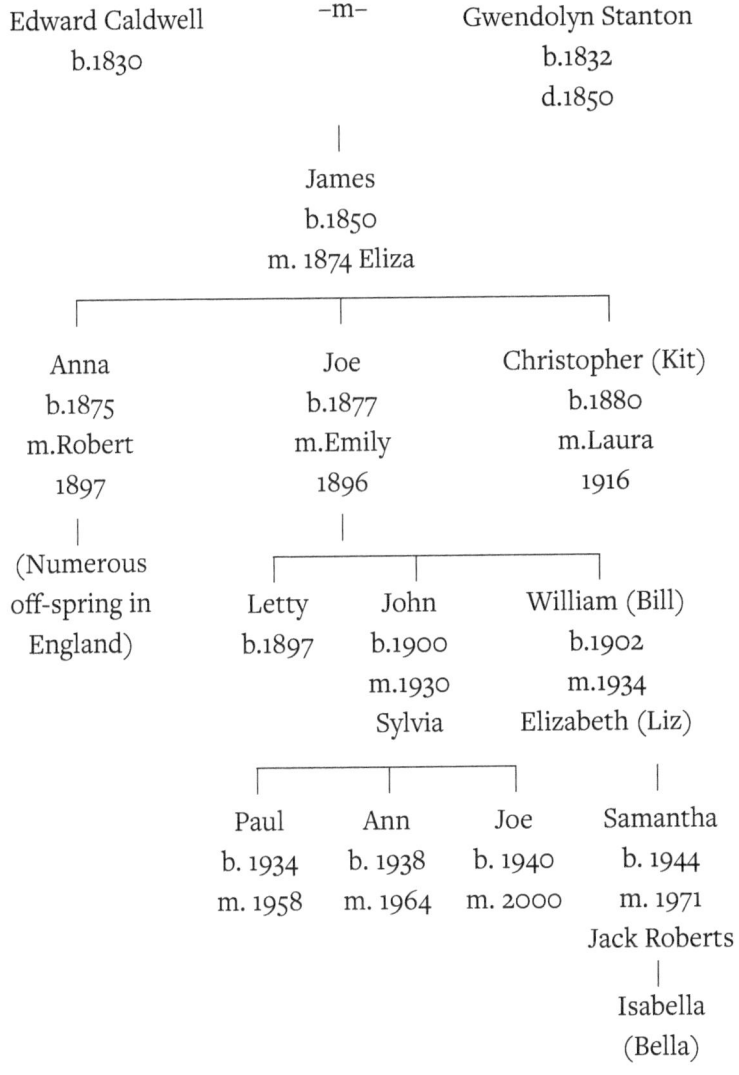

Edward Caldwell   –m–   Gwendolyn Stanton
b.1830

b.1832
d.1850

James
b.1850
m. 1874 Eliza

Anna
b.1875
m.Robert
1897

Joe
b.1877
m.Emily
1896

Christopher (Kit)
b.1880
m.Laura
1916

(Numerous
off-spring in
England)

Letty
b.1897

John
b.1900
m.1930
Sylvia

William (Bill)
b.1902
m.1934
Elizabeth (Liz)

Paul
b. 1934
m. 1958

Ann
b. 1938
m. 1964

Joe
b. 1940
m. 2000

Samantha
b. 1944
m. 1971
Jack Roberts

Isabella
(Bella)

PROLOGUE (1945)

Letty Caldwell left Jane McBride's funeral quickly.

She needed to be back in Providence before the guests arrived at the reception, but she noticed him immediately. He was standing outside the church, waiting to greet her.

He walked towards her and took her hand in his. "I'm so sorry, Letty. She was a wonderful lady, and it was a beautiful service."

"Oh, Austin, she was indeed. I already miss her so much. It's so nice to see you, but I didn't know you were in town."

"I came as soon as I heard. The harvest is over, so we're not so busy now on the farm."

"Thank you, Austin. I appreciate you coming all this way."

They began to walk briskly together back down the lane toward Providence. "Will you join us at the house? We're having a small reception."

"I would be honored."

There was little more to say, so they continued walking in silence. As they approached the driveway, Austin took Letty's hand again.

"There has never been anyone else for me, Letty. I asked you a long time ago to be my wife, and then again after Cal died. Each time you refused, as you felt your life was here to take care of them all, but now ...? You have also lost Granny Mac. And your parents are gone. There is no reason to stay here in Victoria, other than to be near to your two brothers and their families. But we can always come back to visit them. So, I'm asking you once again to be my wife and move to my home in Calgary, if you will have me."

"Oh, Austin—I really can't think about it right now. Please understand."

"Of course. I understand if you need time. You are suffering a great loss right now. But I'm only here for two more days, and I need your answer this time. I will accept whatever you decide, but this is the last time I will ask. I won't bother you again."

"It's not that you are bothering me ..."

"Ah, I know, Letty. It's Stephen, isn't it? Your love for him will always be between us, but I can accept that. I know he was the only man you ever fully loved."

"Well, Austin, you need a woman who can fully love you that way, too."

"I only need you, Letty. I fell in love with you the moment I first saw you in the garden through a gap in the hedge, that day so long ago. I've often thought that perhaps Stephen saved my life that day for you—in case he didn't make it home."

She laughed. "Oh, Austin, you are such a dear man, and a very patient one. I promise I will give you an answer tomorrow, after the reading of the will."

And with that, they both went inside to celebrate the life of the woman who had had such a great influence on all their lives.

The following day, the family gathered in the drawing room, waiting for Letty's brother, William, to read the will. Soon they would know all Granny Mac's wishes. Suddenly Letty remembered the questions Granny Mac had asked her about Cal's girlfriend in England—Maggie, she thought her name was—and after that, she had asked to make her last will.

Soon, Letty would need to give Austin a reply to his proposal. What would dear Granny Mac say? She would probably advise her to grab her happiness where she could. Would Stephen also say that? But she couldn't give it more thought right now. They were all consumed with one thought, and one thought only.

Who was Victoria Jane Blake, and what possible connection could she have to the McBride family?

PART ONE

England (1968)

VICKI
A NEW WORLD

CHAPTER 1

The plane spirals toward the ground. Smoke and flames everywhere. I know instinctively that it will all be over in seconds. I try to scream, but no sound comes out of my mouth. But there is a deafening, roaring, thunderous cacophony all around me. It just won't stop.

I jumped with a start and sat upright in bed, trying to gather my thoughts. Where was I, and what had just happened?

Darn it! I'd had that stupid childhood nightmare again. I hadn't dreamt that for years, but as I grew up, the recurring dream had left me with a deep fear of flying. This morning I also had a headache from hell. I'd wanted to sleep in because it was Saturday. But now, I was wide awake forcing my aching head slowly back down to the pillow.

I couldn't totally blame the nightmare for my headache because it was really because of that third drink last night. I've never been much of a drinker. Alcohol either gives me a headache or makes me sleepy. I didn't need it to have fun, unlike many of my friends who thought over-imbibing was essential to a good time.

I usually drink only Baby Chams or Snowballs, which are quite harmless. But last night after work, when my best friend, Judy, and I had headed to the jazz club on Oxford Street, I'd been persuaded to add a G&T, and that third drink had obviously been my downfall.

"Vic, we must celebrate your new job at P&P's. It's a big promotion, girl," she'd insisted.

"Oh Jude, it's not that big a deal."

But it was, of course, because I'd been promoted to assistant editor at Parker & Parker, the publishing firm I'd worked at for the past three years, so I'd had that third drink because I deserved to celebrate. All my hard work had paid off. After I left school, I'd worked briefly at a bookstore on Charing Cross Road while also taking journalism and short-story writing courses at college. Then I landed a job at Parker & Parker's Publishing House, one of the most prestigious book publishers in London.

Last night, our first choice had been to head to Leicester Square to see *The Graduate* or *Guess Who's Coming to Dinner*. We both also wanted to see *Gone with the Wind* for the umpteenth time. In retrospect that's probably what we should have done, but in the end, we couldn't agree on which film to see, so instead we went to the jazz club with some of the fellows from work.

I belatedly remembered that I'd promised Bee I would help her unpack a new consignment of antiques at her shop next door, so I pulled myself out of bed.

In the kitchen, I poured myself a coffee from our new-fangled machine. Bee, my aunt, God bless her, had already turned on the coffee maker for me. She herself hated coffee and much preferred her usual cup of tea with milk and two lumps of sugar. She was probably next door already, in what had once been my dad's rare books and first editions bookstore. Bee had carried on his work after he died, adding to it her own collection of antiques.

Bee, more formally my Aunt Beth, came to live with us in Grange Park, Essex, after my mother died of pneumonia when I was three years old. Her own husband had been killed at the beginning of the war. We lived in a semi-detached house in the village, and my dad bought the other half of the house for his shop. At first Bee had lived upstairs above the shop, but she moved into our house to better take care of me.

I have no clear memory of my mother, but in pictures she seems beautiful, with a Mona Lisa smile so wistful and sad that it seems to hold some secret sorrow. I grew up imagining there was a mystery surrounding her. So, Aunt Beth became my surrogate mother. I used to call her Mama and then Mama Bee, but she insisted that wasn't proper. My *mother* had gone to heaven. Eventually I dropped the Mama part and just called her Bee.

Grange Park, where I was born towards the end of the war, was then a small village within easy reach of London—thirty minutes on a fast train. Grange Park is halfway between Chelmsford, the county town of Essex, and the centre of London, and was a pleasant place to live. But Essex is not a particularly attractive county. To reach it from central London it was necessary to pass through the squalor of Liverpool Street Station, one of the capital's major train terminals. Liverpool Street left much to be desired in those days, and its drab, dirty atmosphere would put off the hardiest of travellers.

For me, though, it seemed magical. I loved the dirt and the smell of soot. I loved the huffing and puffing of those majestic old trains expelling their steam. I loved the noise, and the hustle and bustle of commuters. To me, the whole atmosphere reeked of adventure.

Bee never argued when my father gave in to me. Instead, she went along with it and almost seemed to encourage it. But she herself was very strict, setting high standards that I was expected to live up to. Despite her disciplinarian nature, however, her love for me was always paramount. She and I were not only like mother and daughter or aunt and niece, but also best friends.

I was barely fifteen when my father had a massive heart attack and died the following day. Bee and I became even closer. I always think of that time as the darkest period of my life. It was Bee who helped me come to terms with death and accept the tragic hand life had dealt me. I still miss my dad so much. He was a gentle, kind man who had instilled in me a love for books and for history.

Despite those unhappy times and the rebelliousness of my teen years, there was much joy in our lives. Bee was fun to be with, never afraid of new ideas, new places, and new people. She was a liberated lady, far ahead of her time, but always made me feel safe and much loved.

There was a special warmth in our kitchen when I came home from school each day and Bee would be baking a cake or preparing dinner as she listened to the popular radio soap, *Mrs. Dale's Diary.*

We would have tea together (I didn't yet drink coffee) and laugh and gossip about our day, or Mrs. Dale's problems with her husband, Jim.

At school, I cultivated a passion for history and writing, both interests being much encouraged by my father and my aunt. Before he died, I had helped Dad after school and on weekends with the store and did the same with Bee now, whenever I could. I loved the smell of all the musty, old books lining the shelves far more than the crisp brittleness of the new volumes. This probably came from my love for anything old, which perhaps I had inherited from Bee. As the years went by, Bee's antiques took over half of my father's bookshop.

And now I finally had a dream job as an assistant editor at P&P's, working in the city I loved with a passion. What could be better, I wondered?

Bee had also instilled in me a love for live theatre. We wallowed in shows like *Salad Days, A View from the Bridge, My Fair Lady,* and so many others, and we knew the words to all the songs in the musicals and sang them, not always in perfect harmony, around the house. We also toured museums, visited art galleries, and tried out new restaurants in Soho. We toured all the tourist spots, too, whatever had survived the Blitz. I never grew tired of wandering old London's cobbled back streets, the aged buildings, the aura and majesty of ancient churches, and all the magic of a long-ago colourful past.

London was in my blood, and my choice in friends reflected my passion for the city. They, like me, were theatregoers and music lovers, enjoying everything from live musical shows to off-beat jazz clubs where we revelled in listening to the likes of Humphrey Littleton and Chris Barber.

As my thoughts came back to last night's fun, I felt my headache easing a little with the aid of another strong cup of coffee. I popped a piece of bread into the toaster and heard the letter box rattle. The post had arrived.

I ambled down the hall, coffee cup in hand, and bent down to pick three envelopes off the mat. They seemed official-looking with typed addresses, so I assumed they were bills. One, however, had an odd return address: a London firm of solicitors. Leaving the other two on the hall table, I headed back to the kitchen with the mysterious envelope and ripped it open.

The contents made absolutely no sense and left me totally confused.

Dear Miss Blake:

We act for the Estate of the late JANE HOPKINS SHERIDAN MCBRIDE.

We are writing to inform you of the contents of the Will of the said JANE HOPKINS SHERIDAN MCBRIDE of Victoria, British Columbia, Canada, that we believe will be of interest to you if you are indeed the said Victoria Jane Blake born 13th May 1945, named therein.

Mrs. McBride passed away in October 1945 and her Estate at that time passed to her two surviving offspring, namely, Albert James McBride and Edward Gideon McBride. A Codicil to Mrs. McBride's Will was added shortly before her death and dated 3rd October 1945. It states that, upon the death of her last surviving offspring, her Estate passes to one Victoria Jane Blake, whom we believe you to be.

Both the above-named gentlemen have now passed away, Mr. Albert McBride on the 31st of December 1961, and Mr. Edward McBride on the 5th day of March 1968. During the past month, since notification of this last-mentioned death, we have been in the process of ascertaining your whereabouts on behalf of the McBride Estate.

We would now like to meet with you as soon as possible to discuss this matter further, as a considerably large inheritance is involved.

We would ask that you kindly contact the writer at your earliest convenience.

The letter was signed *Martin Baxter*, on behalf of the firm of Caldwell & Company from an address in Bedford Square in London.

I read the letter through a second time, but it still made no sense. I had never heard of anyone by the name of McBride and didn't even know of a place called Victoria in British Columbia, Canada. The only connection I could see between myself and the words written on the letter was that my full name was indeed Victoria Jane Blake, and I was born on the 13th of May 1945. Since childhood, however, I had always been called Vicki.

Bee was indeed next door working in the shop, so I immediately went through the adjoining door to find her. Perhaps she could explain the mystery.

I also needed to tell her about my promotion. I know she would be excited.

CHAPTER 2

Bee was kneeling on the floor, carefully unwrapping an antique clock from layers of tissue paper. She looked up when she saw me and smiled.

"Good," she said. "Just the person I wanted to see. I'm glad you're up, Vicki. I really need some help, luv."

"I need some, too. I've had a mysterious letter in the mail that doesn't make a bit of sense. It's from a solicitor in London."

She brushed her hair back from her face. "Oh?"

"He says he wants me to contact him in connection with an estate. I may be a beneficiary in someone's will."

Her attention caught; she sat back on her heels. "May I see it?"

I handed her the letter and watched her face as she read it. I had always been able to understand Bee's reaction to everything. She was always transparent, with an open, honest face that would light up with joy when she was pleased or proud of me or would crumple in despair if I was unhappy or had been treated badly.

But suddenly it was like looking at a stranger. All colour drained from her face. Having read the letter through, she carefully folded it and placed it back in its envelope.

"Well?" I prompted, breaking the silence that followed. "What do you make of it?"

"It's certainly strange, after all these years." She seemed vague.

"You mean because this woman died in 1945?"

She nodded. She was being evasive, though. I had seen the expression on her face as she was reading the letter. I was sure she knew more than she was telling me.

"Have you ever heard of this woman, Jane McBride? Is she someone we know? It seems she died around the time I was born, though. Maybe my mother knew her. Or Dad?"

Bee sighed and suddenly looked as though a great weight had been placed on her shoulders. She stood up slowly and, without replying, carefully closed the lid of the box on which she had been working.

"I'm going to close the shop now," she said. "We'll go back to the house and have a cup of tea, and then we'll talk about it all." A nice cup of tea was Bee's usual answer to every problem in life.

She never closed the shop on a Saturday, so I had a feeling that the letter was very significant, and I sensed that what Bee was about to tell me would not be good.

I followed behind her as she locked the front door, turned the *Open* sign to *Closed* and then headed through the door into our house. Neither of us spoke until we were in the kitchen. Biding her time and perhaps gathering her thoughts, she slowly filled the kettle and placed it on the gas stove while I got out the teapot and two cups. Finally, I could bear it no longer.

"What is it? You look so solemn. You *do* know what this is all about, don't you?"

"Yes, I think I do. But it was just such a long, long time ago."

"What was? And who are these people, the McBrides?"

She sat down with a sigh. "It is hard to know where to begin, Vicki. So many years have gone by. You should have been told this a long, long time ago and ... now ... now, well ... "

"Told me what? Bee, you're scaring me."

"It goes back to 1944, the year before you were born. I was home on leave from Portsmouth, and I was with your Grandma Graham at her house. Your mother was working at the War Office in London then, but she was home too, and for once we both had the same weekend off. That Saturday night we all went up to the Fox & Hounds for a drink. It was sort of a belated celebration. Your Mum and Dad had just got engaged. Harry had been trying to get your Mum to say yes for two years, and she'd finally agreed to marry him. Anyway, the three of us took Grandma for a drink, and we met these Canadian Air Force guys there. One of them fell like a ton of bricks for your mother. His name was Cal Hamilton, but everyone called him Mac."

The whistling kettle interrupted her story. I jumped up quickly, reluctant to have anything stop her story. She never spoke of the war years, especially about her own husband, who had been killed in the Blitz in 1940. I knew she had then joined the Wrens and served in that capacity for the rest of the war, but nothing more. She talked even less about my mother and father's courtship, so to hear her now recalling the incident of their engagement was surprising. And to know that another man had been interested in my mother at that time was remarkable.

Bee seemed to be in a trance-like state as her memories took over. She barely seemed aware of me filling the teapot and placing it between us on the table. I was even prepared to share a cup of tea with her after my two cups of coffee, just so she would be sure to continue the story.

"So, what has all that got to do with this letter?" I pressed.

In a sudden rush of words, she said, "Your mother fell for Cal too, luv. She broke off her engagement to Harry, and she and Cal planned on getting married on September 2nd that year. He was going to take her back to Canada after the war was over, but in August he was killed in a mission over Germany."

"What?"

She paused, and I knew better than to interrupt now. In any case, I was still grappling with hearing that my mother had been involved in another romance when she was engaged to my dad. I had always assumed that she and Dad had been in love.

"Your mother was devastated by Cal's death. We thought she would never recover. In many ways, she never did."

"But ... she married Dad, didn't she? I always thought they were married in the summer of 1944." Even as I spoke, a strange thought was taking shape in my mind.

"Yes, she married Harry ... but not until early in 1945. He loved her so much, and he wanted to make things better for her. He wanted to help."

I knew then that the thought forming in my mind was probably correct. My mother was obviously pregnant when they were married, because I was born in May of 1945. The question was, who had fathered her child? The answer was slowly becoming obvious.

"Dad married Mum knowing she was pregnant with this Canadian's child, right?" I forced myself to ask. "Is that what happened?"

Bee nodded.

"So, my biological father was this Canadian. This fellow called Cal ...?

"Yes, luv, he was."

I digested this in silence but feeling a growing sense of betrayal. Why hadn't I been told? Why had they all lied to me?

"Cal never knew about you, luv. Your mother found out she was pregnant a month after his death. They had planned on getting married, and the wedding was all arranged."

"Oh, right. That was what most of the Canadians and Americans told the gullible English girls, wasn't it?" I said angrily. "Then, after their little fling or one-night stand, he took off into the wild blue yonder. But Mum got pregnant, so she just fell back on good old Dad, I suppose. After all, you couldn't be an unmarried mother in those days, could you?"

"It wasn't like that at all, Vicki. And Cal didn't fly off into the wild blue yonder and leave her that way. He died tragically when his plane was shot down."

"Then what *was* it like? And why did you all let me believe that Dad was my real father?"

"Because in every sense of the word he was your *real* father. And that was the way he wanted it. He begged your mother to marry him after Cal died, even knowing about the baby. She was the one who didn't want to marry him. She felt it wouldn't be fair to him. She was a very proud woman and would have raised you alone as a single parent, despite what the gossips would have said. But Harry loved her and wanted to take care of her and her baby. He loved you very much, Vicki, and always thought of you as his own. Everyone thought you were. Only we four—your mum, Harry, Grandma Graham, and I—knew the truth. Everyone else thought that Harry and your mum got married in a rush because she was pregnant with *his* child."

"So, Grandma knew, too? Why didn't she ever tell me before she died?" I digested all of this, but I still felt angry. I didn't want to be just the result of some fleeting affair that Mum had during the war. I was a romantic. I wanted there to be more. I also could not reconcile the fact that my biological father had been some other man, some stranger and not Dad.

"Grandma was sworn to keep the secret too, luv. Please don't blame her."

"So how does Jane McBride fit into this juicy little story?" I snapped.

"She was the grandmother who had raised Cal in Canada. He was always talking about his home back in British Columbia. His parents had both died tragically when he was a child, and he was raised by his grandmother. He talked fondly about her and their home in Victoria, called Providence. He planned on taking your mother back with him after the war."

I was puzzled by the story. Something didn't quite fit.

"If my biological father didn't know about me, how did his grandmother find out? And why, after all these years, would I learn about an inheritance? It doesn't make any sense. Why didn't they want to know about me before?"

"I can't explain why Cal's grandmother didn't contact us before she died, but I can tell you that she did know about you—at least I now assume she knew."

Bee hesitated, as though remembering something painful. "You see, luv, I went against your mother's and Harry's wishes at the time. Harry wanted to marry your mother, but only if you were raised as *his* daughter, and no one was to know otherwise, not even you. I didn't agree with that. I felt that as you grew older you had the right to know the truth, and I also felt that before your mother married Harry, Cal's family back in Canada had a right to know that his child was about to be born, so I did something without telling either of them. I wrote to Mrs. McBride, the grandmother. I simply addressed it to Providence, Victoria, British Columbia. Cal had often talked about their house called Providence. I knew she must be pretty elderly, but from what Cal had told us, she doted on him and would have been devastated by his death. I felt she deserved to know he had left a child behind."

She paused. "I never had a reply to my letter, nor to the second one I wrote in May, a week after you were born. I told her she had a great-granddaughter. By then, of course, your mother and Harry were married, so I told her that too and that officially your name was Victoria Jane Blake. The letters were not returned to me, so I assumed they had reached her, and she had seen them. Now that I know she died in October of 1945, I'm wondering if maybe she was too sick to reply."

"Or maybe she didn't believe you," I added. "She probably felt you were a fortune hunter. There must have been many English girls who were pregnant and wanted compensation from rich Canadians or Americans."

"It's possible she felt that way." Bee sighed. "But I made it clear in the letters that I was only writing to inform her about your birth and for no other reason."

"What would you have done if she had replied? How would you have explained it to my mum and dad after promising them to keep the secret?"

"Good question. But I just believed that whatever happened, it would be for the best. You've always known I'm a bit of a fatalist.

So, when I didn't hear from the family in Canada, I vowed to forget the whole thing and keep my promise to Harry. I went along with the secret, thinking that perhaps it was all meant to be that way. Then, when your Mum died, I tried even harder to support Harry, I suppose. He was such a good man, and he loved your mum so much. He loved you, too, Vicki, just as if you were his very own."

Her words seemed unreal. *His very own. Well, of course I was.* He was my dad. He always had been—and was to the day he died.

I realized suddenly that the teapot still sat between us on the table untouched. I automatically began to pour out two cups of tea, although the last thing I wanted was to drink anything. I had a million questions racing around in my head. Bee had placed the letter on the table, too, and I reached for it to read it again.

* * *

"I'm supposed to contact this Martin Baxter fellow. What do you suppose it's all about?"

"There is only one way to find out. Make an appointment to see him. The old lady obviously put you in her will at the last minute, after all."

Yes, I thought, *she wanted nothing to do with me herself, and yet she wrote some silly codicil to her will that wouldn't take effect for over twenty years.*

"Were they wealthy people?" I asked. "This letter states 'a considerably large inheritance' is involved. Maybe that was why she thought you were looking for a handout years ago."

"Cal never gave the impression of being rich. He had been well-educated and knew the niceties of life, but he was no snob. In many ways, he was something of a rebel, but he was also just an ordinary man. His grandmother probably felt guilty about not answering my letters, and she decided to make amends for it after the deaths of her two children. Maybe she has left you a piece of antique jewellery or an old book."

I smiled for the first time since we'd sat down. "Bee, you are ever the eternal antique dealer! Oh, and by the way, I just got a promotion at work. I'm now an assistant editor."

"Oh, Vicki, that's wonderful. Good for you!"

Was it wonderful? I couldn't decide. I had so much to digest right now, and I still felt cheated. I accepted Bee's explanation for the way things had turned out, but a sense of betrayal remained. Betrayal from the people who had been my family since birth—people who, by keeping their secret, had lied to me by omission. And betrayal from the people who were apparently my real blood family, many thousands of miles away, who had refused to acknowledge my existence when I was born.

The rest of the day passed in a haze, and that night my sleep was disturbed by confused dreams. One was that old dream from long ago, which had given me nightmares as a child. It involved a plane falling from the sky in a blaze. I had never quite been able to understand why I was so afraid of flying. When I'd travelled to Europe with my friends, I'd always crossed the English Channel by the ferry and then taken the train or driven through Europe. No flying for me.

Sleep continued to elude me, so I got out of bed and walked over to my desk, to search through the drawer where I kept things that once belonged to my mother. For some reason, I felt compelled to look there for some clue, some confirmation. But I came up empty. There were just a few pieces of jewellery, a book of poems she had loved, and a small notebook in which she had pasted newspaper cuttings of events in her life, including her engagement to Dad. I read and re-read them all, but there was nothing that pointed to her love affair with my biological father.

Looking more closely through her jewellery, one piece intrigued me. I had asked Bee about it long ago and she said then that she thought it was some kind of lucky talisman. It was a flat piece of metal that looked like it might be half of a piece that had been broken. There were some words written on it that time had partly erased, but even the words that were legible were in a foreign language. The metal was attached to a thin gold chain, and now I wondered if it had belonged to my mother's wartime lover, my biological father. I held it tightly, convinced it was the secret that would unlock the door to my past. But no answers came to me in the dead of night.

How could Dad not be my real dad? Surely it wasn't true that my biological dad had been someone else.

Eventually I went back to sleep and was immediately thrust back into fitful dreams full of unknown people and places. The next time I awoke, it was with the sudden realization that my middle name was the same as the woman who had refused to accept my existence. In the early hours of the morning, finally exhausted, I fell into a deep sleep.

CHAPTER 3

First thing Monday, I telephoned Caldwell & Company from work and made an appointment with Martin Baxter for Wednesday morning at 9:30. I told my new boss I needed an hour off for a dentist appointment on Wednesday. I didn't want anyone to know about this yet, not even Judy.

Martin Baxter was a middle-aged, slightly balding man who shook my hand vigorously and called me Vicki rather than Miss Blake. He was a Canadian, so, unlike the stereotypical stiff British solicitor, Baxter was warm and casual in his approach. His accent was soft and easy, and he indulged in small talk before beginning on the business at hand. He told me he was born in Toronto and had lived there most of his life. Two years ago, he had moved to the London branch of the company.

"My wife was a Caldwell, and I joined the company once I got my law degree. Caldwell & Company operate in eastern Canada, London, and New York, as well as their head office in Vancouver, and a smaller branch in Victoria," he explained.

He offered me a cigarette, which I declined, and then suggested we drink coffee. I later learned that Canadians prefer that beverage over tea. He pressed a buzzer and requested his secretary to bring us the coffee. After all these pleasantries were finally completed, he leaned back in his chair, placed his hands behind his head and smiled at me.

"Well, Vicki, I have some incredible news for you, but first I would like to complete the formalities. You did bring some identification with you? Your birth certificate and so on?" He had requested that over the telephone, and I now handed my identification papers over to him.

"Yes, these seem to be in order," he said. "It would appear that you are the sole beneficiary of the McBride estate, following the death of Mr. Edward McBride in March."

"The *sole* beneficiary in what?" I repeated.

He nodded. "The McBride estate, yes indeed. Mrs. McBride added a codicil to her will in 1945, just prior to her death, in which she stated that her entire estate would pass to you following the deaths of her two sons, who were at that time both still living."

"But didn't the sons have families?"

"No, they didn't. However, we are talking here about Mrs. Jane McBride's wishes concerning her own fortune and, more specifically, her house, Providence, in Victoria. Prior to her death, she laid down certain conditions as to its future. She also set up a trust fund to maintain that house. Her two sons have been following her wishes, although, as I understand it from the Caldwells, the house has become rather rundown in recent years, due mainly to the ill health of Mr. Edward McBride."

Terrific, I thought. *I have inherited a rundown old barn in the Canadian wilderness!*

"You mention the Caldwells," I said aloud. "Are you talking about the law firm?"

"Yes, the firm, but members of the Caldwell family have also been friends of the McBrides since they first all settled in Canada in the 1850s. I believe they have been associated through four or five generations, and the Caldwells have always looked after the McBrides' legal affairs."

I nodded. "So, tell me more about the house and where it is, exactly."

He leaned forward and smiled as he shuffled some papers and produced a photograph. Handing it to me, he said, "This is Providence, Vicki, taken about ten years ago. I am sure it has become somewhat more rundown since this photograph was taken, though. However, you are, with certain stipulations, now its owner."

It looked very grand to me. A large circular driveway led up to a very imposing structure. I knew little of architectural style, but it

senseless new flying machines,' as his grandmother called them. He was driving her crazy. I do recall thinking he was a very adventurous guy, and I admired him."

I knew he was only telling me this because he wanted to make me feel better. He probably didn't remember my biological father at all.

I began gathering up all the paperwork he had handed me, including my copy of the will and codicil and the picture of the house. "Thank you for explaining everything, Mr. Baxter. I will give the whole matter a lot of thought and get back to you very soon."

He stood up to shake my hand. "Don't leave it too long, Vicki. The estate must be settled as soon as possible."

I returned to work and then, on the pretence of feeling bad after a tooth extraction, I asked to go home. I travelled back on the train to Grange Park in a daze, my mind going in every direction. Did I want to move halfway round the world to claim my so-called inheritance? And if I claimed it, did I really want to live in Canada? What about Bee? I could never leave her behind. And maybe she wouldn't want to come with me?

These questions continued to spin around in my head for the rest of the journey, and even discussing everything with Bee when I got home didn't help. We pored over the photograph and the codicil, and we speculated about the reasons Mrs. McBride had included me in her will after apparently disregarding the letter sent to her in 1945 when I was born. None of it made any sense. But maybe the mysterious letter in her safety deposit box in Canada would explain everything.

Finally, Bee sat back in her chair, ran her fingers through her tousled hair and spoke. "Well, luv, there is only one way to find the truth. I think you should go."

I looked at her for a moment before replying. "And you'll come with me, of course?"

She shook her head. "No, this is something you first must do alone, luv. You must find out for yourself whether you would fit in there, and you don't need me as a distracting influence."

"But ... supposing I decide that I do want to live in the house?"

"Then you would have to follow through with that decision," she replied.

"And *then* you would move to Canada too, right?"

"Well, I would certainly think about it, luv. After all, you're all I've got. You're my family, and—" She didn't finish before I threw myself into her arms in a bear hug. "Oh, Bee, *if* I decide to move there, you must come too. I know I couldn't live six thousand miles away from you."

"Well, first things first. Start making some plans. Why don't you just take your holiday this year and go there for a visit? Look things over. See the house and see this place called Victoria, and then make your decision. By the look of these figures in the trust account, there is more than enough money for a trip and to continue to maintain the house for years to come. Then, if you think you want to move there permanently, we'll talk."

She was always so sensible. I should at least look things over before deciding, and that is what I would tell Martin Baxter. They would just have to wait before settling the estate. After all, moving to another country just to accommodate the wishes of some old lady I had never met who had died over twenty years ago wasn't something one could do overnight on a whim.

I telephoned Martin Baxter the next day and told him that I would not make a final decision until I had visited Victoria. It would take me a while to make travel plans, which would have to coincide with my annual holiday from work in June. It was only April.

"June?" he replied. "Can you make it sooner? I could arrange a flight for you, Vicki, within the next couple of weeks."

"A flight?" I hesitated. My fear of flying was something I had not given a thought to until that moment. "No, I will be sailing. I'll make some enquiries and get back to you when my travel plans are finalized."

Until that point, I had only travelled through Europe, so the thought of undertaking a trip so far away was somewhat daunting. Inspired by Bee's enthusiasm and support, I nonetheless went ahead and booked passage aboard the Canadian Pacific vessel *Empress of Canada*, sailing from Liverpool to Montreal on June 17, a journey that would take almost a week. From Montreal I would travel by Canadian Pacific Rail to the west coast.

Bee frequently tried to persuade me to take a series of flights instead that would get me to Vancouver in less than a day. She almost relented and decided to accompany me, but she was adamant that I should make my decision alone without any input or persuasion from her. At the beginning of May, I let Martin Baxter know my travel arrangements. He assured me that the estate would cover all expenses.

The entire month passed in a flurry of excited preparation. I frequently wondered if I was doing the right thing. Suppose I loved Victoria and the mysterious house in question? Suppose I wanted to move to Canada? It was so far away. What if Bee decided she couldn't leave England? And what about all my friends? How could I leave them all behind?

These questions continued to haunt me, and yet, despite all my misgivings, I could not help but be inwardly excited. I had read about the *Empress of Canada*, and spending a week being pampered in such luxury was something I could not help but relish. And a train journey across 3,000 miles of the Canadian continent would certainly show me a great deal about the country that might eventually become my new home.

CHAPTER 4

June 17th finally arrived.

I was packed and ready to go, and in my handbag, I had placed that mysterious piece of metal jewellery that had once belonged to my mother. Instinctively I felt it might hold some answers for me. It was a cold, overcast Monday when Aunt Beth and I took the train to Liverpool. She had insisted on accompanying me that far. I knew she would miss me. If only she knew how much I would miss her.

My first glimpse of the 650-foot *Empress of Canada* was overwhelming. She was gigantic, all 27,284 gross tons of her. She would be my home for the next week.

I hate goodbyes, so I rather abruptly bade Aunt Beth farewell, hustling her off the ship quickly to avoid tears. We had already inspected my cabin, full of flowers from friends; the first-class dining room, with its spotlessly white tablecloths and sparkling silverware; the cinema; the swimming pool; the shops; and all the other luxuries aboard.

I smiled at the note from Judy that accompanied a large bouquet. "You lucky bugger! But please don't go and marry a Mountie and not come back."

I hadn't told anyone the details of my inheritance—or that I had to live in a house in Victoria and not sell it. I just said I had been left some money by distant relatives. Only Bee knew the size of my inheritance.

After Bee left, I went up to the Promenade deck, where passengers were already gathering to wave to their loved ones on the dockside. The colourful streamers stretching down and blowing gently in the breeze were a stark contrast to the grey buildings of Liverpool, which looked so sombre and overpowering. But it was England down there, I kept telling myself, and I loved England. I didn't want to leave. So, what the heck was I doing here? I suddenly felt very alone.

And then I saw Bee, now just a small speck on the dockside, dressed in her bright yellow outfit. She was waving, her keen eye having picked me out among all the others, and I waved back enthusiastically, pretending I was excited, instead of petrified, with a million butterflies dive-bombing my insides. I tried to ignore the tears trickling down my face.

We finally set sail, heading for Greenock in Scotland, our first port of call, where again other passengers experienced their own sad farewells. The *Empress* majestically pulled out of Greenock at noon the following day, to the poignant sound of bagpipes echoing across the water.

The days that followed passed like a dream. To postpone thinking about all the decisions I would be forced to make once I reached Victoria, I joined in all the shipboard activities with enthusiasm and made many friends. There were deck games, film shows, boat musters, and dancing every night in the Canada Room. And every night at midnight in the ballroom, the captain and crew ceremoniously put back the clock one hour, so that by the time we reached the North American continent we would be five hours behind Greenwich Mean Time.

I somehow felt that the removal of that hour every day was especially symbolic for me. It was like putting off the inevitable. Trying to extend time, painfully stretching it out so that I could make those days at sea last forever. In the evenings, a group of us often sat around until the early hours discussing the Vietnam War, the racial problems in America, and the horror of the Kennedy assassinations.

We were due to arrive in Montreal on Monday, June 24, after first making a stop at Quebec.

On Saturday the 22nd we all stayed up until 3 a.m. to see the icebergs off Belle Isle, but the sea became too choppy to stay out on deck and it was too dark to see anything. We sailed up the St. Lawrence and arrived in Quebec on Sunday to complete customs formalities, and then some of us left the ship and spent the day exploring the old city.

By evening we were off again, reaching our destination early on Monday morning. Montreal was exciting and very French in flavour, and I spent the day exploring, eventually heading back to the Canadian Pacific Railway station to board my train at eleven o'clock that night.

We chugged off into the night, leaving the city behind us as we headed west. It was a strange new experience sleeping on a train, and I began to long for a bed that did not roll, list, or sway.

The next day, June 25, was Canada's Election Day, and I kept hearing the name Pierre Trudeau being bandied about. He had apparently just been elected as Canada's new prime minister, and people were wild about this intellectual bachelor who liked to wear a rose in his lapel. Trudeau-mania was everywhere.

The train, in my opinion, was the 'slowest train going west,' although I suspect this feeling was due mainly to my own impatience. We were due into Vancouver early on the morning of Friday, June 28, and from there I caught a ferry across to Vancouver Island and my destination, Victoria. I was booked in at the Empress Hotel, a hotel situated on the inner harbour, which I had been told was only a short taxi ride away from Providence.

The Empress lived up to her reputation as the "grand old lady" of Victoria. Designed by architect Francis Rattenbury and built in 1908, it seemed to me very British in character, with a classic lobby and ivy climbing up the exterior walls. Once I checked into my room, I threw off my shoes and collapsed on a bed, which thankfully didn't move. I then made a brief trans-Atlantic telephone call to Bee to let her know of my safe arrival. By then, I desperately wanted to hear a familiar voice and to know that I was not completely alone in this strange new world. I told her I liked what I had seen so far of Victoria.

That night, after a pleasant dinner in the Empress's elegant dining room, I wandered around the lobby gazing in the windows of the shops, containing objects far too expensive for my budget. Then I remembered exactly how many zeroes I had seen on that piece of paper. I was suddenly very rich, and I owned a mansion—but first I had to see it and move in!

I slept soundly, thinking I would not have to make any decisions until after the long July 1 holiday weekend. This would give me the next three days to explore the city by myself and get my bearings.

But I was mistaken.

CHAPTER 5

Very early the next morning, the telephone woke me. Not being a "morning person," I was irritated by its abrasive ring.

"Hello."

"Is that Victoria Blake?"

"Yes."

"I'm so sorry if I woke you. This is William Caldwell of Caldwell & Caldwell. Just call me Bill. I'm so pleased you have arrived safely in our lovely city."

How did he know I was already here? I had thought I wouldn't have to contact the lawyers until Tuesday. And this one seemed overly familiar, as though we were old friends.

"Yes, I arrived last night," I snapped back in my early morning voice.

"I wondered if we might meet later today and I could give you a tour of the city and take you out to Providence."

"Oh." I supposed I'd better get it over with. "Yes, all right. What time?"

"How would one o'clock suit?"

"That would be good."

"I'll pick you up in the hotel foyer, then."

"Thank you. Oh, how will I know you?"

"I'll be the grey-haired guy with a rose in my lapel—like Pierre."

"Pierre?"

"Our new prime minister, Pierre Trudeau."

Then I remembered all the talk on the train about Trudeau and his rose habit. "Yes, of course, I'm sorry, I'm still trying to adjust to everything."

"Of course, Vicki. I'll see you soon." And he was gone.

* * *

William "call me Bill" Caldwell was as good as his word.

I was already showered, dressed, and in the lobby, exploring those little boutique-type shops again, fifteen minutes ahead of our arranged meeting time, but I spotted him as soon as he came through the revolving front door. He appeared to be in his early sixties. We shook hands and he smiled warmly at me. "I see a family likeness," he said.

"Oh?" For some reason this shocked me. How could I look like people I had never known?

"Come out and meet my wife, Vicki. She's waiting in the car. She thought you might like some female companionship."

His wife, who introduced herself as Liz, was very sweet. She hugged me warmly, like an old friend, and then insisted I sit in the front with her husband. "You'll have the best view of everything there, Vicki. We'll give you the scenic tour before heading out to Providence."

The scenic tour involved driving through town, where they pointed out City Hall and Eaton's and then swung back around the Inner Harbour, heading for Dallas Road and a drive along the waterfront. It was my first real glimpse of the Olympic Range across the Juan de Fuca Strait, and the mountains looked particularly beautiful that day, with the sun glimmering on their snowy peaks.

We drove through the Uplands, which I was told was the elite part of the city, and then through the Rockland area, past Government House. They pointed out a Caldwell home on St. Charles Avenue.

"My father built that house for his family, and I grew up there with my older brother and older sister. Liz and I live there today. Both my grandfather and great-grandfather built homes in James Bay which also still stand today," said Bill.

Next door to the house he was pointing to on St. Charles Avenue was another equally grand house that had apparently once belonged to Sarah and Ernest Hamilton who I knew from Bee were my grandparents.

"Cal Hamilton spent the first few years of his life in that house," said Liz. "His parents were killed in that terrible maritime tragedy when he was only eight, so he moved to Providence and lived with his grandmother, Jane McBride."

I had no idea what the tragedy was, and most of what they were telling me was going in one ear and out the other. I wanted to digest everything at my own pace and not be given so many facts at once. But I knew they were being kind and were going out of their way to be helpful, so I nodded and smiled and, I hoped, asked all the right questions. Eventually we headed back towards town.

"The bridge ahead is known as the Point Ellice Bridge," said Liz. "In 1896, the old bridge collapsed, and many people lost their lives that day."

Oh no, not another tragedy, I thought.

"Anyway," she rattled on, "the McBride family and many others who then lived along the Gorge Arm came to the rescue and helped those poor souls."

"The Gorge Arm? What's that?"

"It's the waterway heading away from the harbour. There were once many elegant homes like Providence along that area. Now, much of the area has become industrial."

Oh, wonderful, I thought. *Providence is situated in a rough part of town!*

But I could not have been more wrong. The road we turned down was called Pleasant Street, and then it became Primrose Lane, which was quite charming and unique. The surroundings were suddenly very rural. Halfway along, I saw two large stone pillars framing a wrought-iron gate that had been swung wide open.

"The small cottage by the gate is Mrs. Potter's place," said Bill as he drove the car to the left between the pillars, and we began to drive slowly up the long, circular driveway. "It, too, is part of the estate." I had no idea who Mrs. Potter was.

The grounds were massive but terribly overgrown. In my imagination, I could easily picture them in their heyday as carriages drove up to Providence. The gravel crunched beneath the tires on the long driveway. This was an oasis in the middle of a city.

And then I saw the house for the first time. Although it, too, was enormous, I must admit I was not overly impressed. I knew very little about architectural styles, but I knew the house had none of the charm of an English country mansion, the elegance of a French chateau, or the warmth of an Italian villa. Its imposing design was a mixture of many styles thrown together with wild abandon. Any attempt to capture a touch of Italianate or a trace of Steamboat Gothic had been overwhelmed by the wide, extravagant verandas surrounding the house, casting Southern charm in a somewhat incongruous manner. Providence had clearly also been the victim of many years of neglect, so much of its former glory had long since disappeared.

The car drew to a halt at the foot of the wide steps leading up to a massive front door.

"Well, Vicki," said Bill Caldwell. "This is it. I'll introduce you to Mrs. Potter, the retired housekeeper, and she can show you around. We'll leave you for a while and then pick you up in, say, an hour. Unless you would prefer us to stay?"

"No, that will be fine," I said, finally finding my voice. I was longing to explore it all alone, in my own time.

I said my goodbyes to Liz, thanking her for her kindness. Bill walked up the steps with me, and we were about to ring the doorbell when footsteps on the gravel made us both turn. A rather frowsy-looking, grey-haired woman was hurrying up the driveway, obviously short of breath.

"Mr. Caldwell, you're early," she said accusingly.

Bill smiled. "No need to worry, Mrs. P. Don't hurry. We have plenty of time."

She grunted. "Well, I intended to have the house ready before you arrived. People turning up early always upsets me. You said four o'clock, and then, lo and behold, I see the car coming past the Lodge at a half past three."

Bill looked at me and shrugged. "Well, our drive must have taken less time than we thought. Anyway, I'd like you to meet Miss Blake. Vicki, this is Mrs. Potter, who has been at Providence since ... well now, how long has it been, Mrs. P?"

She had her back to us now as she fiddled with the keys to unlock the front door. "Since soon after Master Cal came to live with Mrs. McBride. My 'usband, Arthur, and I arrived from England to be 'ousekeeper and butler in the 1920s, after the Great War. I'm not the 'ousekeeper anymore. I'm retired now. But I tell you, Mr. Caldwell, I'd be in dire straits if Mrs. McBride was here today. You being early and all, and me not being 'ere to greet you. She was a stickler for time."

Bill winked at me. "Now, now, Mrs. P. don't worry about it. I'm sure Miss Blake is not upset."

I nodded. "No, not at all. I just want to look around the house."

"Well, you'd better come in, then. Most of the furniture is still covered with dust sheets." I smiled at the poor woman and muttered my thanks. I had the strong feeling that my being here was a great imposition for her.

"I'll leave you to it, then," said Bill with a smile. "See you about five, Vicki?"

"Thank you, Mr. Caldwell ... Bill," I said. "But please, I can easily take a taxi back to the hotel. I don't know how long I will be, and I may want to explore the grounds too."

He nodded his understanding, but Mrs. Potter seemed irritated. "I can't leave the 'ouse open forever," she said.

"If you want to leave, Mrs. P, you can give Vicki the keys. I'm sure she will lock up."

"Of course," I said, grateful for his understanding. I *really* wanted to be left alone to explore at my own pace. I needed to take in my surroundings without the distraction of Mrs. Potter's voice prattling beside me. Her strong cockney accent sounded like she had just got off the boat from England, rather than having resided in Canada for over forty years. Bill shook my hand warmly and said he would phone me later.

"Take your time before you make your decision, Vicki." He slipped his hand inside his jacket and took out an envelope. "This is the sealed envelope I was instructed to give you. It is from Mrs. McBride and has been in the family safety deposit box since 1945. I was just a young man then but have long wondered how this would all pan out. After you've explored the house, you should read her letter, and perhaps you will understand why she wanted you to be the owner of Providence."

He handed me the envelope. "My goodness, how mysterious," was all I could manage in reply. Mrs. Potter had gone on ahead, so I was glad she hadn't heard what he said.

I watched as his car drove away, he and Liz both waving.

Then I turned back into the expansive hall. The floor was black and white marble, but the first thing that caught my eye was the portrait on the wall at the top of a wide staircase. It dominated the whole house. It was an oil painting of a young woman in a pale primrose-coloured evening gown draped discreetly off her shoulders. Her hair was piled high on her head, with small tendrils escaping on each side of her face. Her eyes were a shade of green, and her face was ...

I stared, open-mouthed. Mrs. Potter was saying something about first taking me into the library to the left, but I didn't hear her. I was still staring at the portrait. I couldn't believe it. Apart from the fashion of that era, it was like looking at myself in a mirror.

"That's Mrs. McBride," she said with a touch of pride in her voice. "Beautiful lady. The painting was done back in the 1860s, I believe."

I nodded, not wishing to spoil the moment. *How could I possibly look so much like someone I'd never known?*

Finally, I said, "I was just surprised for a moment. She looks so familiar."

Mrs. Potter grunted again. "Well, that's as may be," she replied abruptly. She obviously could not see a likeness, or perhaps was not willing to admit to one. I had the feeling she didn't like me. I was the intruder here—the upstart who fancied herself a McBride.

I followed her left into a library with book-lined walls and another portrait of a man in uniform. There was a small fireplace, beside which stood an old-fashioned spittoon.

"This was the captain's smoking room at one time. Mr. Bertie and Mr. Teddy, their sons, were also allowed to smoke in this room, but Mrs. McBride wouldn't allow smoking anywhere else. But the Captain did smoke his pipe on occasion up in the turret."

She informed me that this other portrait hanging over the fireplace was Captain McBride, Mrs. McBride's husband, and my great-grandfather. We continued our tour to the right of the hallway. I sneaked another look at the portrait at the top of the stairs as we walked by. Was I imagining it or did her eyes seem to be following me?

The large drawing room to the right of the hall was very elegant, and I was told that, together with the grand hall, it had doubled as a ballroom on occasion. There were various pieces of furniture scattered about the room, most of which were covered in dust sheets. In the large bay window overlooking a rose garden stood a massive, highly polished black grand piano, dominating the room.

Mrs. Potter saw me looking at it. "That was Mrs. McBride's pride and joy," she said. "The other, smaller piano in the library was the one the captain had shipped here for her after their wedding in 1863. She loved that piano so much. It came around the Horn, you know. This one, he purchased for her later, after Miss Sarah and the twins were born." I nodded. It was obvious that Jane McBride loved her pianos!

French doors with elegant glass panes led into a formal dining room beyond. The oak dining table was capable of seating at least thirty people. Sparkling chandeliers graced all the rooms.

"They're all wired electrically now," muttered Mrs. Potter. "Used to be gas lamps, and before that, candles. There are eight fireplaces in the 'ouse. My poor Arthur had his work cut out for him trying to keep them all going. But Mrs. McBride liked a warm house, and with fourteen-foot ceilings, the house was always hard to heat."

Oh, great! The electricity bill will be enormous!

A back staircase led to the servants' quarters. "Arthur and I used to live there at the back, until we moved to the Lodge," she said. "And before us, there was Angelina, a nanny, and Mary, a maid, plus Dulcie and Skiff, and once there was a Chinese manservant named Ah Foo. The McBrides always had servants."

Was she trying to make a point? Apparently, I would need many servants to keep this house going.

"Then there's the elevator alongside these stairs. Mr. Bertie and Mr. Teddy had that installed during the war for their mother. She was nearing one hundred then and couldn't make it up the large staircase."

My God, a lift in a house!

She then took me into the kitchen, which had two pantries leading off to the rear. It was old-fashioned but certainly would be functional—with a little modernization. There was a wood stove with hot plates and a very ancient-looking icebox, both of which would probably have to go.

We were then back in the hall and about to climb the elegant staircase, the portrait still gazing down at us. I ran my hand along the smooth wood of the banister rail, having noticed the exquisite newel posts on either side, both inlaid with mother-of-pearl.

"Checking for dust?" snapped Mrs. Potter.

I jumped. "No, no ..." I thought she was joking, but her expression was serious.

"I can tell you, Miss, I'd be in dire straits if Mrs. McBride ever found a speck of dust in this 'ouse."

Hadn't Mrs. McBride been dead for over twenty years? Why was this woman still concerned about her finding dust?

"Mr. Bertie and Mr. Teddy liked to keep the house the way their mother had," she said. "I respected their wishes at all times," she added with pride. "This wood is redwood from California, by the way," she added.

The stairs divided to left and right at the top beneath the portrait. I followed Mrs. Potter to the right, which she called the north wing, and was escorted through several bedrooms, a large room that had once been a nursery, and a bathroom that she informed me now had the luxury of a hot-water tank filled by a gravity system. At one time, it housed a cold-water tank, and it was necessary for servants to carry hot water upstairs from the kitchen. The white enamel bath that stood on four clawed feet was charming. *Bee would love that*, I thought.

There was a similar wing to the south with an equal number of rooms and another bathroom with a clawfoot bath. Finally, we were in the enormous master bedroom, which must have measured at least thirty feet by twenty. It had another bathroom off to the left and a small area used as a sitting room to the rear, with French doors leading to its own balcony overlooking the garden. In the far corner of the bedroom was a circular flight of stairs. "Where does that lead to?" I asked.

"That goes up to the captain's turret. Both he and, later, Mrs. McBride, died up there."

That sounded a bit creepy to me.

"The captain used to spend hours watching the boats in the harbour. After he died, Mrs. McBride went up there a lot. It was where she wrote her diaries and read her books, until her poor legs wouldn't let her climb the stairs anymore. Then she spent the summers on the front veranda downstairs in her rocking chair, until the elevator was put in. In winter, she liked the library. It was cosy there, she said."

"May I go up there?" I asked.

"Well, … I suppose …"

"You really don't have to stay, Mrs. Potter. I think I have my bearings now, and I promise to lock up when I leave." I could feel her hesitation. "Is the telephone hooked up?" I asked. "Then, when I want to leave, I can phone for a taxi."

"Of course it's hooked up. We'd be in dire straits without it, wouldn't we?" It seemed to me Mrs. Potter was often in dire straits, no matter what the circumstances. She reluctantly handed over a key ring containing many keys but made no attempt to explain which key opened what. I would obviously have to figure that out for myself.

I was glad to finally see her retreating figure and hear her footsteps heading downstairs. The slam of the front door confirmed that she was gone. I ran to a front window and watched her crunch her way back down the long driveway.

I immediately made my way up the spiral staircase and pushed open the door. The octagonal room had windows all around, with views that could be enjoyed in every direction. I was enchanted by my first real glimpse of the large acreage surrounding Providence. A gazebo stood amidst rolling green lawns that now needed mowing, oak trees, shrubs, and a profusion of rose bushes, leading down to the waters of the Gorge, where a small building stood. To the left, I could look back at the Inner Harbour and in the far distance the ice-capped Olympic Mountains range, shining in the late afternoon sun. No wonder the McBrides had spent so much time up here. The view was breathtaking.

The room was sparsely furnished now—just two white wicker rocking chairs, a desk, and a large trunk. There was a padlock on the trunk, and I wondered if one of the many keys on the ring might open it. I began to try each one individually, but none of them opened the trunk.

I sat in one of the chairs and tried to take everything in. What on earth would I do with a house this big? It was totally ridiculous. Even if Bee came to live here with me, we would just rattle around like two peas in a very large pod. It must certainly have been an elegant house in its day, and in many ways still was, but would it be worth restoring? Now it seemed more like a museum than a home to live in.

Well, perhaps the first thing I should do would be to read Jane McBride's letter and see why on earth she had left this monstrosity of a house and all her money to me.

CHAPTER 6

The letter was dated October 1945.

My Dear Victoria,

If you are reading this letter some day in the far distant future, I know all this will all have come as a terrific shock to you—finding your true heritage at last—and for that I am truly sorry.

However, in that respect you and I are very similar. I never knew where I came from until I was in my twenties. By the time you read this letter, my two sons, Bertie and Teddy, will have passed on, so I have no idea how old you will be. I simply hope you will be old enough to understand how and why this had to happen the way it did.

I believe the only way you will truly understand everything will be by reading my journals, which I kept from the 1850s until now, 1945. Almost one hundred years of history. I wish I could be with you today as you read them. They are locked safely in a trunk up in the turret. I never shared the combination of the lock with anyone but Gideon until now, so no one has ever read my journals—not even Gideon. I am sharing the lock combination with only you—17271862— (these numbers are my age and Gideon's when we first met, and the year we met).

Inside the trunk you will also find some jewellery I have left for you, which you can dispose of or keep as you wish. It might still be very valuable. Some of it was passed to me from my grandmother and some given to me by your great-grandfather. There is also a special piece—a talisman of sorts—which was broken in half when your father left for England. I hope it will be reunited with its other half, though that half might well have gone with Cal to the next life. But then, if he'd still had it with him that day, he probably would have survived and come home safely to your mother.

I would like to tell you more about your father. I raised him from the age of eight after your grandmother (Sarah) died. He was such a stoic, brave little boy, even though he had lost so much—both parents and an older brother who died in the Great War. He grew into a fine young man, full of life and fun. He inherited my talent for playing the piano, but he also loved flying, so I take comfort in the knowledge that he died doing what he loved best. I am sad, however, that he never was able to marry your mother or apparently know about you.

Unfortunately, I will never know the answers to all the questions I have today, and I am too old and tired to find out more, but that is all right. I have finally found my peace tonight after changing my will, and I will die happy, knowing that destiny will undoubtedly take care of everything. Gideon, your great-grandfather, always believed in providence and destiny, and that things eventually happen the way they are meant to.

These are now just the ramblings of an old lady, but once I too was young, with all my years before me. The only way you will truly know me is through my journals, so now they are yours. They begin when I was just six years old.

If I had been able to meet you, I am sure I would love you as much as I loved your father. My last hope is that you will love Providence as we all did, and you will decide to live here. I believe your mother must have named you for the place your father loved best, and for me—and that gives me nothing but joy.

God bless you, Victoria,

Your great-grandmother, Jane (Hopkins-Sheridan) McBride.

I folded the letter slowly and placed it in the envelope. My heart was beating so fast, and I felt very strange. Reading it had been like talking to the dead and, quite frankly, it gave me the creeps. She knew a little about me and she knew about the talisman, a part of which I still had in my handbag, yet I knew nothing about her.

I stared at the trunk. Inside I would perhaps find the answers to everything. My hand trembled as I punched in the numbers on the padlock, and it opened. The trunk lid squeaked as I lifted it. Inside was an array of books that did indeed appear to be journals, each with a different year inscribed on the front. I had unearthed a treasure. Dates ranged from 1851 to 1945. Here in one trunk was someone's entire life. A century of history.

Even though she had given me permission to read them, I felt like an intruder as I quickly flipped through the pages of one of them, admiring the elegant, spidery writing written on pages now yellowed with age. These were documents written by my great-grandmother. Here I would find the story of her life, and perhaps even the secret of my birth. And yet, how could I possibly pry into someone else's private thoughts and feelings? There were also many letters tied in bundles with ribbon. I hastily replaced the one journal I had picked up when something else caught my eye.

It was a small music box, inlaid with sparkling jewels on the outside. I lifted it carefully from its resting place and slowly raised the lid. Music filled the air—something classical—and a ballerina danced in a circle. I think it was *Für Elise*, by Beethoven, because I remembered having to learn it when I took piano lessons as a child. I never could do it justice.

Yet another box contained a small book titled *The Abridged Bible Catechism*, with a crumbling pressed flower inside. The book was inscribed to Jane Hopkins. Its well-worn, leather-bound cover was fading with age. The jewellery box contained a few pieces of jewellery, which she had mentioned, but it was one piece that caught my eye and made my heart race.

An odd piece of metal, identical to the one that had been in my mother's jewellery box at home—the one I had brought with me to Canada. I now took out mine and placed it beside the one belonging to Jane McBride. The two pieces of metal joined together perfectly as one. I sensed something mystical in the air.

This was the final proof I needed. I must truly be the daughter of this man who had loved my mother and grown up in this house. But I needed to know more. I needed to know the whole story. So,

I leaned back in one of the wicker chairs by the window and picked up the earliest journal I could find, dated 1851. The handwriting was more childish.

And I began to read.

* * *

I read for hours. The light dimmed and I stirred only to switch on a small lamp in the corner. My neck and eyes began to ache with the strain of reading, but I couldn't stop. I had to know it all. I realized I was hungry, but it was past ten o'clock before I finally telephoned for a taxi. Even then, I took some of the diaries back with me to the hotel, having carefully locked the trunk and the house before leaving. I was sure I was being watched by Mrs. Potter as the taxi drove down the driveway.

Back at the hotel, I ordered room service and continued reading until the wee hours.

The next morning, I telephoned Bill Caldwell to tell him I still had a lot to think about and would contact him again on Tuesday. I didn't tell him about the diaries or the letters. I wondered if anyone else even knew about them—although Mrs. Potter had mentioned Mrs. McBride writing her journals up in the turret. But I suspected that no one could have opened the trunk if my great-grandmother had never divulged the lock combination.

I finally completed reading them all, up until the last diary written in 1945, the year of her death. I now knew her whole story. Some of it had shocked me. Parts had brought me to tears. I felt a mysterious bond with Jane Hopkins McBride, a fiery-spirited child who had suffered so much as an orphan. I suspected that only she and I now shared some parts of her story. I ached for my grandmother Sarah's sad and tragic love story, but I was glad she found peace and happiness before she died with my grandfather, Ernest Hamilton, and their son—my father.

Two days later, I returned to the house. Then I really *saw* Providence for the first time. During those two intervening days, I had explored a century of memories in the world to which the house had once belonged. A world of which I now felt sure I was a part, for I knew beyond a shadow of doubt that I was the missing piece in this family mosaic.

I could then look beyond the peeling paint, the chipped wood, and the somewhat unique ugliness in the style of Providence, and see instead years of joy and sorrow, laughter, and tears, lived by generations of McBrides. I could hear their voices echoing within the walls. I finally saw the house for what it really was. Not simply a building, but a symbol—a symbol of the future. But, most of all, it was what it had always been—Jane's immortality. It was her house of tomorrow, and it was my job to preserve it now.

I telephoned Bill Caldwell again early Tuesday morning.

"Bill," I began, "I have decided. I will be claiming my inheritance." I thought I heard him sigh with relief.

"But before I return to England, I would love to meet your sister Letty. Did she ever marry?"

"She did indeed marry Austin Harris, after Mrs. McBride died, and she went back to Calgary, where he lived. Sadly, Austin died of cancer five years later. Letty returned to Victoria to take care of the two uncles at Providence until earlier this year."

"Is she still in Victoria? She seemed to love my father and his older brother so much."

"She did indeed, Vicki, but I'm sorry to say that Letty died earlier this year. She was only 71."

"Oh, I'm so very sorry."

"Yes, it was tragic. She could have told you so much more about your father, as she knew him better than I did. She helped raise him, as both a mother and big sister. After a lifetime of service to others as a nurse and taking care of Mrs. McBride until her death in 1945, our own parents until their deaths in the 1950s, and her new husband and the two uncles until earlier this year, she lost her own battle with cancer and passed away just two weeks after Edward McBride did, in March. Her last words to me were, 'My job here is now done.'"

"How very sad. And yes, I would love to have met her. She sounded like a wonderful person." I sighed before adding, "I will be staying in Victoria a bit longer to conclude all the business arrangements with you, and then I'll return to England to finalize a few things there."

"Of course, I completely understand." He paused for a moment. "But I am curious, Vicki. What was it that made you finally decide to stay? And you seem to know so much more about your family and the Caldwell family now."

"I can't explain it, Bill." I didn't want to tell him about all the diaries, which were so personal. "It was the letter she left me, I suppose. I now know she was my great-grandmother and Cal Hamilton was my father. It all came together."

He was silent at the other end, but I sensed he was pleased with my decision.

* * *

During the remainder of my time in Victoria, I re-read some of Jane's journals and went through her many letters and other mementos that had helped me piece together her story. I no longer felt like an intruder. I felt like her soul mate, and in many ways, I became her.

The day after talking to Bill, I even decided to move to Providence for the remainder of my stay in Victoria, to get a better feel for the house. I must admit it felt quite eerie on the first night, staying on my own in such a large house, but for some reason I didn't feel alone or frightened. I did feel surrounded by the past everywhere I looked. Mrs. Potter had popped in to remove some dust sheets and make up a bed for me with fresh linen in the master bedroom.

"I'm only doing this as a favor to Mrs. McBride," she insisted. "I'm retired, you know."

"Oh, of course, Mrs. Potter, but really I can fend for myself."

She looked at me and shook her head as she muttered to herself. "Little bit of a thing like you, managing in this big house on your own .... Humph!"

She was probably right. But I'd worry about that problem later because I knew I had to move into Providence, one way or another.

I spent a lot of time wandering around the garden. The profusion of trees and plants overwhelmed me. I breathed in the scent of wisteria climbing over the trellis and admired the bougainvillea draped over walls. I tried to picture my great-grandmother and great-grandfather as they stood on their land before building this house so long ago. I thought about Ah Foo and his fellow workers building the boat house and sleeping down there after a hard day of work.

I sat for long periods of time in the gazebo, inhaling the perfume of the flowers and shrubs and thinking about my grandmother, Sarah, and her tragic love affair with Etienne Dupont. They were now all real people to me.

I also hired a car with my international driver's license and drove around Victoria. I knew that, once I moved here, I would need to take another driver's test for a B.C. license, but even driving on the right side of the road came easily—as though I had always lived here. I passed by other Caldwell and Hamilton homes again and was invited to Bill and Liz Caldwell's house for dinner on two occasions. I met their daughter Samantha, who was about my own age, and we got along well. She lived in Vancouver but was planning to move back to Victoria at Christmas, having finished an interior design course at university. I looked forward to spending more time with her and maybe asking her for ideas about designs for my new house.

Their house had once belonged to Bill's parents, Joe and Emily Caldwell, and stood alongside Hamilton House, the place my father had lived for the first eight years of his life. Hamilton House had long since been sold, but I gazed at it, trying to imagine all that had happened there and the secrets perhaps only Jane and I knew.

It was strange to feel so much a part of the McBride family, having never met any of them, but slowly I was immersing myself in the past and felt I was living in another era. The time I spent in Providence drew me back to that other time, which was both comforting and welcoming.

I had tried to explain this feeling to Bee in a telephone conversation after my first visit to Providence, but I had left her in a state of complete amazement. She was puzzled by my feelings. I knew I needed to see her in person soon to explain, and because I still wanted more answers from her.

I was looking for more details about the love affair between my mother and Cal Hamilton that had produced me in 1945.

CHAPTER 7

I was on a plane heading for Calgary, the first step on my way back to England, before I fully realized what I had done.

I'd purchased an airline ticket, boarded a plane and was flying back to England! My fear of flying had miraculously disappeared, enabling me to get back to England quickly so I could tie up the loose ends of my life. I had finally overcome my paranoia in order to start my new life.

After talking with Bee about everything again once I arrived home, and convincing her to move to Canada with me, she was easily able to fill in the missing pieces now, and I was once again thrust back into the 1940s and the horror of my father's last flight.

"What happened, Bee, on that last operation he went on?"

"Well, it was apparently a successful mission by all accounts, but on the way back they encountered unexpected flak from the Germans and at least fifteen planes in that sortie were shot down, Cal's being one of them. Your mother waited patiently for news, and of course, not being next-of-kin or family, it was days before she heard that Cal had been killed. It was a member of his squadron who finally came to see her, out of the kindness of his heart. Apparently, Cal had confided in this guy, Peter Pegrum. He knew Cal was going to marry Maggie on September 2nd. Fortunately, Peter was with another crew on that mission and his plane made it home."

"How awful it must have been!"

"Well, luv, now that you have told me the story about that talisman Cal wore around his neck, I realize why it must have been even more terrible for your mother!"

"How do you mean?"

"Well, when she first heard the news that he had been killed, she became quite hysterical and kept saying it was all her fault. I never could understand what she meant, but I am assuming now that because you have that half of the talisman that she had kept in her jewelry box, Cal must have left it behind on that final mission when he left her in London."

"But if he just forgot it, how could she blame herself?"

"Who knows? Maybe she had asked him about it, and he took it off for some reason that night. I do remember that he always wore it round his neck, and he said it kept him safe."

"Yes, I discovered it had initially belonged to his Scottish great-grandfather who died at sea in a storm, supposedly because he wasn't wearing it that one time. But maybe it was all meant to be this way, because in the end it was the one thing that finally convinced me Cal Hamilton is my biological father. The two halves fit together perfectly as one. That's how I came to understand the puzzle."

She smiled. "Yes, fate is a funny thing, luv."

"How sad my mother must have felt—and how frightened when she first discovered she was pregnant."

"It was bittersweet for her. Of course, she was happy to be having Cal's child, but still devastated by his death. I honestly believe she never really got over it. She was still a sad woman when she died, but Harry was such a wonderful husband to her and loved you dearly, as though you were his own child. But Maggie—well, she seemed to live those short years after Cal's death in a trance, as though she was never here, just going through the motions. She was certainly not the same woman ever again. Theirs truly was a great love story, Vicki." It made me feel good to hear that, now that I really knew for sure where my roots began.

"If only she hadn't died, Bee. Perhaps after Dad died when I was fifteen, she might have tried to find the McBride family, like you did."

"Perhaps, luv. But we will never know that for sure."

The next day we decided to put the house and shop up for sale, then packed up our home and planned to ship most of our belongings halfway around the world.

The hardest part for me was leaving my job, but my boss asked me if I would be interested in writing a book about the amazing story of my inheritance and the house on the far side of Canada. They would be willing to publish it, he said, as they were impressed with my writing skills. I wasn't quite ready to write a book yet, but they also offered to put me in touch with a magazine that might take travel articles about Canada. That was exciting, and I could not have been happier. Judy even promised to visit me the following year.

I admired Bee's sense of adventure, which matched my own. "I may be past my prime, luv," she said, "but I'm still open to new adventures."

So, I realized, was I.

We celebrated her forty-ninth birthday two days before we left England, flying back to Victoria in late September of 1968.

*   *   *

Bee loved Providence, just as I knew she would, and we soon settled in with the help of Bill and Liz Caldwell, and of Mrs. Potter, who offered to "temporarily come out of retirement, or else you two women will be in dire straits!" I think she secretly enjoyed organizing the house once again and seemed to have finally accepted the fact that I was who I purported to be—a member of the McBride family.

We soon realized, however, that a great deal of money needed to be spent on updating and modernizing the house for it to be livable in today's world. It was still stuck back in the 1940s. The grounds were terribly overgrown and neglected, despite their great beauty, so I also needed some landscaping advice. I hired a gardener to mow the large lawn and weed some beds. Now that I was the new owner of Providence,

I intended to maintain it the way Jane would have wanted. The house and grounds should be restored to their former glory.

It was strange how I found myself mentally consulting my great-grandmother over the coming weeks. It was almost as though I had become her, though I knew that was ridiculous. When I was alone, I talked to her and asked her advice about things. Bee said I was going bonkers and accused me of being obsessed with my great-grandmother, because I seemed to sense her wishes and felt her hand guiding my decisions on so many occasions. One in particular.

It concerned my decision as to which heritage architectural firm I should hire. I wanted one that specialized in heritage reconstruction and restoration, and the Yellow Pages contained a couple. It seemed, however, that my grandmother's voice was telling me to consult a firm by the name of Foster & Associates, so Bee and I decided to make an appointment with a member of the firm to come out to Providence and go over some ideas with us.

Our top priorities were modernizing the bathrooms and the kitchen while still retaining their heritage. We also wanted to close off one of the wings, as the house was already far too big for just the two of us. We knew we needed some expert advice on knocking out walls, stripping down wood, and repainting walls.

"Let's wait until after Christmas before we do anything drastic," suggested Bee, ever the cautious one.

"Okay, but we could call someone now so that at least we'd know what we can start on in the new year," I said.

So, in late November, we arranged for someone from Foster & Associates to come to Providence for a meeting.

His name was Ryan Foster.

CHAPTER 8 (RYAN)

I was about four years old when I first visited Providence, and I will never forget that day.

My grandmother's friend, Letty Caldwell, lived there, looking after an old lady and two elderly gentlemen. We were invited for tea one day. I don't really remember much about the tea, but I do recall that the old lady, whose name was Mrs. McBride, terrified me. Both my grandmother and Letty Caldwell called her "Granny Mac."

She was dressed in black and sat in a high-backed chair in the living room. Another lady came in and served us tea. The chair was large, and Mrs. McBride was very small, but she still commanded the room with her presence, and her eyes pierced into me as though she was summing me up. I also knew that I was fascinated by her enormous house.

Later that same year, my grandmother told me that the old lady had died, and her dear friend Letty had moved to Calgary, so we never went back there for tea again.

Loving architectural heritage the way I did meant I often drove past the house in later years, but I knew it had deteriorated greatly recently. I assumed the two elderly gentlemen still lived there, but I'd heard a rumor that a distant relative of the McBride family in England had inherited the house, so they too must have died. When my office received a call about Providence, I was immediately interested.

"Hey, Ryan, guess what?" My partner, Joe, walked into my office one morning with a spring in his step. "Apparently, we just had a call from someone up at Providence, the old place on Primrose Lane. They were asking for an estimate on doing a restoration project there."

"What? When did this happen?"

"Just now. Sue gave me the message. They want someone to go out there and look. We were both on another line when the call came through."

"Well, that job, my friend, is mine. I've been itching to get back inside that place for years." I replied.

"It's all yours, pal. The house must be falling apart by now. Restoration will be a nightmare."

"What's the name of the new owner?"

He looked at the message again. "Someone called Victor Blake, I think."

I buzzed for Sue, and she came right in. "Sue, call the person at Providence back and tell them I can come out on Monday around ten."

"Sure thing, boss." And off she went.

The appointment was confirmed. I couldn't wait to see Providence again.

* * *

I drove slowly up the gravel driveway, arriving promptly at ten as arranged. I rang the bell on the enormous oak front door and waited.

An attractive woman who looked to be in her forties opened it.

"Good morning," I said. "I'm Ryan Foster and I'm here to see Mr. Victor Blake, the owner. Are you Mrs. Blake?"

She laughed as she shook my hand. "Oh, nice to meet you, Mr. Foster. I'm so glad you were able to make it out here. I'm Beth Winters, but the new owner of Providence is my niece ..."

"And my name is *Victoria* Blake!" said another voice from behind her.

The woman who had spoken was coming down the enormous staircase. She was much younger, probably in her twenties and very cute, and was wearing a bright pink top and matching pink miniskirt that showed her legs off to perfection.

She was smiling as she walked towards me, extending her hand. "I'm *Vicki* Blake, Mr. Foster. Your office must have thought I said *Victor* Blake."

"Oh, I do apologize, Vicki. I should not have assumed the new owner was a man. And please call me Ryan."

"No, you shouldn't have!" she said with a twinkle in her eye, which for some reason I found very attractive.

I began to remove my shoes before stepping on the exquisite marble floor, and both women looked surprised. "Well, *Miss* Blake, what can I do for you?"

"My aunt and I want to do some updating, and I believe your company works on heritage homes. We want to restore many of the heritage features, but the bathrooms and kitchen badly need some modernizing. We have no idea what we're looking at here or where to start."

"Maybe we should give Ryan a tour first, Vicki," the aunt said.

I couldn't wait. I wanted to see the whole house before giving any advice. I did remember the expansive main hall we were standing in, with its black and white marble floor.

As we wandered from room to room, Vicki Blake chatted constantly about how she wanted the house to look. For someone who had no idea what she wanted to do or where she wanted to start, she sure had some strong opinions. The aunt was more reluctant about making too much change and seemed to realize how much all this would cost.

"I'd like to look around outside, too," I finally said. "I think there must be a cellar entrance from the outside. I want to see the bones of the house and what would or would not be possible."

"Oh," she added, "that reminds me. I want to have some landscaping done too, in the spring. Do you know of a good heritage landscaper?"

Good grief. This is going to cost her a fortune. What kind of money does this woman have?

"Yes, of course. I can put you in touch with the heritage landscaper on our staff. He's an expert on restoring grounds."

"Thank you. Now, would you like me to show you around outside?"

I really wanted to go on my own, so I replied, "No, it's fine. I'm only walking around the perimeter of the house to see the foundation and the cellar. I'll be back in a few minutes." And with that I put my shoes back on and headed outside.

The house had good bones and a strong foundation. It had been very well constructed over a century ago.

They were both waiting in the entrance hall when I returned.

"So, what do you think, Ryan?" Vicki asked.

"Well, before we could start on any changes inside the house, you will need to have completely updated electrical circuits, and the plumbing is antiquated, from what I can see, so that would also need to be updated. Rewiring and plumbing can be very expensive. It will also mean a whole lot of dust inside the house, so you might want to move out while that work is being done."

She shook her head, as though irritated by what I'd said. "I understand that, and it's no problem. I worked with my dad when he turned our two houses into one in England, so I know about renovations. And the money is no problem."

The aunt immediately intervened. "Vicki, perhaps we should first get an estimate from Mr. Foster for those basic things, plus a rough idea of how much it would cost to modernize the kitchen and the bathrooms and doing any landscaping."

I could see she had more common sense than her niece, who obviously wanted everything done yesterday.

"Yes, I can easily do that and bring back some figures for you to consider. There are always incidentals, too."

"Incidentals?"

"Additional expenses for things that can go wrong. When you're working with a house this old, there are always the unknowns."

"Well add your *incidentals* into your price, and we can go from there."

"I should also warn you that once word gets out that there is a new owner living here, you will be inundated with real estate people who would probably like to demolish the house and buy this valuable land. It's prime industrial land."

She looked aghast. "Well, that's not going to happen! The house will certainly NOT be demolished. I thought you would understand that being a heritage architect."

"I do indeed, and I'm delighted to hear you say that. I'm just warning you. I'm all for preserving Victoria's heritage. There's a new group of people in town who want to form a heritage society to stop heritage homes being demolished, and you will probably hear from them, too."

"Good! This is my home now, and I intend to keep Providence, so please let me know what you think we can do to restore it and live here comfortably."

"I will indeed. I'll consult with my partner, Joe Caldwell, and get back to you as soon as possible."

"Caldwell? Did you say *Caldwell?*"

"Yes, Joe joined me two years ago."

"Is he any relation to my lawyer, Bill Caldwell? Or to all the other Caldwells that seem to live in this town?"

I laughed. "Yes, Bill is his uncle."

"So, his father must be John Caldwell?"

"Yes, he is. You seem to know a lot about the Caldwell family."

"Well, I know that most of them are lawyers. So how come your partner is an architect?"

The aunt immediately interrupted. "Vicki, I'm sure Mr. Foster doesn't need your curiosity."

"That's fine, Mrs. Winters. I don't mind. Joe is the black sheep in the Caldwell family. He and I went to school together—elementary and high school—and we played soccer with the Gorge League. After school, I went to UBC and studied architecture, but Joe did one year of law back east and absolutely hated it, so he then took off to Italy for a year, studying architecture there. When he returned, he switched courses to architectural science, which was his real interest. His father was not happy. He told him that law was supposed to be in his blood."

"How awful—to be expected to do something you hate."

"Yes, but Joe is happy now. He made the right choice, but he's rather cut off from the rest of his family. He joined me in a partnership two years ago, and we make good business partners."

"Well, consult with him and come up with an estimate. Oh—and one other thing. This black and white marble in the hall drives me crazy. Our heels will ruin in, so I'd much prefer wall-to-wall carpet. My aunt and I are unlikely to hold balls in the house as they did years ago."

My heritage-loving heart sank. "Vicki, this is Italian marble, and it's priceless. It would be a crime to cover it over." I felt like saying: *Just take your shoes off in the house, like I did!*

"Maybe so, but it's rather ugly and keeping it clean will be a nightmare. Plus, the gravel on the driveway is always being tracked inside, so I would like to have the driveway paved eventually."

"Well, perhaps a couple of area rugs for now?"

She shook her head. "I think I'd like the new wall-to-wall carpeting."

I sighed. "Well at least I hope you don't like shag."

She laughed at that. "I'll think about it," she said.

"Please do. This floor is a valuable treasure."

I couldn't believe this girl. She owned a heritage treasure in Victoria and seemed to want to preserve it but had no idea what this would involve and how much it would cost. As I walked to the door and donned my shoes again, they showed me out.

"You don't need to take off your shoes every time," Vicki said.

"Just trying to preserve your marble flooring." I laughed.

"That's why I want carpet!"

"I'd still remove my shoes," I replied. "That's what we do in Canada."

I hoped the aunt would knock some sense into her about the floor. And I couldn't help but wonder how she fit into the McBride family. She was certainly feisty, and I'd been told the old lady had been, too.

But what was their connection?

CHAPTER 9 (VICKI)

Bee glared at me once we were alone, and I knew that look of hers only too well. She was about to lecture me.

"Vicki, how do you propose paying for all this?"

"You know how much money there is, Bee. There are millions in the trust fund. It won't be a problem."

"But money doesn't last forever. Don't you think you should just concentrate on getting the electrical and plumbing work done first and leave the rest until later?"

"Well, I have the money now. Why wait?"

"Yes, but you will have to live on the interest for now—unless you plan on getting a job."

"No, I want to concentrate on my writing and work from home. I'll start doing magazine articles for that travel magazine in London. I thought about turning the turret into my office. What do you think?"

"That sounds wonderful, luv, but please take things slowly. I certainly intend to work, too. I have already applied for a job in one of those lovely antique shops on Fort Street."

"Oh Bee, you don't need to work. Between my inheritance and the money we have from the sale of the house and your antiques, we could survive for years."

She laughed. "Yes, but I would soon go crazy not working, and you would, too."

"I suppose I would," I relented.

"I've had another idea too, Vicki. Tell me again how many acres are in the estate?"

"Twenty-five."

"Well, you certainly don't need that much land, so you could sell some of it off. Ryan said it's very valuable land."

"I agree, but I don't want to be surrounded by industry like there is on the other side of the Arm."

"Well, you could sell off some of the land to the north, beyond the little church, to a private developer, to build homes along the waterfront."

"I suppose I could." This idea rather appealed to me. If I were to live here forever in this big house, I might one day marry and have children, so it would be nice to have some other young families and maybe a school nearby.

"And you could still keep about six acres or more around the house," Bee added.

I nodded, but my mind was already going in a million different directions. Life had suddenly presented me with so many options. I found myself mentally consulting my great-grandmother again about what I should do. It seemed ridiculous. She had been dead for over twenty years and had lived in a completely different world.

But I knew I was becoming obsessed with her and her poignant story, which took her from rags to riches.

* * *

Ryan returned a couple of days later with a rough estimate for the plumbing and electrical work, and I told him to go ahead with it in the new year. Bee had by then started to work at an antique store in town called Vintage Arts, and even she agreed that the estimate was reasonable. Ryan had also drawn up plans for changes inside the house, which were amazing.

He was also very attractive, and, although he was all business when we discussed the restoration, I felt sure that most of the time he was also flirting with me.

Bee seemed to have noticed this, too. "I think you need to meet more young people your own age, Vicki. Maybe Ryan could ..."

"Could what?"

"Well, he's probably only a bit older than you, but maybe he could introduce you to some young people. Why don't we have a housewarming party on Christmas Eve, and we could invite Bill and Liz Caldwell and Ryan and maybe his partner, Joe Caldwell. And I'd like to invite Mary from work and her husband, Geoff. I know you will love Mary."

"Yes, that sounds wonderful, Bee." I had already begun to like the idea. "Bill's daughter, Samantha, will have moved back to Victoria by then, so we could invite her. She seemed nice. And we could ask Mrs. P to help us prepare but invite her to be a guest, too."

And so, we started to plan. We purchased a very large artificial Christmas tree and boxes of decorations from a Christmas store on Government Street. We dragged the boxed tree into the house and erected it in a corner of the hall, feeling rather pleased with ourselves. I would have preferred a real tree but thought it might die before Christmas, and this one would be easier and need less care. Standing over six feet tall, it was also the biggest we could find.

I phoned Liz Caldwell and told her about our housewarming, and she was delighted to accept. "Bill and I would love to come, and Sam will be here, so I know she would love to see you again."

I then phoned Ryan.

"We're having a house-warming party on Christmas Eve, Ryan. Bee and I would love you to come—and you can bring a plus-one." *Why did I hope he didn't have a plus-one?*

I'm sure I heard him chuckle at the other end of the phone. "Vicki, is that your way of asking me if I have a wife or girlfriend?"

"Well, do you?"

"No, I don't have a wife."

"A girlfriend?"

"Not currently."

"So, just come yourself," I said, perhaps with too-obvious relief in my voice. "And ask your partner, Joe, if he'd like to come too."

"I'll ask him, but I think he's going skiing over Christmas. He usually does. He has friends in Vancouver, and they head up to Whistler. I'll let you know." He paused before adding, "My brother Todd and his wife Ruth will be here for Christmas, though, so do you mind if I bring them?"

"Not at all—the more the merrier. And bring your parents, too," I added.

"You might regret saying that!" He was laughing.

"Why?

"Because I'm sure they'll ask you a million questions."

"About what?"

"The house you've inherited. And whether we're dating."

"Well, we're not, are we? I'm just asking you to a party. I'm your client."

"Of course you are." But I felt he was still laughing at me.

Why did he always unnerve me? Yet at the same time he made me feel excited each time I saw him.

I told Bee the latest tally of guests we should plan for. With Bee and me, Bill and Liz, Samantha, Ryan, Bee's friends Mary and Geoff, Ryan's brother Todd and his wife Ruth, and his parents, plus Mrs. Potter, it came to thirteen guests. Thirteen had always been a lucky number for me. After all, I was born on the thirteenth. So, I felt the party would be a success even if thirteen was supposed to be unlucky.

But that same night, I had a very strange experience. As I lay in bed, before falling off to sleep, I distinctly saw a shadow coming down the spiral staircase from the turret. As the shadow grew closer, I could see it was a woman in a long, flowing gown. She stood at the foot of the bed and appeared very angry. Was it Jane? Before she disappeared, I heard her say: "It should be fourteen." And then the apparition faded.

Had I seen a ghost or was I dreaming? Did I imagine it?

Who was she? And what did it mean?
What should be fourteen?

* * *

Mrs. Potter came up to the house early on Christmas Eve to help with preparing the hors d'oeuvres. She had made vol au vents and cocktail sausage rolls, and we made pineapple and cheese on sticks. We also had a large fruit platter and a cheese and cold meat platter, and the whole thing looked like it would feed an army. Another table held bottles of wine, some gin and rum, with various mixes. I even had a bottle of Advocaat, in case I made some Snowballs. Bee prepared a large non-alcoholic punch, and we would make some hot apple cider later.

"I don't mind helping prepare, Miss, but I wouldn't feel right being a guest at your party. Mrs. McBride wouldn't agree with that at all."

"Oh dear, Mrs. P, we're not living back in those days. I'm the owner now, and I am inviting you. You can't be alone on Christmas Eve. Bee and I want you here with us."

"Oh miss, that is so lovely of you, but it just doesn't seem right."

"Well, my aunt and I insist. You must come."

She finally agreed, and when all was ready by six o'clock, she walked back to her cottage to change. "I'll be back in time to serve," was her parting shot.

* * *

Bill, Liz, and Samantha were the first to arrive, soon after seven.

"Oh Vicki," squealed Sam. "The house looks so Christmassy, doesn't it, Dad? I can't wait to see it all." Bill and Liz agreed.

"It will look much better after all the restoration is complete. I'm getting Foster & Associates to start after Christmas. You'll meet Ryan Foster tonight."

Bill nodded his agreement. "Well, you got the best company in town. I know Ryan, and of course my nephew Joe works with him. Is Joe coming tonight too? It would be good to see him again."

"I'm afraid he couldn't make it. Ryan said he'd gone skiing on the mainland over the holiday."

"Oh, what a shame," replied Liz. "He's cut himself off from his father, and we're the only ones in the family he stays in touch with. I'd love to have seen him. He's such a nice young man."

As more people arrived, the subject of the missing Joe Caldwell was dropped.

Bee's friends Mary and Geoff were fun people and very friendly as they admired our house. Finally, Ryan arrived with his brother Todd and his wife, Ruth, followed by Ryan's parents, Ken and Dorothy.

Ryan's mother thanked me profusely for inviting them, as did Todd. I really liked them all, but I found Todd's wife, Ruth, a bit overwhelming. She was very flirtatious with all the men, especially Ryan, and she gushed over everything in the house, including the grand piano and the grandfather clock in the hall.

"How absolutely darling," she said. For some reason she didn't seem completely genuine, and I was wary of her.

Everything was going well, with everyone mingling and enjoying themselves. Mrs. Potter handed around trays of goodies while Bee and I served drinks.

"I think I should leave now, miss," whispered Mrs. P after a while.

"No, please stay and enjoy yourself. Everyone can help themselves to food from the table now. You can relax."

She didn't have a chance to reply, as Ryan's mum suddenly tapped her glass with a spoon and spoke. "Well, Vicki, I'm sure everyone is charmed with Providence but also curious to know your connection to the McBride family. I'm sure only Bill Caldwell, your lawyer, knows."

Ryan, who was standing beside me, whispered, "I warned you, didn't I?"

I laughed. "It's quite simple really, and even Bill doesn't know the whole story," I said. "My mother died when I was three and my father when I was fifteen." There were a few sympathetic noises around the room. "Then, earlier this year, I received a letter from a lawyer in London saying I had been left Providence by Jane McBride, whom I'd never heard of. It's a long story, but luckily Bee was able to piece the story together, and it seems my biological father was really Cal Hamilton, Mrs. McBride's grandson. He met and fell in love with my mother during the war. They planned to marry, but he was shot down in a bombing raid, so he never knew about me."

"Oh goodness, how romantic and sad," gushed Ruth.

"I met your dad on a couple of occasions, as you know," said Bill. "But my sister Letty helped raise him. She could have told you so much more about him, but I do know he grew into a fine young man."

Everyone began chatting at once, all intrigued by what I'd said.

Ryan looked down at me. "Can we escape for a while so I can apologize for my mother?"

"Ryan, you don't need to apologize. I'm sure everyone was curious. I would have been, too."

"Well, I'd still like to sneak off with you to somewhere more private."

"To discuss the restoration?" I teased.

"Not entirely," he replied as he took my hand and led me across the hall into the library, closing the door behind us.

"I know this isn't professional, but I've wanted to kiss you since I first got here tonight. May I kiss you? You look so tempting."

"Tempting? Really?"

"And I hope you want to kiss me, too."

He didn't wait for my reply before pulling me towards him and placing his lips firmly on mine. I felt very warm. Perhaps it was the drinks I'd had. But then again, hadn't I only had some non-alcoholic punch?

"What was that all about?" I managed to gasp.

"I was just preparing you for my mother's next question, asking if we are dating." He grinned.

"So, are we?"

"You are such a tease, Miss Blake. I think you know by now that I would love to date you."

Someone tapped on the door and Bee's head popped around the corner. "There you two are, Vicki. I thought I saw you both come in here. Samantha is playing the piano, and we're going to have a sing-along. Come and join us."

Ryan coughed. "Sorry, Bee—may I call you Bee?—but I was just telling Vicki about some more ideas I'd had, uh, for renovating the house."

"Oh, of course." She smiled, but I knew she didn't believe a word of it.

We joined the others, but Ryan was still holding my hand and I felt somewhat embarrassed by his attention in front of everyone. I'm sure his mother noticed and was now convinced that something was going on between us. And now I knew for sure that there probably was.

Sam was brilliant on the piano and had a wide repertoire of songs. The whole evening was a wonderful success as we sang, drank, ate, and played charades until well after midnight. As everyone gathered up coats, jackets and shoes from the hall cloakroom, Ryan managed another quick kiss—somewhat more respectable this time—as he left. "I'll call you," he whispered.

I felt sure Bee wanted to chat as we closed the door on our last guest, but I immediately told her I was really tired and headed upstairs. "We can clean up in the morning," I said over my shoulder.

"Okay, luv," she replied. "I'm tired, too."

Jane came to me in a dream that night. This time I knew it was her, and it was a dream and not a vision. She was very animated and appeared happy. "So nice to have McBrides and Caldwells together again, enjoying themselves in Providence," she was saying.

And then she added, "There was just one missing. Should have been fourteen tonight."

Did the dream mean there should have been fourteen guests? But who was missing? Was she referring to Joe Caldwell? Or someone else?

* * *

The phone rang early on Christmas morning. It was Ryan, and I felt my heart beat a little faster.

"Merry Christmas, Miss Blake," he said.

"And a merry Christmas to you, too, Mr. Foster."

"I wanted to thank you and your aunt for a great party last night."

"I'm glad you enjoyed it."

"And I was hoping we could spend some time together today."

"Well, that would be nice, but Bee and I are going over to Bill and Liz's for the day, I'm afraid. They invited us to have Christmas dinner with them."

"Aw, what a shame. I was hoping to escape the family here." He chuckled. "I'll ask you out on a proper date after Christmas, and then I'll really have something to tell my mother."

Much to my surprise, Bee didn't ask me any questions about Ryan that day, and we had a lovely time enjoying dinner with Bill and Liz Caldwell. Samantha and I got to know each other better. I soon felt we would become close friends. We made plans to get together again the following week. I felt at last that I was really fitting in to my new hometown and was making new friends.

But late on Boxing Day, it began to snow heavily and the whole city shut down. Within a few hours, about two feet of snow lay outside our door, and no one was going anywhere. Victoria, we were told, had never seen a snowfall like this one. I hoped not, because I thought the winters here were better than eastern Canada and more in keeping with English winters.

The next day, it was still snowing, and the world around Providence became a sparkling white wonderland, with roads on the outside quite impassable. Were all Canadian winters going to be like this?

Ryan phoned me a couple of times, concerned that we might be isolated at Providence, and asked if there was anything he could do. While we waited for a thaw to happen, Bee and I cleared some paths down the driveway ourselves and one across the lawn towards the gazebo, which we inspected. The storm had not been kind to it, and it would now need a completely new roof as far as I could see.

After that, we cleared one more path towards the building that once housed the stables, and we explored inside. Sometime at the turn of the century, part of the building had been turned into a garage, and an old 1930 Porsche occupied that side. Bill Caldwell had told me it had belonged to one of the twins—Teddy McBride. It, too, was now mine as part of the McBride estate.

It was obviously a classic, vintage car in good condition, but I had no idea what I would do with it. I intended, once I had passed my driving test, to buy a Mini Minor or a Ford Prefect, both of which I'd driven in England. Then I realized that with the money I now had I could probably afford a Ford Mustang or a Lamborghini—not that I wanted either—but the thought overwhelmed me. When you are a middle-class, working girl and suddenly become an heiress with millions of dollars in your bank account, it is overpowering and hard to think about. Money and assets take on a whole new meaning.

When we had first moved into Providence in early October of last year, I had started keeping a journal—yet another thing I felt compelled to do, as Jane once had. Keeping a day-to-day account of things would also be a good reference for when, and if, I ever wrote a book.

Now, while the snow lasted, I spent hours up in the turret, sitting at the desk and comfortable chair that I'd purchased before Christmas, surrounded by some of the books we had moved up from the library downstairs, which had now become our television room. Bee and I had also bought a brand-new colour television—the latest rage—and called it our Christmas present to each other. We loved staying up late watching *The Tonight Show Starring Johnny Carson* in living colour. There was another small black-and-white television in one of the twin uncle's bedrooms in the north wing.

But the intensity of being confined to the house, just the two of us, during the many snow days after Christmas began to irritate both of us.

"You need to get out and meet young people, Vicki," Bee constantly told me.

"And how am I supposed to do that unless we at least get the long driveway cleared?" Clearing those other small paths had totally exhausted us. And every time we did it, it snowed again.

Finally in February, Ryan hired a plow for us from a nearby building company to come out and clear the long driveway, and by the end of the month he sent out electricians and plumbers to begin stage one in our restoration process. The snow had finally stopped, and things were slowly getting back to normal.

After putting some of the most valuable pieces in the house into storage, Bee and I moved into town on March 4, allowing the work to begin.

By then, Ryan and I were officially dating.

CHAPTER 10 (RYAN)

Once the work began at Providence, I saw Vicki almost every day. I wondered if I was falling in love with her. She intrigued me more than any other woman ever had.

By early February, Joe and I were also working back in our office again. He'd immediately asked me about the job at Providence on his return from the mainland.

"You're spending a lot of time there, Ryan. How's it going?"

"Well, the electricians and plumbers are still in there right now. Vicki and her aunt have moved into town."

"Oh, *Vicki*, is it?"

"Yep, the mysterious Victor Blake turned out to be the very attractive Victoria Blake. You should come and meet her."

"I will, but I'm busy catching up on jobs right now. Maybe later."

"I should also let you know I'm dating her, Joe."

"What?! But she's a client, Ryan. That could be awkward—especially knowing your record with women."

"I realize that, but she is pretty darn cute. I love her English accent."

"But can English accents afford all the restoration work needed on that old monster of a house? Is she likely to bounce a cheque?"

"You're such a pessimist, man! She listens to her aunt, who is very sensible, and I'm sure they have the money. Vicki tells me they are thinking of selling off some of the land, too, so that should bring in some extra cash for her. I gave her a very rough estimate of how much the interior work will cost, and she didn't bat an eye."

"Well, I hope you're right—but dating her? What if things don't work out and she still owes us money?"

"You worry too much. Joe."

I dismissed it without another thought. Every day, I headed out to Providence to oversee the work and continued to meet Vicki there. We also went out two or three times a week on dates—to dinner, a show or for long drives—and we enjoyed each other's company. Despite being a client, I couldn't see anything going wrong. She wrote cheques at regular intervals to cover the completion stages of the electrical and plumbing work, and nothing bounced.

By May the restoration work started inside the house. The bathrooms and kitchen began first, and by June, Vicki and Bee moved back to the house and didn't object to the rest of the work going on around them.

I did begin to wonder about her finances, though. She and her aunt had spent almost three months in a hotel, which could not have been cheap. And now there were all these expenses. Her aunt was working, but Vicki wasn't—other than what she described as dabbling in writing.

One night in July, we drove up to the top of Mount Tolmie to look down at the city. We loved going up there and making out. It was a beautiful spot.

I had helped Vicki buy a car at a local dealer. She decided on a modest 1969 Ford Taurus in bright red. She obviously felt comfortable with me by now, because that night on Mount Tolmie she suddenly pulled away from me and said, "I suppose you're wondering just how much my great-grandmother left me, Ryan?"

"Not at all," I replied, although I did really want to know. "I just hope you're not getting in over your head with the restoration and buying a car. Are you planning to sell Providence when it's all completed?"

"Absolutely not!" She looked at me in horror.

I knew that the McBride family had been very wealthy, but it was "old money" from the 1940s at least, and I had wondered how long it could last in today's world.

"Well, I just assumed that was why you were restoring the house."

She laughed. "I would have done that when I first heard about my inheritance, but one of the conditions of accepting the inheritance was to NOT sell the house. I have to live there forever. My great-grandmother put all her other money into a trust fund for me, and it's been accumulating interest ever since she died in 1945."

"Oh ..." This surprised me.

"Yes, shocking, eh?

"It's an enormous house for you and your aunt, though, and the upkeep—whew, it will be enormous."

"My thoughts exactly. I know it sounds totally ridiculous, but ever since I first saw Providence and read the story of the McBrides and my great-grandmother's early life, I felt compelled to carry out her wishes about the house. Eventually I might get a job, and we have already had offers from building contractors for the acreage to the north for a subdivision. That will keep us going for a while."

"You *read* something about the McBrides?"

She seemed hesitant at first but then said, "Yes, my great-grandmother had kept diaries, and she wanted me to read them. I admit I have become somewhat obsessed with her ever since."

"Well, as I told you, I met her when I was about four, and she terrified me, but my grandmother's friend was Letty Caldwell, and they both loved her."

"I know. I wish I had met your grandmother and Letty Caldwell."

"I'm afraid I don't remember them much. I was about ten when my grandmother died."

"You're lucky to have had her that long. One of my grandmothers was Sarah Hamilton, who I never knew, and the other was Grandma Graham, my mum's mum, who died when I was quite young. And of course, I never knew my biological dad."

"Well, he sounds like a great guy."

"Yes, like my dad Harry, who raised me. So, I guess I shouldn't complain. I was lucky. But, getting back to the house: it is a bit of a problem, as of course it is far too large for Bee and me. We could make a suite in the north wing and rent it out, I suppose."

"Or ... you could get married and have children to fill up all the rooms?" *Why on earth had I said that?*

"Oh yes, masses of children," she replied with a giggle.

"What about me?"

"What do you mean? What about you?"

"As a candidate for a husband to help fill up the rooms with kids?" *Good God, am I losing my mind?*

I disliked children and had never thought about having any of my own.

"Is that a proposal? Because if it is, it's lame."

The car radio had been playing "Hey Jude" by the Beatles, and as it switched to "Moon River," I pulled her back into my arms. "I agree it was a pretty lame proposal. So, is this any better? I'm in love with you, Victoria Blake. Will you be my Huckleberry friend and marry me?"

"I think you're supposed to go down on one knee, Ryan."

"I'll do that when I get you a ring and we make it official."

"That sounds good to me," she whispered as I leaned in and kissed her again, and we made it official.

By the time I drove her home, I think she had said yes.

CHAPTER 11 (VICKI)

After Ryan drove me home and we said goodnight, I was far too excited to sleep, so I went to the kitchen to make myself an herbal tea. Bee was in there reading the newspaper.

"I didn't know you were still up, Bee."

"Old habits, I guess. I can never sleep until I know you're home safely."

"Well, I'm glad you're up, as I have something to tell you."

She put the paper down and set down two cups. "Oh? What's up, luv?"

"Ryan asked me to marry him tonight, and I said yes," I blurted.

"Wow!"

"What do you think?"

"I think it's great if you're happy and that's what you really want. He seems like a good chap, and he's been so good to us ... but ..."

"But what?"

"Well, it is a bit quick, isn't it? You haven't been dating for long."

"Six months, Bee."

"But your life here is still very new, Vicki. Everything might seem exciting right now and—"

"I know, Bee. I thought about that, but I'm sure this is what I want. Ryan and I can make it work."

"Well, if you're sure he's the right one, then I'm happy for you, luv." She stood up and gave me a hug.

"I assume he'll be moving in when you get married, so I'll find a place of my own then."

"NO! You can't move. We won't be getting married until next year at least, and you will *not* move out ... *ever*. We'll convert the north wing into a self-contained suite for you, with a separate entrance from the stairs down the back of the house. How would that be?"

She laughed. "Oh Vicki ... bless your heart. I will think about it. But don't worry about me. I'll be just fine whatever happens. I love Victoria too, and I'm glad I moved here with you."

"Good, because I'll talk to Ryan about starting the north wing soon. Oh, and to put your mind at rest, he told me that before we get married, he's going to put his James Bay house on the market, and he'll put that money into Providence—so he's not just marrying me for my money!"

She laughed again. "I admit that makes me happy, but I didn't believe he was after your money. He seems to be quite well-to-do himself."

We drank our herbal teas, hugged again, and then I went upstairs to bed, feeling happy. All of Bee's concerns seemed to have been ironed out, and I could only see happiness ahead.

Nonetheless, I had a very restless sleep, and Jane came to me again in a dream. This time she seemed really agitated. I couldn't figure out why.

On the following Sunday, July 20, Ryan and I were watching television together in the library as Neil Armstrong landed on the moon and began to take a step.

As we heard him say, "That's one small step for man and one giant leap for mankind," Ryan suddenly went down on one knee and officially asked me to marry him, a ring in his hand. It took my breath away.

"This," he said, "is my one giant leap, Vicki. Will you leap with me into a new life and be my wife?"

It seemed the most romantic proposal ever. "Yes, yes, of course I will," I said as I flew into his arms, and we kissed passionately. That night, we went outside and looked up at the moon.

"There really is a man up there on the moon, Ryan. Can you believe it?"

"I'm still trying to believe that you are going to be my wife. I'm the luckiest guy on earth right now."

* * *

The rest of the month passed in a blur for me as Ryan and I made plans for our future. One day I went to the office to meet Ryan for lunch. I still hadn't met Joe Caldwell or any of the other staff, other than the landscape architect who had come out to Providence earlier. I'd talked to Sue, the receptionist, many times on the phone.

She told me Ryan was on the phone but would be free soon. She invited me to wait in reception and offered me a cup of coffee. As I sat down in a comfortable chair, a man rushed down the hallway, clutching a briefcase while attempting to put on his jacket at the same time.

He nodded to me politely as he flew past Sue. "I'm late for my appointment at city hall, Sue. Can you give them a call and let them know I'm on my way?" He was gone in a flash.

"Who was that?" I asked Sue. "He seemed in a big hurry."

"Oh, sorry, I thought you must have met Joe before. I should have introduced you. That's Joe Caldwell, the other partner. He's usually the organized one and never late for an appointment, not like Ryan—oh, sorry, Vicki."

"Don't apologize. I agree Ryan is always late." I was still intrigued by the mysterious Joe Caldwell, so I added, "So that was Joe Caldwell, eh? Quite the Speedy Gonzales, wasn't he?"

She laughed, and at that moment Ryan came into reception and greeted me with a kiss and I completely forgot about the brief glimpse of Joe Caldwell.

Ryan told me at lunch that he had put his house on the market and had already had an offer. The closing date was October 1. We decided it made perfect sense for him to move into Providence then, but, knowing Bee and her old-fashioned values, I figured this would not go down

well with her, even though Ryan was already supervising the work on
a restored north wing as a private suite for her. The large room that
had once been a nursery had been converted into a kitchen and family
room. One of the bedrooms became a living room, and there were still
two other bedrooms and two bathrooms. Bee loved how it was going to
look, with a private front door leading to the landing and steps down
to the back of the house. It would be completely self-contained, but
she would still be close by.

"I still don't think he should move in with you until you're married,
luv. I know I'm old-fashioned, but it doesn't seem right. Harry and
your mum wouldn't have wanted that for you," Bee said one night.

"Bee, I'm almost twenty-four. Did they expect me to still be a
virgin when I got married?"

"I don't know, luv. But they left me to take care of you, and I want
everything to be perfect—and right this time."

"It is perfect, Bee. It's not like the other time. I am sure I want to
marry Ryan. I love him very much, and he loves me. You know I don't
sleep around and never have."

"Then I suppose I must get with it and move into the 1970s and
accept all the changes going on in the world with young people." She
laughed.

She was only being protective of me because of that one other
serious relationship when I was nineteen that had been so wrong and
had left me with a broken heart.

She didn't want that to happen again, but when Ryan's sale went
through, she accepted him moving into Providence, and she moved
to her suite.

Ryan brought more antique furniture from his house in James
Bay, and together we placed it around Providence to complement
what was already there.

The move and then all the plans for the wedding in 1970 occupied
my thoughts most of the time, and for a while I forgot about Jane and

the way I had earlier been obsessed with her. When I was alone up in the turret, I did occasionally re-read her diaries, but other than that I gave her little thought.

Ryan wanted a spring wedding, so when I said I wanted to get married in September, he said he didn't want to wait that long.

"Why September?" he asked. "That's months away."

I then made the mistake of telling him the reason I wanted September, and that it had to be September 5th.

"My great-grandmother Jane and Gideon were married on that day in 1863, and I'd like it to be our wedding date, too."

"Good grief, Vicki, do you have to do everything she did?"

"Of course not. I just like the idea of September 5th."

He looked at his calendar. "Well, it is Labor Day weekend, and it will be all booked everywhere."

"We don't have to book anything except for the church up on the hill. The reception can be here in Providence. We have plenty of room."

"Use the church? You don't *own* the church, Vicki!"

I was being a bit foolish, I know, but I really wanted my wedding date to be the same as Jane and Gideon's.

"If we give people enough warning, they can make plans. It will be no problem for me, having Bee to give me away and Sam as one bridesmaid. As you know, my friend Judy is coming from England this summer and is just waiting for me to let her know the wedding date. I've asked her to be the other bridesmaid. I guess you'll ask your brother to be your best man?"

He still didn't seem enthusiastic, but I put it down to the fact that men never enjoy wedding preparations, and we dropped the subject. But I was determined to have September 5 as my wedding day—come what may.

* * *

That night, Ryan came home very late from work. I had already gone to bed, but I knew as soon as he came into the bedroom that he'd been drinking. His words were slurred, and he was unsteady on his feet.

"Sorry I'm late, babe," he said. "Went for a drink with a client and I think I lost track of time."

I sat up in bed and switched on the bedside light. "And wasn't there a phone where you were? It would have been considerate to phone me to tell me you'd be late. I was worried."

He tripped over something as he tried to unbutton his shirt and remove his pants. "Oh my God, are you going to turn into a nagging wife once we get married?"

He had never spoken to me like that before, and it frightened me.

"I said I was sorry, for God's sake," he murmured as he climbed into our big four-poster and tried to put his arms around me.

I pushed him away angrily. "You smell of booze. Get away from me!" He continued to touch me and even tried to pin me down.

I had never seen this side of Ryan before. Usually, he didn't drink much and our lovemaking had always been mutual and very loving. Now he was trying to force himself on me, and I didn't like it. What was wrong with him?

I kept pushing him away, and then he started laughing, suddenly turning from an angry drunk into an asinine one, who seemed to think everything was funny. But I certainly didn't. I wanted to hit him.

"Vicki ... I'm sorry ... I guess I'm a little bit tipsy."

"A little bit?! You're drunk. Where the hell have you been all this time?"

He fell backwards and didn't answer. Within seconds, I was thankful to see he had passed out. He was snoring loudly, with his mouth wide open. I pushed him away and jumped out of bed, leaving him there. I moved into a guest bedroom because I couldn't bear to see him like this and my reaction to his behavior concerned me. I was repulsed. Okay, he was drunk—but why did it make me feel this way?

I didn't like this other side of him. He had tried to force himself on me before passing out. Could this be described as rape? I immediately thought about Jane and what had happened to her when she was in service.

Stop it, Vicki. That was a whole different situation, I told myself. *I love Ryan.*

But I still wondered if I had made a mistake by letting him move in before the wedding. Had he got drunk simply because I wanted to get married on a specific date? Was this some kind of punishment?

I barely slept as these questions floated around in my head while listening to his snores down the hall. I was glad Bee had moved into the north wing last week, as I didn't want her to know we had argued.

Eventually I fell into a fitful sleep, anxiously waiting for morning.

* * *

The next morning, he was standing over me, holding a tray.

As I looked up at him, I saw the old Ryan, the one I had fallen in love with. His hair was ruffled, and his eyes were sad.

"I'm so sorry for the way I behaved last night, Vicki. Can you forgive me?"

"Why didn't you let me know you would be late, Ryan? And why did you have to drink so much? You don't usually have more than a couple of beers, but last night you smelled like a brewery, and I'm sure you'd been drinking hard liquor. I hope you didn't drive home."

"I got a cab, and you're right," he replied sheepishly. "I should have called you, and I shouldn't have drunk so much. I've made you breakfast to apologize, and if you want to get married on September 5th, that's fine with me. I'll talk to Todd about being my best man, and I'll let my parents know the date. I'll also ask Joe to be an usher. Maybe we could take him and his girlfriend out for dinner one night and discuss it—anything you want, my love."

So maybe he *had* done this as some sort of punishment because of my insistence about the wedding date. Was I driving him crazy, always talking about my ancestors and what they had done a hundred years ago? I decided not to go there right now, as he had at least agreed to the date I wanted. After that, I would be more careful about talking about the McBrides' past.

"Ryan, it was more than that. I didn't like the way you acted and spoke to me. I know you were drunk, and I'm glad you finally passed out, because you were trying to force yourself on me."

He looked genuinely ashamed. "I'm so sorry, Vicki. I really am. Can you please forgive me?"

I looked down at the breakfast tray he had prepared. A slice of burnt toast sat alongside a very watery soft-boiled egg. But at least the coffee looked good.

Suddenly we both laughed. "Pretty pathetic breakfast, eh?" he said.

"Yes, it certainly is. But it is Saturday, so you can take me out somewhere for a decent breakfast."

"Am I forgiven, then?"

"I guess you are."

We kissed and I got up to shower. I noticed a bruise on my shoulder, which must have come when he pinned me down on the bed. As I dressed, my head was in turmoil, and before going downstairs, I glanced out the window. Ryan's car was down there, parked at an odd angle in the driveway. Didn't he say he took a cab home? Had he lied to me?

But then I told myself that he must have woken up early and walked over to get the car wherever he'd left it, before he made me breakfast. But for some reason I didn't ask him or press the issue any further. The crisis was over for now. In fact, it was anything but over. It was simply the first of many times when I allowed myself to be manipulated and to believe his lies.

CHAPTER 12 (RYAN)

The following week, I called my brother, Todd, and asked him to be my best man. He said he would take that week off work and he and Ruth would fly in from Toronto.

I then talked to Joe about it. "For some reason, Vicki wants to get married on September 5th, which happens to be Labor Day weekend, so I guess we won't have to close the office. That's good because she's inviting all the staff. And we hope you'll be an usher. I wanted you as my best man, bro, but I guess Todd would have his nose put out of joint if I didn't have him."

Joe laughed in his usual easygoing manner. "Don't worry. I understand. But I would like to meet the bride before the big day! Or are you going to keep her hidden forever?"

"She says she saw you when she was last in the office, but you were rushing out in a big hurry."

"What? Was that her in reception when I was late for an appointment at city hall the other day?"

I nodded.

"She must think I was very rude."

"Oh yes, she was devastated!" I laughed.

"I would certainly have made time to introduce myself if I'd known. I was just in such a rush."

"Well, let's go out one night this week for dinner and I can officially introduce you. Bring your latest girlfriend ... what's her name?"

"She's not exactly my girlfriend, Ryan. We've only had a couple of dates, and her name is Sally. But let's do it."

"You're on. I'll talk to Vicki."

* * *

We arranged to have dinner on Thursday night at the Century Inn in town. The restaurant was called The Persian Room, with a Middle Eastern theme and a steak and lobster dish on the menu to die for.

Vicki and I had been there a couple of times before, and she loved it. Joe and Sally arrived shortly after us, and we ordered drinks. Vicki had her usual Snowball.

"That's an unusual drink, Victoria," Joe remarked after the introductions.

She laughed. "Yes, it was my old favorite in England, and not many places here know how to make it."

"Advocaat, eh? Looks interesting," he said. "And by the way, I must apologize to you for not introducing myself the other day. I was very late for an appointment that day, I'm afraid, and I didn't realize it was you in reception."

"That's fine," Vicki replied.

"Well, Ryan said you were devastated."

"Did he?" She had a twinkle in her eye, and Joe seemed to be lapping it up. I felt a bit sorry for Sally, who appeared to be bored with us all. She and Joe didn't connect in any way. I tried to bring her into the conversation as Joe and Vicki started to discuss Providence and other heritage houses in Victoria.

"I love old houses," Vicki was saying. "That's why I wanted to restore Providence. I'm working on a series of heritage home articles to send to a magazine in London."

"Are you a writer?"

"I am," she said.

"That's incredible. You should get Ryan to take you on a tour of some of our best heritage homes in Victoria. Not nearly as old as you have in England, of course."

"I hear you spent time in Europe, Joe," she replied. "Did you visit England then?"

"I was mostly in Italy, but I did visit England, and I loved all the buildings and architecture."

They then rambled on about London and places they both knew. Neither I nor Sally had been to England, so the two of them monopolized the conversation.

By the time the food arrived, I was feeling a bit neglected, so to change the subject I remarked about the waitresses, who were all dressed in Arab costumes. The head waiter was the Sultan, and the girls were dressed as harem ladies.

Vicki looked at me. "Ryan! I can see you ogling the harem girls and the belly dancers," she said.

"I only have eyes for you, my love," I said and then tried to bring the conversation around to our wedding.

"So, Joe, I hope you've marked your calendar for September 5th."

"I wouldn't miss it," he replied.

"I had hoped the wedding would be this spring, but Vicki wanted that date."

"I love spring weddings," Sally chipped in, possibly because she thought she wouldn't still be dating Joe by September.

"Well, sorry, but it's going to be September," Vicki said.

The rest of the evening was a reasonable success, and we got along well. This was especially true of Joe and Vicki, who seemed to find a lot to talk about. I was glad Joe liked her and that she got along with my best friend.

"Please come out to Providence soon, Joe," Vicki said. "You must see all the wonderful work Ryan has done."

I was surprised when he immediately agreed. "I would love that—maybe this weekend."

"I've been asking this guy to come out to Providence for weeks, and he always says he's too busy. Vicki asks you once and you agree."

"She's better looking than you, Ryan." Sally glared at Joe, but Vicki smiled her gorgeous smile, which always melted my heart.

By the looks of it, her smile had won Joe over, too.

And for some reason that irritated me.

* * *

That night, I made passionate love to Vicki. It was odd, but I somehow felt the need to claim her as mine and mine alone. Perhaps I had suddenly realized how lucky I was to have this woman in my life. I felt very possessive of her and glad she was mine.

The conversation between Vicki and Joe had flowed so easily, and for some reason, their instant connection bothered me. I knew Vicki loved me, but I also knew I needed to be more careful in future. I could easily lose her if I continued to behave badly. I had already destroyed her trust in me once, when I got drunk and tried to force myself on her that night.

She was a woman to be cherished, and even though her obsession with her ancestors who had once lived in Providence irritated me beyond words, I realized I must not let it get between us. I loved her and I wanted her to be my wife.

My past life of drinking and womanizing needed to stay in the past.

CHAPTER13 – (VICKI)

On Saturday morning, Joe drove out to Providence, and I enjoyed showing him around the house and grounds.

When we came back inside, Ryan had made coffee, and because it was a warm morning we sat outside on the veranda. "You've done a great job here, Ryan. The house has come to life again."

"Well, it was originally very well built, so we were able to work from a masterpiece of engineering."

"I can't believe how hard the Chinese labourers in those days must have worked without all the modern tools builders have today," I said. "In my great-grandmother's diaries, she described how their future houseboy Ah Foo and his fellow countrymen worked long hours on Providence after they'd built the boathouse at the bottom of the lawn. That was where they all lived, in bunks, while the house was being erected."

"Here she goes again," said Ryan. "Vicki is obsessed with the McBrides and everything about them."

"Well, so she should be. I would be proud of this house and my family, too. The McBrides did a lot for Victoria."

"Thank you, Joe," I said, glaring at Ryan. "I am extremely proud of Jane McBride, and I'm honored she left this house to me."

I turned towards Joe again. "Maybe, being a Caldwell, you might have heard the story of how she grew up in an orphanage and didn't know her true parentage until years later. It's a wonderful story of a strong woman rising from nothing to such a rich life in the new world."

"You should write a book about her," said Joe. "And yes, as a child, I do remember my grandfather telling us stories about her."

"I intend to write her story one day."

Joe seemed really interested in the idea, but I could see how the fact that Joe and I were in complete sync about so many things was annoying Ryan, so I quickly changed the subject. The book wasn't my top priority right then, whereas our wedding was.

* * *

The months flew by, and I was getting desperate about finding a wedding dress. The church was booked, and we had found caterers for the wedding reception to be held in Providence, but I couldn't seem to find a dress that I fell in complete love with.

After yet another futile shopping expedition with Sam one Saturday in early June, we returned to Providence totally exhausted.

"I'm going upstairs to change, Sam. Can you put the kettle on or, better still, open a bottle of wine? We both need it." Over the last few months, I'd developed a love for red wine.

She laughed. "Absolutely."

She headed for the kitchen as I ran upstairs to my bedroom. I kicked off my shoes and began rummaging around in the large wardrobe.

For no apparent reason, my eye caught the back panel, which seemed to be loose. I pushed it slightly. Much to my amazement, it fell backwards, revealing a large space in the wall behind. It was very dark and dusty inside, so I grabbed the flashlight beside the bed, which we kept there in view of the frequent power outages that happened whenever a tree came down across a power line.

I could hardly believe what I was seeing inside the large space. It appeared to be another closet, with at least two large garment bags hanging on a rack.

I ran down the corridor and yelled from the top of the stairs. "Sam! Sam, come quick!"

Bee's apartment door opened on the north wing, and she rushed out. "Vicki, whatever is wrong?"

"Come and see what I just found. You won't believe it!"

They both hurried behind me.

"Look!" I screeched. "There is another closet behind this one, and there's stuff in there. What could it be?"

"Wow!" said Sam.

Bee was looking at it very intensely. "Be very careful how you take these out. First, draw the curtains so it's dark in here. It looks like two very old muslin garment bags, and there are obviously clothes inside. Muslin is non-acidic and moth-resistant, and it provides some kind of buffer against light or humidity. But I'm not sure about temperature."

The three of us gently carried out the first bag and laid it on the bed. It was very heavy and was buttoned at the front. Bee, with her archival knowledge, suggested we put on gloves before touching what was inside. Once that was done, I started to unbutton the bag from the top.

"Oh my God! It looks like a wedding dress. Was this Jane's wedding dress?"

"There's a note attached on the front of the bag," Bee said.

Wedding Dress of Jane McBride worn in September 1863. Packaged and stored away by Letty Caldwell in June of 1930 at Mrs. McBride's request.

Sam had run back to the dark closet. "There's a similar note on the other bag," she said, "but it reads *Primrose yellow dress belonging to Jane McBride as seen in her portrait. Packaged and stored away by Letty Caldwell in June of 1930 at Mrs. McBride's request.*

My heart was beating so fast. All I could think was *Jane knew. She guided me here today. She wants me to wear her wedding dress. Why else would that back panel have dropped out after all this time?*

Bee seemed to be reading my mind. "Vicki, this might be very impractical for your wedding gown, if that is what you're thinking. There are yards of material here, and it's very fragile now. It would need to be preserved by a garment archivist before it sees the light of day. And I think it was once a crinoline, so there must be a hoop somewhere."

"There is a wire contraption on the floor back here," said Sam.

"Bee, could I just use the design and some of the material for a wedding dress? The satin is so soft, and it's beautiful. There is a daguerreotype photo of Jane and Gideon on their wedding day downstairs, so perhaps a designer could work from that."

Having touched that soft material, which Jane had described perfectly in her journals, I was determined.

"I have a contact at the Victoria Costume Society," Bee said. "I'll see what they think. I'm sure there would be no problem for a designer to make you a dress, but it's just a case of making sure the material is preserved."

I began to dance around the room. "Oh, this must be fate, ladies. I finally have my dress. It's a miracle that this extra closet was never found when all the renovations were done."

We all agreed, but of course only a few changes had been made to our bedroom, mainly to the ensuite bathroom, so it was not surprising.

Bee shook her head. "I guess you do have your dress, Vicki. No stopping you when you know what you want."

We carefully examined the yellow dress, too, and then placed them both back inside the closet until Bee could make some enquiries.

I replaced the panel and decided not to say a word to Ryan about my discovery of Jane's dresses. After all, a wedding dress was supposed to be a secret from the bridegroom.

* * *

The following day, the dresses in their garment bags were spirited out of Providence to a costume society that would preserve them. Part of the wedding dress was then given to a designer to design a replica of Jane's dress—without a crinoline skirt. Within two weeks, my dress was slowly taking shape and I was having fittings.

But by the end of July, Bee still hadn't decided on her own dress as "aunt of the bride." She wanted something special, as she would walk me down the aisle and give me away. So, on the first weekend in August, she and her friend Mary decided to go over to Vancouver to shop.

She phoned me from Vancouver on Saturday night to say she'd found something beautiful. "But I won't outshine the bride, I promise." She laughed. "We're coming back on an early ferry in the morning, and Geoff is picking us up at the terminal." I was relieved that Bee had found a suitable dress, and everything seemed to finally be falling into place.

On Sunday morning, Ryan and I were sitting on the patio, enjoying coffee. Music was playing on the radio, and I felt very relaxed. Suddenly an announcement on the radio disturbed our thoughts. The Queen of Victoria ferry from Vancouver to Victoria had collided with a Russian freighter in Active Pass, and there were unconfirmed injuries.

"Oh my God, Ryan! Bee and Mary were on that ferry."

"Are you sure it was that one?"

"Yes, I'm sure! They were getting in at eleven, and Geoff must be out at Swartz Bay right now, waiting for them."

I began to shake violently, and I thought I was having a panic attack. "Find out, Ryan," I screamed.

He held me tight. "It's okay, Vicki. We don't know anything for sure. I'm sure they're all right."

I screamed at him, "How can you be sure?"

Suddenly the phone rang, and Ryan ran to pick it up. "It's Geoff," he indicated to me. "Yes, we just heard, Geoff. Do you know anything more out there? ... Okay. ... okay ... keep us posted."

He came back to me. "There has just been an announcement at the terminal that the ferry is delayed because of an accident. They are being updated and he will phone back when he knows more."

"I knew it was their ferry. Oh Ryan ... what if ..."

He held me tightly again to soothe me. I think he was rubbing my back, but my mind was a blank. "Don't go there. Bee will be all right, I'm sure," he said.

"She's all I've got. She must be all right."

CHAPTER 14 (RYAN)

I tried everything I could to calm Vicki down, but nothing helped.

"I want to drive out to the ferry, Ryan. Right now," she said as she grabbed a jacket and started to run towards the front door.

"Sweetheart, Geoff said he will phone us back. We must stay by the phone until we know what's happening. Once we know more, we can perhaps go and wait with Geoff."

"You don't understand, Ryan. How could you? Bee is all I've got."

"You have me."

She ignored that. "I mean blood family. My mother died when I was three. My dad when I was fifteen. My biological father died before I was even born. I only have Bee left in the whole world. "

I grabbed her in my arms and made her sit down in the library by the phone. "I know. I know. And you still have her. Calm down, Vicki."

"NO, you don't understand," she insisted. "You have parents and a brother. You have a family."

Good grief, she sounded just like her great-grandmother, who had always wanted a family. She had told me that damn story so many times. Well, for God's sake, she did have a family now—the McBrides—and a bloody big house to boot. If something has happened to her beloved aunt, I thought, the next thing she'll do is cancel the wedding!

But I knew I shouldn't voice those thoughts. It would only make her angrier. But I could tell her she was wrong, so I decided to tell her my own long-buried secret truth, which I had never shared with anyone.

"You're wrong, Vicki. I don't have a biological family. My parents adopted me when I was a few weeks old."

"What? What are you saying?"

"I've never told you this before, Vicki. After my mother had Todd, she was told she couldn't have any more children. They waited a few years and then decided to adopt a companion for Todd—me—so you see, I don't know my roots, either."

"I'm sorry, Ryan ... but I didn't know. Why did you never tell me this until now? It makes no difference to me, though. They have been wonderful parents, haven't they?"

"Oh, wonderful," I replied with a touch of sarcasm.

"Why do you say it like that? I don't understand."

"I was always second best—the companion for wonderful Todd. He was the brilliant one who became an economist and worked for the government in Ottawa and Toronto."

"But you became an architect, with your own company. That's something to be darned proud of, too."

At least I'd taken her attention away from obsessing over Bee. "Well, you'd think so, wouldn't you? But didn't you notice how pleased my mother was when you and I began dating? At last, in her eyes, I'd done something she could boast about—landed myself a girl with pots of money."

"What!! But that's ridiculous, Ryan. I've never seen that side of her. She has always been very nice to me and seems to love you very much."

The phone rang and interrupted our conversation. Vicki grabbed the receiver.

"Geoff, do you know anything more? Are they okay?"

They talked for a while, and all I knew was from Vicki's end of the conversation. As she put the phone down, I could see tears in her eyes.

"Oh, Ryan, it was terrible. There are a few minor injuries that are being attended to by paramedics ... but apparently a young mother and her baby were on the car deck where the other ship sliced through, and they were killed. And another younger woman on a higher deck was also fatally injured. That's all they have been told. Geoff asked us to stay here, because everyone waiting at the terminal has been told it will be hours before most passengers will be transferred to another ferry and brought back to Swartz Bay."

"I'm sure he will let you know when they arrive."

"Yes, he will phone us again, and he said he will drive Bee home, too—"

"There, I told you she would be fine."

"But how do we know, Ryan? She might have an injury."

"Vicki, she'll be fine. They'll be here before you know it. Stop worrying."

But I knew my words were going right over her head. She was determined to look on the dark side, and she kept concocting a million scenarios in her head until I couldn't stand it anymore.

"We're going for a walk, Vicki. We both need some fresh air. Then I'll make us some lunch. It will help pass the time."

"Oh Ryan, I can't eat a thing until I know she is safely home. And I'm going to stay right here by the phone until then."

I could not change her mind, so I shrugged and left the house alone.

CHAPTER 15 (VICKI)

After Ryan left, I phoned Sam. I needed to talk to a friend who I knew would understand what I was going through. For some reason, Ryan didn't seem to appreciate my sense of fear, despite his own disclosure about being adopted. I was still surprised he had chosen this time to reveal that.

"Sam," I said after giving her details of what we knew so far. "I hope to God she is okay. We only know there were some injuries, and there were those three fatalities."

"Look, Vicki, try and be positive. I'm sure she and Mary will be fine, and you can take care of Bee once she's home. I know how worried you must be. I will talk to Dad and see if he can find out anything more."

"Thank you, Sam. I just needed to talk to you."

"Where's Ryan? I hope he's there with you."

"Yes, he's here ..." For some reason, I couldn't tell her he had left and gone out for a walk.

We chatted for about ten minutes, and then I told her I better hang up in case Geoff called again.

But it was hours before we heard anything more from Geoff. When the phone finally rang, I could hardly speak, I was trembling so much.

"They're here, Vicki, and they are both safe," he said. "Both a bit shaken up, and Mary has her arm in a sling, but Bee has no injuries. We're heading for the car and will be there in about forty minutes."

"Thank God, Geoff. We'll be waiting."

When Geoff's car drove into the driveway forty-five minutes later, I flew down the stairs and flung myself into Bee's arms as she stepped out.

"Vicki, I'm fine. Please don't fuss. We are both okay, although Mary was told to get her wrist x-rayed tomorrow. I'll tell you all about it ..."

She turned to Geoff with a smile. "Thank you so much for bringing me home, Geoff. Now take your lovely lady home and give her a cup of tea to make up for the ones she spilled all over the place on the ferry." Both women laughed. They seemed all right, but I was sure they were still in shock. I know I was.

While Ryan took Bee's luggage up the stairs, I linked arms with my aunt. "You can stay in a guest bedroom with us tonight, Bee."

"No, dear, take me to my suite. I'm fine, honestly."

"Well, I'll stay with you then—just to make sure you're okay."

Ryan turned and glared at me when he reached the landing. "Vicki, Perhaps Bee wants to be on her own. We know she's safe, and we are nearby."

"Well, I'll get you settled, Bee, and put you to bed. Maybe I'll make you some chamomile tea to help you sleep."

Bee laughed. "She'll never give in, Ryan," she said. She gave him the key to her suite, and we all went in.

"Bee, I'll put the kettle on while you get undressed and into bed. Then I'll bring you the tea." I turned to Ryan. "I'll see you soon," I said as I gave him a peck on the cheek. He still looked angry as he left us.

* * *

When I returned to Bee's bedroom with her tea, she was tucked up in bed.

"Thank you, luv," she said. "You can go home to Ryan now. I am fine, really."

"Bee, you've had a horrible experience. I'm sure it was very scary, so I'm going to stay with you until you've finished your tea and fallen asleep."

She started to sip her tea. "Vicki, please don't fuss. Yes, it was frightening, but we were lucky. I was looking after our cases and the garment bag with my dress, and Mary had gone to get us something to drink and some sandwiches. She was just heading back towards me when the ship was struck so, she dropped the tray, fell over, and slid across the floor with many others. I was still sitting down, hanging on for dear life to our luggage. Mary hurt her wrist, but hopefully it's not broken. So, luv, there is no need to worry about us. We'll laugh about this one day. I just feel so sad for that poor young family and the other woman who was killed. There were many others injured far worse than Mary, but I was simply shaken up."

"It was awful waiting for news, Bee. I thought something bad had happened to you ..." My eyes began to fill with tears.

"Oh, Vicki, I know it must have been terrible for you all, not knowing what was happening—but all's well that ends well, so now I'm going to turn over and go to sleep, and I want you to get a good night's sleep, too."

I took the tray away. "All right, Bee. I'll turn off the light."

But then I lay down on top of the duvet beside her and closed my eyes for just a moment, thinking how relieved I was to have Bee home.

* * *

The next time I opened them, I sensed Bee was looking at me. It was morning.

"What on earth are you doing here still, Vicki?"

"I must have dropped off. I can't believe it's morning already. I'll get you some breakfast and then go home."

"You will do no such thing! I had a lovely long sleep, and I feel fine again. I want you to go home to Ryan and stop fussing."

She was ordering me around, so I knew she felt better. I smiled at her and headed out her door to the landing, where I came face to face with Ryan, looking glum.

"So, you decided to come home at last?" he said.

"I'm so sorry, Ryan. I only intended to stay a while and get her settled in bed, but I lay down for a moment and must have immediately fallen asleep. I only just woke up."

"You've got to learn to worry less, Vicki. She was fine."

"I always worry about the people I love." *Why can't he understand that? And why do I have to explain it?*

"Well, you can worry about me now. I'm starving and need some breakfast before I go to work."

His tone was harsh, but I didn't want to irritate him even more, so I kissed him on the cheek and headed downstairs towards the kitchen. "Coming right up," I said.

Only later did I wonder again why I was the one who always capitulated whenever we argued or there was tension between us.

CHAPTER 16 (VICKI)

Things soon settled down again, although the newspapers were full of the ferry tragedy for weeks. Mary had her wrist examined, and the good news was that she hadn't broken it. It was simply a severe sprain. Poor Geoff was stressed about the whole incident, though, and he was the only one, apart from Sam, who seemed to understand my anxiety.

But once we all became preoccupied with wedding plans again, I began to relax. My wedding dress was finished and looked amazing, and I loved the dress Bee had chosen for herself—a most elegant sky-blue satin ensemble. Sam and I had picked out two dark blue dresses for her and Judy to wear as my bridesmaids, and when Judy arrived ten days before the wedding, she approved of our choice.

As everything seemed to be under control, it allowed me time to show Judy around Victoria. She loved our beautiful city, but she was more impressed with Providence than anything else we saw.

"Vic, this house is amazing, but it must cost a fortune for upkeep. How will you manage?"

"Well, Bee and I had money from the sale of our duplex, and when Ryan sold his house, he put money into Providence."

"And speaking of Ryan—wow, what a catch, Vic! He's gorgeous, and such a gentleman."

I laughed. "Yes, he is handsome, eh? Everyone loves him when they first meet him."

"And he's so much in love with you."

But within a few days of Judy being here and the two of us spending a lot of time together catching up on our lives, Judy made a strange observation. "Ryan is very possessive of you, isn't he? He wants to keep you to himself all the time. He doesn't seem to like you spending so much time with me."

"Oh no, he's fine, Jude. And he'll have me all to himself on our honeymoon. We'll be away for about a month."

"How did you get Bee to agree to him moving in with you and you two living in sin?"

We both laughed. "It wasn't easy, believe me. But I told her this is the '70s and she'd have to get used to it."

"Well, my latest chap, Tony, is wonderful, but my dad would have a fit if we moved in together!"

"Is it serious?"

"I think he might be the one. He said he's going to miss me like crazy while I'm here. He's already popped the question, but I said I'd think about it while I'm away."

"Well, absence makes the heart grow fonder."

"It already has. I miss him so much."

"Well, you both must come over together on your next visit, or we'll come to England for *your* wedding—if you get married."

"Oh, I hope so."

* * *

Suddenly it was September 5th.

The night before, Ryan had stayed over at his parents' house. I was glad he'd had his stag party a week earlier because the morning after that he was very hung over. I knew he'd had a lot of fun, so I understood his over-indulgence that night. Judy and Sam had given me a combined shower and bachelorette party last week, but it was much tamer than his stag party.

When I woke up on the morning of my wedding day, Bee and Judy brought me breakfast in bed, but I was so excited I could hardly eat anything.

"I wish Dad was here to give me away," I said to Bee.

"Harry would have been so happy for you, luv."

I wondered why I had really been referring to Cal Hamilton, my biological dad, at that moment, because I knew that Harry Blake had always been my only real father. Or did I? I was so immersed in this house and all my ancestors, I couldn't think straight today.

Then my bedside phone rang, and it was Ryan.

"I hope you haven't changed your mind," he said. "You'll still meet me at the altar, right?"

I laughed. "Of course, I will, silly. I love you and still want to marry you."

"That's all I need to hear. I love you, too."

We chatted for a while, and Bee and the girls left me alone. After I hung up the phone, I gazed at my beautiful dress, and I thought about my great-grandmother on her wedding day so long ago. There was something magical about that dress—an eternal aura surrounding it.

* * *

The church was full, but I couldn't distinguish any faces as Bee escorted me down the aisle towards Ryan.

He looked so handsome standing alongside his brother Todd and Joe Caldwell, and he was smiling at me with that same loving smile I had grown so used to. I knew beyond a shadow of a doubt that our marriage would be a happy one.

I was sure I was making the right decision, even though it had all happened so quickly—being left a fortune, leaving England forever for a new life in another country, moving in with a man I had only known for a few months, and now marrying him—all within less than two years.

We made our vows solemnly, and I inwardly promised I would make my marriage the best. My mother never got the chance to marry her true love, so I would do it for her. After we were pronounced man and wife, I began to relax a little.

We kissed then, and everyone clapped. "We did it!" Ryan said, and I laughed as we walked to the vestry to sign our marriage certificate. We had indeed done it!

Then we turned to walk back down the aisle together. That's when I really noticed Joe's face for the first time. Todd was escorting Judy behind us, and Joe was putting out his arm to escort his cousin Samantha, but he was looking at me strangely. I couldn't really discern his expression. It was a mixture of hope, kindness, and sadness, but then it changed, and he smiled at me, and I thought maybe it had been my imagination.

I also noticed Todd's wife, Ruth, sitting in the front row beside Ryan's parents, and she looked far from happy. I wondered briefly what was bothering her. Was she upset that I hadn't asked her to be part of the wedding party? But I don't think it was that. It was something more.

I quickly forgot these two impressions as Ryan and I walked out of the church to the sun shining, bells ringing and a bagpiper waiting to escort us back to Providence for the picture-taking and the reception.

Friends came up to congratulate us. Most of them were Ryan's friends and family. I thought about Ryan's comments concerning his parents, and I still found it hard to believe. His mother was so kind and loving towards me and to him. I could not believe she would put Todd first and treat Ryan any differently, but I hadn't pursued the subject again with Ryan since that night when he first told me about being adopted.

Todd and Ruth's children were there also, and I noticed again how Ruth was clinging to Todd protectively while flirting with every other man, especially my husband!

"My goodness, Vicki," she said, "now that you've taken this very eligible bachelor off the market, what *will* all the single girls do?"

"They'll survive," I replied. "They'll have to." Everyone laughed, and then she said, "May I kiss the groom?"

I was pleased that Ryan offered a cheek even though she attempted to place her lips on his. What was the matter with her? Was she just naturally flirtatious with men in general, and how could Todd possibly tolerate that kind of behavior? There must be something else going on in their family dynamics.

The reception and dinner were fun and the speeches funny and very moving. After that, the music started playing and Ryan and I had our first dance. I noticed Joe leaving in a hurry, without even saying goodbye. He hadn't brought a plus-one with him, which for some reason made me happy, but he had been a perfect gentleman to Judy, Sam, and Bee, taking turns talking to each of them. But somehow, he seemed sad. I wondered why he had left early and mentioned it to Ryan.

"He's just a very quiet guy," Ryan said. "He doesn't like these kinds of affairs."

"Well, at least he could have said goodbye." I felt hurt.

"He did congratulate us earlier, so leave it at that."

The music grew louder, and everyone was having a good time. But by ten o'clock I sensed that my husband wanted to leave. We were planning to stay the night at the Empress Hotel and then catch an early ferry to the mainland to begin our epic journey south from Seattle and along the Oregon coast. I went upstairs with Bee, Judy, and Sam to change out of my wedding dress, though I didn't want to take it off.

"Don't worry, sweetheart, I'll take good care of it for you," Bee said with a laugh. "And we'll also look after Judy until she flies home, so don't worry."

Sam was very teary and more than a bit tipsy. "Have fun, Vicki. We'll miss you."

But it was my farewell to Judy that was the hardest. "We'll try and make it next year for your wedding, Jude, so do keep me posted. Thank you for coming to be my bridesmaid." By then, I had tears running down my face, too.

"Oh, Vic, I just want you to be happy ... not just today, but always."

I felt sure I would as I stood at the top of the staircase in my going-away outfit—an elegant green jacket and matching dress with a cheeky Beatles-type cap in a darker shade of green. I made sure both Sam and Judy had run down the stairs to stand with all our guests before I turned to throw my bouquet. My eyes came to rest on Jane's portrait. Was it my imagination, or had her usual serene smile turned to a look of concern? I hesitated, staring at her, sensing the silence of everyone down below, waiting for me to throw.

I quickly pulled myself together. I mustn't do this again. My great-grandmother had died years ago. She could no longer influence my choices in my troubled dreams or her strange appearances and those changing expressions in her portrait. That was all fantasy, pure fantasy. It was simply my overactive imagination at work.

Bill Caldwell, who had served as our master of ceremonies with charm and humor, now tapped his glass to get everyone's attention.

"The bride is about to throw her bouquet," he said. "After that, she and her groom will leave on their honeymoon, folks. Are you ready, Vicki?"

"Yes ... yes, I'm ready." And with that, the bouquet flew and landed just where I wanted it to—in Judy's hands.

Everyone laughed and applauded, and my inexplicable and somewhat perplexing moment as I peered at Jane's portrait passed.

"Let's wish Mr. and Mrs. Foster all the happiness they deserve," Bill shouted above the laughter, and as we descended to the main floor we were suddenly showered with confetti raining down on us.

"Oh, poor Mrs. P will be in dire straits cleaning all this up forever," I whispered to Ryan as we ran through the crowd to our car waiting to take us to our new life.

I dismissed all the little things nagging at the back of my mind because at that moment I was determined to not have a care in the world.

CHAPTER 17 JANE

Our honeymoon was magical. On that first night, we stayed in the bridal suite at the Empress and early next morning drove to the ferry at Swartz Bay to cross over to the mainland. The weather was perfect, and the crossing was smooth. Once on the mainland, we drove leisurely towards the border into the States and headed for Seattle, where we stopped for lunch before continuing on the Pacific highway south, a trip that Ryan had planned meticulously.

He was the most romantic lover imaginable and was constantly surprising me with special little treats along the way. As the weather was so warm, we sometimes camped on the beaches in our small but cozy tent. Other nights, we just slept under the stars.

Whenever we arrived in a larger city, such as Portland, Ryan had booked us in at a penthouse suite, and we ate in all the finest restaurants. On other occasions, we ate hot dogs or hamburgers on the side of the road. Wherever we stopped for the night, we made mad, passionate love like two horny teenagers. Being married made it all seem new, even though we had lived together for a while. This was different, and I loved being Mrs. Ryan Foster.

I adored San Francisco and Los Angeles and sent postcards back home from all the sights we saw. Once we reached San Diego, we headed inland to Arizona and admired the majesty of the Grand Canyon.

On the way back north, we stopped in Reno for two nights, and only then did I begin to feel concerned about all the money we were spending. I assumed Ryan was paying for everything, but I was alarmed on our second night there when he also began drinking and spending a lot of time at the casino tables. He won some money but lost a lot, too, and I challenged him about it.

"Oh dear, are you going to turn into a nagging wife?" he said.

"Of course not. I'm just worried about all the money we've been spending."

"Why are you worried? The old girl left you a fortune, Vic."

"Is it *my* fortune you've been spending? It won't last forever, you know."

"You know I've paid for our entire honeymoon, so why do you say that?"

I could see he was angry, and I felt I had misjudged him. If he was spending and losing his own money at the casino tables, who was I to question that? But it still felt very reckless to me. I must have inherited more of Bee's caution about money than I realized.

He then came over and put his arms around me. The angry expression I'd seen had disappeared from his face, and the old, familiar, loving one had returned. I couldn't believe how his irritation and anger could turn back so quickly to kindness and love.

"I'm sorry about what I said about your great-grandmother's fortune. Honestly, I was just having fun, and we might not come here again any time soon."

"You're right," I replied, and once again the moment passed.

* * *

We were both tired by the time we reached Victoria late on Friday, two days later.

It felt good to be home again, and even better when Bee came over with a casserole that she'd prepared for us.

"I heard you pull up. It's so good to see you again," she said, giving me a hug. "You both look tired, so I won't stay, but I thought you might like something to eat. Just need to warm it up."

"Oh Bee, thank you so much. That's so thoughtful. But please stay and join us. You don't have to rush off. We have lots to tell you, and I want to hear all your news."

I could see Ryan scowling at me behind Bee's back. "Well," he said somewhat sourly, "it's kind of you to bring this, Bee, but we are tired so I hope you understand that we want to head straight to bed."

Bee laughed. "Oh, still in the honeymoon mood, I see."

Ryan said something under his breath that sounded like, "No, we just want to be left alone ..." but I wasn't sure. I coughed loudly to try to cover up what he might have said.

"Don't worry," continued Bee. She seemed to sense some tension. "I won't stay now, but I will come over in the morning, as I need to tell you about poor Geoff, Vicki. He's had a few more heart scares and was in the hospital for a while, so I've been driving Mary back and forth. He seemed to get worse after the stress of the ferry collision in August."

"Oh Bee, that's awful. I'm so sorry. Is he home now?

"Yes, he is ... but I'll tell you more in the morning. Just enjoy the casserole."

"We will, and let me know if there is anything I can do to help Mary."

We hugged again and she left.

Ryan said nothing but seemed happier once Bee had gone.

"I'll pop this in the oven to warm it up and then go upstairs to have a shower and change."

"Or we could just skip the casserole and jump in the shower together," Ryan said.

I was really exhausted and just wanted to get cleaned up and changed into something more comfortable. The last thing I was thinking about was having sex in the shower, but I could tell he was irritated by Bee being there the minute we got home. And he hated that I had invited her to stay and join us, so I decided to appease him, and we both went upstairs.

I guessed the casserole could wait until tomorrow, even though I was hungry.

* * *

First thing on Saturday morning, the phone rang. It was Sam.

"Can I come over, Vicki? Bee told me you were home, and I have lots of news. And I want to hear all about your wonderful trip."

We were still in bed. "Who is it?" Ryan growled.

I covered the receiver. "It's Sam. She wants to come over—"

"Good God, can't they all leave you alone?"

I whispered, "Darling, you've had me to yourself for over a month. I really want to see Sam ... and Bee."

He grunted and turned over.

"Yes, Sam. Come on over, but give me an hour to shower and get dressed."

Ryan stayed in bed while I showered and dressed quickly. On my way downstairs, I knocked on Bee's suite door and told her to come over.

They both arrived soon after, and I made coffee while we pored over the wedding photos, which had arrived after we'd left on our honeymoon. It was fun to chat with them both, but I could tell that Sam was bubbling over and eager to tell us something. After Bee had finished telling me about Geoff and I had related all but the X-rated parts of our honeymoon trip, Sam couldn't wait any longer.

"There's going to be another wedding next summer," she announced. "Jack asked me to marry him, and I said yes!"

Bee and I let out screams of joy. We both liked Jack, the man she'd been dating since the spring.

"Oh, Sam, that's wonderful news. You must have your reception here at Providence. And I'd love to give you an engagement party. Gosh, I bet Bill and Liz are thrilled, as I know they like Jack."

Suddenly the kitchen door burst open, and a disheveled Ryan glared at me. "What the hell is all the noise! It woke me."

"Sorry, Ryan," I said in embarrassment. Was he going to have one of his temper fits in front of Bee and Sam? "We were all so excited to hear Sam's news. She and Jack are engaged and getting married next summer."

"Oh, I guess congratulations are in order," he mumbled. "Is the coffee pot on?"

"Yes, yes," I said, pouring him a black coffee, which I hoped would improve his mood.

Bee and Sam could obviously feel the awkwardness between us, so they both said they were leaving.

As I went to the door with them, Bee hugged me extra hard. "I'm sorry we woke Ryan up with our screams," she said.

"Well, he needn't have been so rude," I said.

"No, he shouldn't have been," Sam agreed. She always spoke her mind.

Her response made me want to defend his mood. "Well, he was very tired last night. It was a long drive yesterday."

Sam hugged me. "It's okay, Vic, I understand."

Did she? Had she witnessed his anger before, or did he just save that for me?

Ryan was on the phone when I got back to the kitchen. He hung up and turned to me.

"Vicki, I've just checked in to the office to tell them I'm back."

"Are you going in on Monday?"

"No, I've decided to take another week. It's almost Thanksgiving, so why don't we drive up-island for a few more days?"

"Really? I was rather enjoying the thought of being home and sleeping in our own bed again."

"Well, if we stay here, they'll never leave you alone."

"Who?"

"Your friends and your aunt, of course. Wait until I go back to work for all your visiting. Pack a small suitcase for us, and we can leave tomorrow. There's lots of Vancouver Island you haven't seen yet, and it will be fun to show you. And the fall colors are spectacular."

I had hoped we could have a Thanksgiving dinner with everyone at Providence. I wanted to use some of our wedding presents, such as the table linen and bright orange woven place mats, which would be so appropriate for Thanksgiving. But I nodded because I didn't want to disagree with him and see his temper flare up again. But why was he being so possessive?

Nonetheless, I was flattered that he wanted me all to himself for another week.

CHAPTER 18 VICKI

I felt relaxed, enjoying the scenery, and listening to music on the car radio. Ryan kept looking at me with such a loving expression. Occasionally he placed his hand on my knee, which made me feel warm inside. He was still the man I loved, even though his anger needed managing sometimes.

Suddenly, the music on the radio was interrupted for a special announcement. Prime Minister Trudeau was making a statement. Ryan pulled over to the side of the road so we could listen.

I didn't really understand everything he was saying, but it was about the FLQ—the *front de liberation du Quebec*—situation again, which had now reached a crisis point. After a series of terrorist attacks in Quebec, and now the kidnapping of a British diplomat, James Cross, and the provincial labour minister, Pierre Laporte, the prime minister was prepared to do more—hinting at even invoking the War Measures Act.

"What's the War Measures Act?" I said. "What does this all mean?"

"Shush ..." Ryan was listening intently. "My God, this is terrible!"

"Tell me, Ryan. I don't understand what it means ..."

Ryan's expression changed. He now looked angry as he glared at me. "For God's sake, Vicki, if you're going to be living in Canada, you'd better learn a few things about Canadian history. The War Measures Act has only been brought into force twice before: the first time during World War I and then again during the Second World War. It provides for the declaration of war, invasion, or insurrection. It's a very serious decision to have to make."

A reporter was now asking the prime minister just how far he would go, and he replied, "Just watch me." I felt a tingle of pride down my spine, as his strong words reminded me of Churchill during the war, in all his famous speeches.

Nonetheless, I was surprised by Ryan's violent reaction. These things were all happening in Quebec, but by his anger, you would imagine we were about to go to war right here in British Columbia. Nonetheless, I did understand the seriousness of this situation.

Ryan switched off the radio and turned to me. "Vicki, I think we should cut our trip short and go home."

"Why?"

"Isn't it obvious?

"Not really."

"It's a tense situation, Vicki.

"I realize that, but—"

"We can carry on up to Parksville and spend one night there, and then we'll go home."

I was secretly delighted to go home, as perhaps now Bee and I could do a Thanksgiving dinner for everyone together at Providence. But Ryan's next words put a damper on that, too.

"I promise I'll take you out for a lovely Thanksgiving meal somewhere in town, Vicki—to make up for this."

It seemed our new table linen would not be used.

* * *

Bee was surprised to see us back so soon and offered to cook Thanksgiving dinner for everyone, but Ryan had already booked a meal for just the two of us at a fancy restaurant in town. It seemed he still did not want us to be with my family and our friends.

The next few days were tense in Canada as the War Measures Act was indeed invoked. Eventually, negotiations led to James Cross being released, but Pierre Laporte was murdered, his body found in the trunk of a car. These anxious moments continued until the end of December, and Ryan seemed constantly obsessed by it all.

Meanwhile, his words about my learning more about Canada made me realize that perhaps I should become a Canadian citizen, so I talked to Bee about it one day while Ryan was at work. She agreed and said she would like to also, but we discovered that to attain citizenship, we would need to have lived in Canada for at least five years.

So, in the meantime, I began to study and immerse myself in Canadian history. This was easy for me because I had always loved studying history in England. I soon realized that the history of Victoria and British Columbia was just as fascinating, though somewhat shorter, not counting the many centuries that First Nations had lived on this land before the arrival of European colonists.

Guided by my great-grandmother's diaries, I could now add color to the early history they had lived through. I began to think seriously about writing the story of their lives and how I became the missing piece in their story. I remembered that Joe had suggested this to me when we first met.

Ryan, however, told me I was becoming obsessed with the past and my family tree again, so I put the book idea on the back burner. My so-called "obsession" with anything other than him made him angry.

By early December, I had forgotten all about the idea anyway, because I was feeling a little strange. I was always tired, and two mornings in a row I had thrown up. So, without saying anything to Ryan, I decided to make an appointment with my doctor.

* * *

After a thorough examination and giving blood and urine samples, the doctor confirmed what I already suspected. I might indeed be pregnant. His nurse said she would confirm with me the following day and she would make a follow-up appointment.

Ryan had left for work when the telephone rang the next day. It was the doctor's nurse with the test results, telling me I was indeed pregnant and that I would need to set up monthly appointments.

I could hardly believe the news or contain my excitement but decided not to say anything to Ryan just yet.

As I walked home from my follow-up appointment the next afternoon, I was practically dancing on air. Even though I had been on the pill, somehow this miracle had happened. I felt sure Ryan would be as thrilled as I was. After all, he had once said he wanted to fill all the rooms at Providence with our children.

Last year, we had started a tradition of giving one another one gift on Christmas Eve and the rest on Christmas morning. I still hadn't found anything for Ryan's Christmas Eve's gift, and it was now December 10.

Could I wait until the 24th to tell Ryan and give him this incredible gift then? It seemed the perfect idea, even though I was bursting with joy and wanted to tell him immediately.

CHAPTER 19

Christmas Eve finally arrived. We had planned a party for friends, with Mrs. Potter and Bee helping me. Mary also came over for a while but didn't stay long. Geoff was having more heart problems and was going into hospital the following week for surgery.

As Ryan and I got ready in our bedroom, he seemed particularly happy. I decided this would be the perfect moment to give him his Christmas Eve gift.

Before I had a chance to say anything, he handed me a small box wrapped in Christmas paper. "I hope you like my Christmas Eve gift, honey. You can wear it with that beautiful dress tonight."

"Oh, Ryan, I'm sure I will love it, just as I know you will love mine to you."

I unwrapped the box and inside it was the most exquisite emerald necklace, which matched my dress perfectly. It must have cost him a fortune. He knew I intended to wear this dress tonight, so he must have gone out of his way to find this necklace.

He turned me around and helped place it round my neck as I looked at it in the mirror. It was so gorgeous; I couldn't believe it was mine.

"It suits you perfectly," he said as he kissed me tenderly.

"And now for my gift to you, darling," I began. "It's not wrapped, exactly, but it is quite priceless, I'm sure you will agree."

He looked puzzled. "Okay, Vicki, where is it?"

I placed his hand on my stomach. "Right here. You are going to be a dad. We're pregnant."

He looked astonished. "How could you be pregnant? You're on the pill."

"Yes … but these things happen."

"Did you forget to take the pill?"

"No ... but there was a gap of a few days when Dr. Phillips changed me over to the new one. Remember, the first one didn't agree with me? Anyway, aren't you pleased?"

"Pleased? Vicki, I thought we agreed to wait. You know I don't want kids yet. How could you have gone a few days and not tell me you were off the pill?" He looked so angry; I couldn't believe his reaction.

"Well, I wasn't exactly *off* the pill. The doctor was just changing me over to another one."

"Same thing if there was a gap. Vicki, I can't believe how careless you were! How far along are you?"

"About two months. Our baby is due in late July."

"Oh my God! But perhaps it's not too late to do something."

"*Do* something? What on earth are you saying?" Tears were welling up in my eyes. This was not at all the reaction I had expected. Why was he so angry?

"An abortion, of course. We're not ready for kids, Vicki."

"What are you talking about? We have enough money, and we live in a beautiful house. I can still work at home writing, and you have a good job. Why aren't we ready?"

He raised his voice, shouting back at me. "Because I don't want a kid now. I refuse to share you with a squealing little brat. It's too soon. Why did you do this to me?"

"I didn't *do* anything to you. We both made this baby, Ryan, and I won't have an abortion."

"I know it's dodgy, but we have the money to get you a safe one, even if we have to go to the States."

I broke down and began to sob. "I don't understand. I thought you would be happy." I knew I sounded pathetic.

"Well, I'm not!"

I could hear the doorbell ringing. People were arriving. "Ryan, please don't say that. Let's ... let's just talk about it later."

He glared at me. "Get yourself together, Vicki. We're going downstairs. Try and look happy as we greet our guests."

Happy? How was I supposed to look happy when he had just broken my heart?

* * *

I wiped my eyes and dabbed some powder on my nose before following him down the stairs.

Our grand hall looked so Christmassy, and everyone was in high spirits as the evening progressed—everyone but me, that is. My misery must have been obvious, because at one point Sam drew me to one side.

"What's wrong, Vicki?" she whispered. "Are you feeling all right?" Although our friendship was relatively new, she could always spot when something was wrong.

"I'm fine, Sam, really I am."

Across the room, Ryan now appeared to be enjoying himself as he laughed with some of his golfing buddies. He had left me alone in my despair, appearing to have completely forgotten our conversation. My Christmas Eve surprise for him had gone terribly wrong.

Everyone was soon talking about Sam and Jack's wedding the next summer. They announced the wedding date, in early July, and Sam declared she wanted me to be one of her bridesmaids. The other two were to be Jenny, her friend in Vancouver, and her cousin Ann, Joe's sister. Suddenly this made me think of Joe, but once again he was absent from our Christmas Eve open house, as he had gone skiing with friends. All I could really think about was that by the beginning of July, I would either be as big as a house—or in total anguish because my husband had forced me to have an abortion.

Sam and Jack remained the center of everybody's attention until suddenly Ryan came over to me, clinked his glass with a spoon and grabbed my hand.

"Sorry to interrupt the festivities, but I just wanted to thank you all for coming tonight and to hear some news that Vicki and I want to share."

I looked at him in amazement. What was he doing?

"Ryan?" I spluttered. Was he making a mockery of my announcement?

He simply laughed as he continued. "My beautiful wife just gave me an early Christmas present this evening. The absolute best gift. We're expecting a baby in July!"

Our guests let out a joint screech of joy.

Words of congratulations and hugs floated around me, but I was hardly aware of what was happening. Why had he changed his mind? Did he enjoy torturing me this way? One minute he was talking about me having an abortion, and now this—describing my pregnancy as the absolute best gift?

His golfing buddies were making lewd remarks like, "Well done, Ryan. You found the right hole," and "Hey, buddy, you made a hole in one!"

This was not the way I had intended it to go. This was a special gift I had first given to Ryan, and then I wanted to tell Bee privately and then our friends.

"So," said Sam, "that's why you looked a little peaked. Are you having morning sickness?"

I nodded. "Yes, I am. I wanted to tell you and Bee the news first. I didn't think Ryan would make the announcement tonight!"

Bee had joined us in the corner. "I suspected something was up, luv. You've been a little bit off-color lately."

"Afraid so," I said, trying to make light of it and enjoy the rest of the evening.

I felt so overwhelmed at how things had gone that at one point I escaped to the kitchen to pour myself a large glass of water. My roller-coaster of emotions had travelled from pure joy to incredible despair and then back to joy again, so when the door opened behind me and Ryan came in, I wasn't sure how best to react.

"I saw you leave the party, Vicki. Are you okay?"

"Yes, but I'm just ... surprised."

"I changed my mind, that's all. We'll get through this, I suppose."

I stared at him. The anger had disappeared, and he was looking at me lovingly again.

"But are you happy about it?" I pushed.

"Leave it alone, Vicki." And then he added ominously, "Just don't surprise me this way again. One kid is enough."

Much later, I wondered if he had simply made the announcement to take the attention away from Sam and Jack and place it squarely on him. Or was I being paranoid?

In any event, we rejoined the party together and, somehow, I managed to get through the rest of the evening and the remainder of the Christmas holidays.

CHAPTER 20

I knew I loved my husband. I just did not completely understand him. His moods were often beyond comprehension, but over the first months of 1971, I excused everything he said and did; even the fact that he seemed to find me less attractive, which on many occasions was very hurtful, as he frequently made fun of my size in front of people. Even his mother reprimanded him for that. She was always very supportive of me, and I remained puzzled by Ryan's constant criticism of her.

I tried not to argue with him, as it usually threw him into a violent rage. He hated to be proved wrong about anything, so it was easier to agree with him. I had to admit that on occasion I was afraid of him. He continued to be very possessive of me and disliked me having my friends around.

He was undoubtedly a very sexual man, but my quickly expanding body appeared to repulse him. We were going to be parents in a few months, so I tried instead to concentrate on the miracle that was happening inside my body. Everything else, I ignored. I knew it was wrong, as I felt my personality being swallowed up. I was becoming a shell of my former self.

One Saturday, Joe Caldwell stopped by unexpectedly, which also appeared to annoy Ryan. Joe told me I was glowing and congratulated us both again. It made me feel valued—and somehow guilty. Why did another man make me feel special, while my own husband never said anything remotely nice about me? *Is this how it's going to be now? Is he still punishing me because I got pregnant?* After Joe left, he told me I looked beautiful, something he had not said for weeks.

In the spring, news came that Pierre Trudeau, Canada's most eligible bachelor prime minister, whose name had been linked with many famous women through the years including Barbra Streisand, was dating a young girl in her twenties from Vancouver. Her name was Margaret Sinclair, and she looked like a '60s flower child. He was over twenty years her senior, so gossip was rampant. Things quieted down when they married in March, and that May, the couple visited Victoria with Queen Elizabeth, Prince Philip, and Princess Anne. It had just been announced that Margaret was expecting, so, when I saw them all, I felt a certain kinship with this young woman who had been thrust into the limelight.

Bee and I, being loyal monarchists, decided to go into town to catch a glimpse of the important visitors at various locations. We especially wanted to see the Royal Yacht *Britannia* anchored in the harbor. The royal visitors were touring the province to celebrate British Columbia's 100th year in Confederation, and it was a momentous occasion.

We watched the cavalcade of cars travelling through town and later saw Princess Anne leaving the Empress Hotel. On their final day in Victoria, even Ryan joined us at the harbour that night. An enormous crowd had gathered to watch the royal party arrive from a farewell dinner at Government house and then board the Royal Yacht before it departed the city. I felt quite emotional as the drone of bagpipes drifted across the water and the Queen and her husband waved to the cheering crowds.

Maybe it was simply my hormones running riot, but that night I was imagining my ancestors, Gideon and Jane—he first arriving here more than a century ago, about to go into business, and she in 1862, the year Victoria became a city, an orphan hoping to better herself by becoming a governess—and suddenly I felt tears escaping my eyes and running down my cheeks. They had both worked so hard under terrible conditions to come to the new world. And in the momentous year of 1871, when the province joined Confederation, their daughter Sarah (my grandmother) was born. Now I was continuing the McBride line, exactly one hundred years later.

I knew that if I tried explaining my thoughts to Ryan it would only annoy him and draw more complaints about my "obsession." So I turned to Bee, who I knew would understand. "What a beautiful sight," I whispered. She nodded as she, too, wiped away a tear.

But the next day, I started to make notes for the book I wanted to write about Jane and Gideon. Ryan had constantly belittled the idea, but this was one thing I knew I needed to do for myself, and one day I would.

* * *

In April, Geoff passed away. Bee was occupied with helping Mary cope. Mary decided to sell their home in Oak Bay, and Bee suggested she could move into the suite with her if we agreed. I was happy to agree, and Mary insisted on paying rent. Being together was good for them both. Eventually they became known as the "merry widows."

As spring turned into a very hot summer that year, I spent my days up in the turret that had been converted into my office. I mailed many short articles about Victoria and British Columbia to an international magazine, while at the same time continuing to make copious notes from Jane's journals.

My biggest regret was that we would no longer be able to travel to England for Judy's wedding on July 24. My baby was due on July 20, so the timing was not good. I had really wanted to be there for her as her matron of honor, but she said she completely understood, and instead the two of us began planning a trip for the following year. By then, our baby would be a year old, and I hoped that Ryan would agree. Meanwhile, he had insisted I could not be Sam's matron of honor on July 10.

"But why?" I asked. "I hate to turn her down, too."

"Well, she has her cousin, Ann, and her Vancouver friend Jenny as bridesmaids, so she doesn't need you, too. Anyway, you'll be too big by then." He added, "There won't be a dress to fit you!"

"Thanks for reminding me." I was hurt by his remarks. "Well, we're still going to the wedding," I insisted.

But he was right. I was as big as a house by then, and the heat was really getting to me. I had offered them Providence for their reception, and we had a marquee tent erected on the lawn. They held the wedding ceremony at Christ Church Cathedral, and I felt a pang of jealousy seeing my friend being led down the aisle on the arm of her father, Bill, towards the man she loved. I'd had two fathers, neither of whom were able to escort me down the aisle on my wedding day. Somehow it seemed unfair.

A week before my due date, I began to have false contractions and Doctor Phillips said the baby was dropping into position. Everything was perfectly normal and going well, and apart from the discomfort of being so large and having constant backache, I felt healthy. However, on my final checkup, my blood pressure was extremely high, so I was admitted to hospital on July 18 and put on a salt-free diet. I kept thinking of my great-grandmother, who had lost two babies with miscarriages. I knew my thoughts were ridiculous. Medicine had advanced so much since the 1860s, and I was being well taken care of. But would I lose my baby, too?

For the first time, I saw genuine concern in Ryan's eyes when he visited me that night, even though our doctor informed us both the baby was fine.

Was Ryan concerned for the baby? Or was his concern just for me? I couldn't decide.

* * *

My blood pressure returned to normal, and I was told I could go home the next day, as the baby might take another week to arrive. But, in the middle of the night of July 20, real labour pains began. By six o'clock on the morning of July 21, the centenary of British Columbia entering Confederation, our son was born, weighing in at a healthy eight pounds.

Ryan visited me a few hours later, with an enormous bouquet of roses. "At least it's a boy," were his first words. When the nurse brought in our son, Ryan barely looked at him.

"We have to think of a name for him," I said as I admired his tiny hands and counted his little toes. "He is so beautiful, isn't he?"

"He's a boy, Vicki. Boys should be *handsome* and not called beautiful. Right now, he looks like a miniature Winston Churchill."

He had to be joking, so I laughed. "Yes, I suppose he does, but I'm not calling him Winston."

"Call him whatever you like, Vicki."

"How about Cameron? I've always liked that name for a boy."

"That's fine with me. It sounds manly."

Thinking it would please my husband, I added, "How about Cameron Ryan Foster, then?"

He said nothing for a moment.

"Do you like Cameron Ryan, then?"

"Oh yes ... that's fine. I'll see that he's registered as Cameron Ryan."

"Did you let Bee know he'd arrived?"

"Yes, and of course she couldn't wait to see him—and you."

"When is she coming?"

"Probably any minute. I had to rush to get here first."

"I can't wait for her to see our little boy."

At that moment, the door burst open and Bee, wearing a big smile and carrying more flowers, came in.

"I went to the nursery first, but they told me your little man was with you in your room. Congratulations to you both." She gave me a big hug and turned to hug Ryan, but he walked away from her, around to the other side of my bed.

"I'll leave you two to bill and coo over Winston," Ryan said. He bent to kiss me, and I held onto him tightly.

"Come back soon," I whispered. I was on the point of crying, as I didn't want him to leave.

"Of course. I'll be back in a couple of hours. Bye, Bee." And he was gone.

Bee sat in the chair beside the bassinette. "Oh, I hope I didn't scare him off."

"No," I replied, and, trying to excuse his strange behavior, I added, "He had things to do, like registering the baby's birth. We're calling him Cameron Ryan."

"That's a wonderful name. So, who is Winston?"

"Oh, that's just a joke. Ryan thinks our son looks like a miniature Winston Churchill."

"He does not! He's beautiful, Vicki. Absolutely perfect."

But he is handsome, not beautiful, I thought.

CHAPTER 21 (VICKI)

After a wonderful week of rest and being pampered in the maternity ward at the Royal Jubilee Hospital, plus a constant stream of visitors, I went home to Providence with our son.

That's when everything changed. Ryan didn't seem at all thrilled to have a son and took little interest in him. We had turned the room opposite ours into a nursery so I could hear Cameron in the night, but even though I was exhausted, Ryan never offered to get up and change him at night. He wore ear plugs instead, so he didn't have to listen to him crying. As far as feeding him was concerned, his excuse was always, "You're the one who's nursing him, so what good would I be? When you decide to bottle-feed him, I'll help more." But he never did.

And although it was ridiculous, he even resented me nursing him. I often caught him watching me as Cameron sucked on my breast and we rocked together in the rocking chair. "Lucky little bugger," he said one day. Was he even jealous of our son?

So, though I had more than enough milk to feed two babies, to appease my husband I decided to change Cameron over to formula when he was three months old. Unfortunately, the radical change turned him into a very colicky baby, whereas before he was always content.

After a while, something about Ryan's attitude also put off any friends stopping by. Even Bee or Mary always phoned before coming, despite being just down the hall in the suite, and then they only came when Ryan was at work. I began to feel very lonely. I never left the house, other than to stroll in the garden with Cameron in his buggy.

One day, Ryan came home early while I was in the garden, talking to our gardener. He waved me over to the front veranda.

"What are you talking to Parker about?" he asked.

"We were just discussing the vegetable garden for next year and if it could be extended. He also wanted to see Cameron."

"Vicki, I deal with Parker about everything in the grounds. You don't need to be discussing that with him."

"Well—I—er ..."

"Come inside now. Let's have a drink. I need one. It's been a bitch of a day."

Although I certainly didn't feel like a drink, I agreed to join him. I lifted Cameron out of his buggy to carry him inside with us.

"Can't you leave him in the buggy? He should be okay on the veranda. Nobody's going to run off with him, Vicki."

"Well, he's woken up now, so I need to feed him his bottle anyway. Perhaps you'd like to feed him, Ryan, while I get you a drink."

He hesitated for a moment and then, much to my surprise, agreed.

I hoped that holding his beautiful little son and feeding him in his arms would perhaps bond the two of them. He rarely picked Cameron up.

* * *

It worked. For the next couple of months, Ryan took a much greater interest in his son. Now he loved to show him off to people, and one day we took Cameron into his office.

By three months, Cameron was very alert, watching everything and smiling. I assumed that Ryan's earlier lack of interest was simply a case of men not being particularly intrigued by newborns, who do nothing but eat, sleep, cry and need changing.

He even welcomed Bee into our lives again, mainly to babysit, which she willingly did on a regular basis so we could have time alone together on a date. Bee was the only one I felt comfortable leaving our son with. I was still the paranoid mother of a newborn, but now that he had settled into bottle feeding, life was better. I still felt guilty for not nursing him, but as usual I agreed with Ryan to keep the peace.

While I had been nursing him, I hadn't gone back on the pill, as I believed I would not get pregnant. But now I had to decide about the wretched pill again, so at my October appointment with Dr. Phillips, I decided I would discuss it with him. Ryan had long since renewed his vigorous sexual interest in me.

On the morning of my appointment, I woke up feeling very weird. Ryan had already left for work and the baby was sleeping, so I had gone back to bed. I had to get up quickly and rush into the bathroom, where I threw up.

"Oh God no!" Surely I couldn't be pregnant again.

I staggered out of the bathroom and headed down the hall to Bee's suite.

"Bee, are you home?" I called out frantically.

She immediately opened the door. "What's wrong, Vicki? Are you sick?"

"Yes. I've just thrown up again. I have a doctor's appointment for me and Cameron this morning, but I doubt I can drive right now. I feel awful. Could it be the flu?"

She felt my forehead. "Well, you don't seem to have a fever. I can drive you both to the doctor, and I'll come in with you."

"Oh, thank you, Bee—" And then I had to run back to the bathroom again in a hurry. Bee followed a few moments later with dry crackers and water. She helped me back to my bed and said, "Do you think you could be pregnant again?'

I started to cry as I nodded my head. "That's what I'm afraid of. I feel just like I did when Cameron was on the way."

"Why are you afraid, luv? If you are pregnant, it's wonderful news."

"But Ryan will be furious," I whimpered.

"Why on earth would he be furious?"

"Because—because it's too soon, and I promised."

"Promised what?"

"That I wouldn't get pregnant again. He didn't want children in the first place, even Cameron."

"What? Well, if that's the case, he should have had one of those new vasectomies that men are getting."

"He says it's my body, so it's my responsibility."

"Good grief, Vicki. It's a joint responsibility you decide together. Didn't you want children, either?"

"God, no. I'd love to have two or three ... but not so quickly. It's my fault if I am pregnant because I haven't gone back on the pill yet. I was going to ask the doctor today about starting again. While I was nursing, I didn't think I could get pregnant."

"Well, luv, that's a bit of an old wives' tale. Anyway, the doctor will take a test, and if you are pregnant, I'm sure Ryan will be just as happy as you are. He seems to have come around with Cameron."

"So, you noticed how disinterested he was at first?"

"Yes, it was obvious. Don't worry. It will all work out. But first, let's get you ready—if the nausea has worn off—and then wake up Cameron and we'll head to the doctor."

As if on cue, Cameron started to cry. "I'll take care of him, luv. If you feel able, you jump in the shower and get dressed."

What would I do without her, I thought. "I feel a bit better now. Thank you, Bee."

With the help of the crackers, my stomach settled down and the shower refreshed me. I still felt an inner dread, though. How could I possibly tell Ryan another baby was on the way, and how on earth would I manage two infants only a year apart in age?

We drove downtown to Dr. Phillips' office, and after I told him my symptoms, he took a urine sample and examined me. The nurse brought the results back immediately this time.

"Well, no need to go back on the pill just yet, Vicki," the doctor said with a smile. "The sample is positive. It appears you are about six weeks pregnant. Your second baby should be here in early August next year."

CHAPTER 22

I was silent in the car all the way home, despite Bee's assurances that all would be fine. I dreaded telling Ryan, and this time I knew for sure the conversation would be difficult.

For once, he was home early and seemed in a good mood. "How is my beautiful wife and our handsome little boy today?"

"We're both fine," I said.

"Any chance we could get Bee to babysit tonight? I'd like to take you out for dinner, so stop whatever you are preparing and go and get changed while I play with Cam."

"That sounds lovely, Ryan, but I need to tell you something first. We could go out for dinner and celebrate after that."

"Celebrate? What are we celebrating?"

I paused. It was now or never. "I was at the doctor this morning," I began.

"Oh right, your checkup. How did it go?"

"It went well. Cameron is healthy and doing well and I'm—"

"Are you all right?"

"Yes, very all right."

"Well, that is definitely something to celebrate, Vicki."

"I'm also—pregnant again."

"WHAT?"

"The doctor took a test, and it was positive. Oh Ryan, I'm so sorry. I didn't mean for this to happen. I know you didn't want another baby—not so soon, anyway—but maybe it could be a good thing. Get it over with, and we'll have two children close in age—maybe two boys." I knew I was babbling, my words running together like water over a waterfall.

He glared at me for the longest time. "How could you possibly be pregnant again? What kind of a stupid pill are you taking that allowed this to happen?"

"I haven't gone back on the pill yet," I admitted. "That's what I was going to ask the doctor about today, but then this morning I threw up again, so—"

"You threw up again? Why didn't you tell me before? And you aren't on the pill? What the hell is the matter with you?"

"I thought I couldn't get pregnant again while I was nursing."

"But you stopped nursing weeks ago!" He was shouting now.

"I'm so sorry, Ryan. I didn't mean for this to happen. I know we agreed to wait."

"Well, I thought we agreed not to have any more children."

I didn't know how to respond to that, because deep down I knew Ryan had said he didn't want any more. I had just hoped he would change his mind, as he had about Cameron.

"If you felt that strongly about it, you should have had a vasectomy!" I retorted.

"Oh, is that right! It's your body, Vicki, so it's your responsibility."

"It's both our responsibilities," I sobbed, repeating what Bee had said. "And I was an only child, so I don't want to inflict that on Cameron. It can be a lonely life for a child."

He turned away from me and began pacing back and forth. "You sound like my mother, who couldn't have another child after Todd, so she adopted me to be his playmate. I was just the substitute."

"What are you talking about, Ryan?"

"You planned this all along, didn't you? It seems I only have to look at you and you get pregnant! So, you didn't bother to take any precautions. Despite what I wanted, you just went ahead and made the decision to have another baby!"

"NO! No, it wasn't like that at all. I am as surprised as you are. I didn't plan this, I promise you. But now that it's happened, I admit I am happy about it."

"So, you wouldn't consider an abortion."

I gasped. "*No*. Why would I?"

"Because I asked you to."

"How can you ask me that, Ryan? I thought you loved me. And you love Cameron, don't you? Why would we kill a perfectly healthy baby?"

"Because—because that's exactly what MY birth mother should have done, instead of having me and then giving me away!"

With that, he ran out of the kitchen, calling behind him, "Forget about going out for dinner. I'm not in the mood now. I'm going for a drive to clear my head."

I suddenly realized that my husband was obviously sick in the head to have said such a thing. Something was making him very illogical. Did he imagine his "sickness" could be inherited? Was that it? But that didn't make any sense, because before now he had always believed he was right about everything. Even when his temper got out of hand and I suggested taking an anger management course, he said there was nothing wrong with him.

I knew I couldn't fight this because I simply didn't understand it. I sat, speechless, at the kitchen table for a long time and cried until I had no more tears left.

* * *

Two hours later, he returned. He had calmed down considerably but still didn't look particularly happy.

"Okay, Vicki. I've decided we'll have this child. But that is it. NO MORE!"

I breathed a sigh of relief. "I swear, Ryan. No more. I'll go back on the pill right after the baby is born. I promise."

His moment of vulnerability had disappeared, and he was back in control. I didn't question him this time but simply accepted what he said, because I desperately wanted this baby that was growing inside me. I was determined that Cameron would not be an only child.

The next morning, I had a phone call from Sam that overjoyed me.

"Guess what!" she began.

"I know by the sound of your voice that it must be something good," I replied.

"Oh, Vicki, it is. I'm pregnant."

"WHAT? Sam, that's wonderful. When are you due?"

"August."

"No! That's incredible ... because I'm pregnant again too, and I'm due in late August as well. Sam, this is wonderful. Our children will be best friends."

"Wow. You guys didn't waste much time having another baby. Is Ryan happy about it?"

"Of course, why wouldn't he be?" I snapped. "Isn't Jack happy?"

"Yes, he's delirious, but ..."

"But what?"

"Oh, nothing ..."

"But what?" I insisted.

"I just got the impression he wasn't happy about you becoming pregnant last time, but perhaps I'm wrong."

I sighed. She always somehow could see the truth. "You're right, Sam. He's not into newborns but look how he is with Cam now. He adores him."

"But another one so soon?"

"Get it over with quickly is the idea."

"Is it?"

"Leave it alone, Sam!"

"Sorry, Vic. I just hope everything is all right. Sometimes you seem a bit down."

"Don't worry. I'm fine. I think it was a bit of postpartum depression last time, that's all. I'll be fine with this one."

I hoped that I was right. Sam sounded so happy about her news. She knew that Jack supported her and was just as happy as she was. I wished I could be that confident about Ryan.

CHAPTER 23

The next months passed quickly. I was glad I had Sam and Bee to talk to about the baby's arrival, because Ryan ignored the whole thing. As I grew larger, he lost interest in me again. But at least he was spending more time with Cameron, and this pleased me.

As a wet spring turned into another very hot summer, Sam and I often sat together on the veranda at Providence, comparing notes about our pregnancies. Bee was very handy with a sewing machine, and she made us both some long muumuus and loose peasant blouses for our expanding bodies. With the addition of headbands and long beads, we looked like two pregnant hippies, even though the Swinging Sixties were over.

During my seventh month of pregnancy, I began to suspect that Ryan might be having an affair. I had absolutely no proof, just a suspicion, as he began to come home later and even take overnight trips to Vancouver, ostensibly on business. I closed my eyes to it and made excuses to myself. I was sure I must be paranoid.

Early on the morning of August 3, Jack phoned us to say that Sam had delivered a baby girl weighing a healthy seven pounds, and they were both doing well. Ryan had left for work already, so I asked Bee to drive me to the hospital to visit Sam that afternoon.

The baby was to be called Isabella (Bella) Susan, and she was beautiful.

"I hope mine is a girl too, Sam," I said. "Then they will be best friends, I'm sure."

I had to wait until the end of August before I went into labour, and on the very last day of the month, I also delivered a daughter. She came into the world very quickly, and the delivery was much easier for me than last time.

"You must be happy now you have one of each," were Ryan's first words when he came to the hospital.

"Yes, I am. I hope you are, too."

"As long as this is the last kid we're having," he replied. "Maybe you should get a tubal ligation now."

I was only in my mid-twenties, and, although I was sure I would have to be content with just two children, I did not want to make that decision right now.

"I'll think about it, Ryan," I replied. "Now, what shall we name our daughter?" We hadn't discussed names before she was born, but I wanted to include Ryan in the decision. Once again, he showed no interest in names.

"Choose whatever you like."

"I like Kaitlyn, with a 'k'. Do you?"

"That'll be fine."

"How about Kaitlyn Victoria Foster? It sounds very grand."

He nodded as he gazed out of the window. He had barely looked at our baby. "I'll go home and get Cameron from Bee and bring him in later."

"Oh, yes. He will love to see his baby sister."

* * *

For my second birth, I remained in hospital for only five days. Kaitlyn and I were doing well, and I soon recovered. I went back on the pill immediately and started Kaitlyn on formula. I felt guilty about not nursing her, but again, I wanted to please my husband. It all seemed to work best that way, and Ryan seemed happier as time passed. He spent even more time with Cameron once he started to walk and say his first words. Ryan was content to leave me alone with Kaitlyn.

One weekend in early January 1973, after a heavy snow, Ryan took Cam outside to play in it. They were laughing as they made snow angels together, and I finally felt at peace. Perhaps it was simply newborn babies Ryan disliked. I was convinced that once Kaitlyn grew up, he would also show interest in her.

However, the next morning, when I came downstairs to breakfast, Ryan had folded the newspaper on the table at my place. The headline read: *Roe v. Wade: Women allowed legal abortions in the U.S.*

"Read it," he said. "Just in case you happen to get pregnant again!"

"Oh, Ryan, not that again. I won't get pregnant, I promise, but accidents sometimes happen."

"Well, get your damn tubes tied, then, and then there will be no accidents!" His anger was back.

He picked up the coffee pot and threw it across the floor, narrowly missing Cam sitting in his highchair. Both Cam and Kaitlyn, who I was holding in my arms, started to bawl.

Just as quickly as his anger had arisen, it disappeared. Ignoring me, he ran over to Cameron. "Cam, I'm so sorry," he said. "I dropped the pot. I didn't mean to throw it like that." His words calmed Cameron down. Figuring this was some sort of game, he picked up his bowl and threw it down on the floor. They both started laughing.

I felt a fury of my own enveloping me, though I'd been conditioned by now to accept these outbursts. Kaitlyn was still crying, and I left the kitchen with her. It seemed the best thing to do.

I wanted to retort, but I knew it would be pointless.

* * *

After that outburst, things got better again, so I chose to let it pass.

During 1973 and 1974, Bee and I studied for our Canadian citizenship. We took the test, which turned out to be relatively easy, and at the end of 1974 we were invited to the Citizenship Court in the city to be sworn in as citizens.

Ryan said he had to work that day, but Mary and Sam both offered to come to the ceremony and bring all the children with them—which was quite a handful. Keeping a three-and-a-half-year-old boy and a couple of two-year-old girls happy through the whole ceremony was quite a feat, but they succeeded, and it all went well. I was now a Canadian—something I wished my husband had been there to witness and be a part of. Swearing allegiance to Her Majesty the Queen seemed a no-brainer. I had always been a monarchist.

I was grateful that the next few years were reasonably good. As Cameron grew, his interest in all sports became apparent, and this delighted Ryan. He wanted to encourage him to play football, or soccer, as it was called in Canada. They both loved to kick a ball around on the lawns of Providence.

Kaitlyn, however, was not particularly interested. She loved to dance and play the piano, and I decided that once she was old enough, I would enroll her in lessons.

In the outside world, after years of anti-war protests and a 1973 peace accord that took the U.S. out of the fight, the Vietnam War finally ended in April 1975 with the south's capitulation.

It wasn't until Sam visited one afternoon with Isabella that I realized I had been closing my eyes to so many red flags in my marriage.

* * *

Our two daughters did not like each other. Little Bella obviously wanted to play with Kaitlyn, but every time she offered her a toy, Kaitlyn threw it aside and ignored it. I was embarrassed by her behavior and reprimanded her.

"Don't blame Kaitlyn," Sam said. "She just doesn't know Bella and probably feels threatened by her. They haven't had a chance to really get to know one another, as we aren't allowed to come over much ..." Her voice trailed off.

"What? But I'd love you to come over more."

"Well, Ryan has made it clear we are not welcome. Bee thinks the same, Vicki."

"That's not the case, Sam."

She looked at me a long time before replying. "Vicki, we're worried about you."

"Why?"

"Because you are in denial, sweetie."

"Denial about what, for goodness' sake?"

"Your husband."

I felt she was being unreasonable. I saw her so infrequently that I didn't want to turn this visit into an argument. "My husband! Whatever do you mean?"

"Vicki, he's turned you into a different person. When you and I first met, you were full of life and so much fun—but now ..."

"Now what?"

"Vicki, I love you, but I simply have to say this. Ryan is treating you so badly. He's monopolizing you and controlling everything you do. I hate to say anything, but I'm honestly worried. Bee has tried to talk to you too, but you have shut her out of your life. And we've both seen Ryan's temper flare-ups. Has he ever harmed you physically? Or the children?"

"Good grief, *no!*" I was almost screaming at her. "Why are you saying these crazy things, Sam?" But I remembered only too well Ryan's temper outbursts and the day he threw the coffee pot across the kitchen, narrowly missing Cameron.

"I'm not trying to hurt you, honey, but Ryan's behavior is very strange. Often the person living with a narcissistic partner cannot see it."

"What the hell do you mean by that? Ryan and I are fine. We understand one another, and we're happy."

"But are *you* really happy?"

"Yes, of course," I replied, bewildered by her insistence. I could feel a tear escaping, so I turned my head away.

"You are a dear friend, Vicki, so please talk to Bee about your feelings. She wants to help you without interfering."

I pulled myself together and turned back towards her. "There is nothing to help me with. I'm fine."

But that night I looked up narcissism in one of our encyclopedias. I realized I knew nothing about it. I discovered that a British essayist and physician named Havelock Ellis had identified it as a mental disorder as far back as 1898. It was described as a "God-complex." The narcissist is filled with self-importance or self-admiration and lies about many things, believing they are always right.

The disorder, Ellis said, could be the result of genetics, or a parent-child relationship where they were over-compensated, but it was always characterized by an inflated ego and a constant need for attention.

Many of the symptoms in the definition exactly described Ryan. The sad part, I learned, is that narcissism can't be cured.

I decided I could handle it. I had to, because I loved Ryan, and I couldn't bear the thought of leaving him. I desperately wanted us to be a happy family, so instead I turned into an enabler.

* * *

Things continued smoothly for a few more years as our children grew. In mid-August 1977, news came that rock legend Elvis Presley had died at Graceland. He was only forty-two. This depressed me, and I wrote a long letter to Judy in England, as I realized we had also grown apart. We had both loved Elvis Presley's music, and it was part of our early friendship growing up. We never had made that trip to England as a family, mainly because Ryan had no desire to go there. So, my friendship with Judy had lapsed through the years.

That piece of world news on August 16 became, for some reason, the last thing I really remember clearly before the next storm came in and destroyed my peace of mind.

* * *

One morning in mid-September, I woke up feeling sick. I barely made it to the bathroom before I vomited. Nothing would stay in my stomach except some ginger ale and a few crackers. I couldn't eat any breakfast. I was also ten days late!

Oh no, I thought. *How could this be happening? I can't be pregnant. Ryan will be furious.*

But by the end of the month, I knew I should make a doctor's appointment. Without telling Bee why, I asked her to babysit the children and headed downtown. As usual, she agreed without question. Mrs. Potter had died two years earlier, and Bee and Mary had moved into the vacant Lodge. With our permission, they had converted the upstairs into a two-bedroom suite, with an antiques store below. It was a charming addition to the Providence estate, and Ryan had been pleased simply that they had left the house and moved—even a short distance away. But I had missed them being close by.

The doctor confirmed my suspicions. My third baby was due the following May.

That night, I knew I could not put off telling Ryan any longer. I waited until both the children were asleep, and we were in our bedroom watching an episode of *The Beachcombers* on television.

"Ryan, I need to tell you something, and I don't think you will be very happy." My heart was beating fast. Would he fly into a temper? Would he hurt me? Would he insist I have an abortion this time? I was now thirty-four, so my pregnancy was already considered "geriatric"!

"What is it?"

No point in beating around the bush. "I'm pregnant again."

"WHAT?" He leapt up off the couch and glared down at me. "How the hell did that happen? Is it mine?"

"Ryan, how can you ask me such a thing? Of course it's yours. I have been on the pill, so it is a miracle ... "

"A MIRACLE! Goddamn it, it's a catastrophe. How could you do this to me again? You promised it would never happen again. I asked you to get your tubes tied, but you refused." He was shouting now.

"Well, if you felt that strongly about it, you should have had a vasectomy, like I told you before."

"I told you, it's YOUR responsibility, not mine."

He was pacing around the room now, still shouting while spewing his anger at me. "I need to get some air." He opened the bedroom door and began to run down the corridor. I trailed behind him, with tears pouring down my face.

"Quit whining, Vicki. Get an abortion! Don't bother me again about babies, babies, babies. I can't stand it. You know I never even wanted Kaitlin." He ran down the stairs and out the door, slamming it behind him, leaving me sobbing on the landing.

That's when I heard a sound behind me. Our shouting had woken Kaitlyn. She was rushing towards me in tears. She had overheard everything.

PART TWO

Finding Strength

(1979-1996)
(KAITLYN, VICKI, CALEB)

CHAPTER 24 (KAITLYN)

Mummy was crying because Daddy had left us. Their loud voices woke me up. Cam always slept through everything, but I didn't. The wind blowing in the trees, winter thunderstorms, heavy rain and their arguments always woke me up. And so, without thinking, I jumped out of bed and went outside to see what was happening. Daddy was running down the stairs by then, saying he didn't want another baby and he had never even wanted *me*, and mummy was crying, so I cried too.

I flung myself at her, hugging her tightly as she bent down to comfort me.

"Kaitlyn, it's okay," she said, hugging me back. "Go back to bed, darling."

"But Daddy left. He said he never wanted me, and that makes sense, because he never pays any attention to me or anything I say or do. He must hate me, so I hate him, too."

"Oh, Kaitlyn, he didn't mean it. He doesn't hate you. He loves you. He was just upset about something else."

"Was it about you having another baby, Mummy? I heard you say that. I hope so, because I want a little sister. Cam never plays with me. Brothers stink!"

"No, they don't, sweetheart. And yes, I am having another baby. It's a bit of a surprise for us both, as we didn't plan to have any more babies, but it will all be fine. We will all love this baby too, whether it's a boy or a girl."

"Is the baby in your tummy now?"

"Yes, but it's still very tiny."

"How did it get in there?"

"I'll explain that to you when you're a lot older, but for now we should go back to bed."

"I'm going to have nightmares, Mummy. I don't want to go to sleep. Can I stay with you in your bed? You'll be lonely if Daddy doesn't come back."

"All right, Kaitlyn," she said.

We cuddled together under the covers, but I knew she was still crying quietly because I could hear her sniffles. How could Daddy do that to us? I decided that I really did hate him.

* * *

The next morning, when I woke, I was back in my own bed. I don't remember being carried back, but maybe Daddy had come home and was in their bed.

I crept out of my own bed into their room, but the bed was empty. Had they both left me? I ran next door to Cam's room, but he was still sound asleep. Oh no, we had both been left. We were orphans.

I ran down the stairs, calling out frantically, "Mummy, where are you? Are you still here?"

I found her in the hall below. "It's okay, baby. I'm right here. I was just making our breakfast in the kitchen."

I followed her into the kitchen, and I was surprised to see Daddy sitting at the table, eating scrambled eggs and bacon.

"Daddy, you're here!" I didn't know whether to be pleased or disappointed.

"Of course I'm here," he said. "Come and sit up at the table and eat your breakfast, Katy girl."

He was acting as if nothing had happened last night, and neither was Mummy. I couldn't believe it. Did I imagine it all? And he had called me 'Katy-girl,' which he rarely did.

I decided I would ask Mummy later. Perhaps there wasn't even a baby coming after all.

* * *

However, as time went by, Mummy's tummy got bigger, and as the weather got warmer the following spring, she had to go to hospital to have the baby taken out of her stomach.

Later, Aunt Bee took Cameron and me to the hospital to meet the new baby, my baby brother. Mummy called him Caleb Harrison, which seemed a very fancy name for such a little fellow. Cam was thrilled he had a brother and said he couldn't wait until they could play ball together, but I was disappointed.

When Mummy brought him home to Providence, I spent a lot of time sitting beside his cradle, singing to him, which he seemed to like. I'm not sure if he was smiling or passing gas, but he certainly seemed happy. I was fascinated by his tiny hands and fingers and those little toes. Every day I grew to love him more. I decided that if Mummy and Daddy didn't want him, he would become my baby.

"Little Cally," I said to him one day, "I will take care of you always. If Mummy or Daddy don't love you, I will be here for you always, I promise."

It was true that Daddy spent very little time with him, but Mummy made excuses for that. She said Daddy just didn't like newborn babies. *Then why doesn't he like me much, either? I'm not a baby anymore.*

I was fascinated by Cally. He was so tiny and helpless. All he did was cry, eat and sleep. I often fed him his bottle, and although I was not yet quite seven, I was the only one who could quiet him. I hated it when I had to leave him to go to school, so I asked if I could take him for "show and tell."

"Maybe when he's a bit older, Kaitlyn," Mummy said. "When you go into Grade 2 next September, we can bring him in. He'll be a few months old by then."

I had to be content with that. At least I would be home to protect him all summer when school was out.

CHAPTER 25 (VICKI)

Kaitlyn had finally fallen asleep in my arms on that dreadful night I told Ryan about being pregnant again.

Thankfully he had returned to the house soon after midnight in a much better mood, so I carried Kaitlyn back to her own bed, and Ryan and I talked for a while. He made me promise him faithfully that once this baby was born, I would have a tubal ligation. At that point, I would have promised him anything rather than face his raging temper again. He seemed satisfied after that, and peace reigned once again.

By the time Kaitlyn came running down the stairs for breakfast, Ryan was in a much better mood. Not only had he accepted the situation, but he seemed to be happy about it. Why had his mood changed so quickly? I wondered. He was such a challenging man to understand, with all these mood swings. Was he sick? Did he have some kind of mental illness? But once again, I ignored the red flags and simply enjoyed the good moments on a day-by-day basis.

When the baby arrived on May 5, 1979, it was another boy. Before I left the hospital, I had a relatively easy tubal ligation surgery, just as I had promised Ryan. We had three beautiful, healthy children, and I was happy.

This time, I chose a name without consulting Ryan, given his lack of interest. I named him after my two dads, Caleb (my biological father) and Harrison or Harry (the father who raised me). Kaitlyn was disappointed at first that she didn't have a sister, but as the months passed, she became obsessed with Caleb. She called him Cally, a nickname we all eventually adopted. She called him *her* baby and spent hours sitting beside his crib, singing and chatting to him. It always calmed him down after a crying fit, so I was grateful for her help.

I convinced myself that we were indeed a happy family again. But as the months went by, I knew Sam and Bee were probably as puzzled about our marriage as I was. Bee called on me occasionally, but never when Ryan was there, and Sam simply stopped coming. I didn't really blame either of them, even though at one time we had all been so close. But it made me sad, as I was lonely most of the time. My only company seemed to be Ryan and the children, which obviously suited him.

The following year, on one particularly hot Saturday in April, I was sitting outside on the veranda feeding Cally when the phone rang. Ryan had gone fishing with a friend. Cameron and Kaitlyn were playing soccer on the lawn but were having an argument about whose turn it was next to be in goal. Kaitlyn was screaming at her brother, and Cally was being fussy in my arms.

I reached for the remote phone beside me while trying at the same time to tell all my children to be quiet. "Hello."

"Hello there. Is that Victoria Hamilton?" The voice had what sounded like an Australian accent.

Who was this? I had never used the name 'Hamilton.'

"No, this is Vicki Foster. Maybe you have the wrong number."

"No, I don't think so, not if you live in Victoria in a house called Providence. I'm sorry, I didn't know your married name, and I apologize for interrupting you like this." She laughed briefly. "Sounds like you have a brood of children around in the background."

"I do, so I don't have time to talk right now."

"That's fine. I wondered if I could come and meet you and see Providence while I'm over here in Victoria. Maybe on Monday morning, if you're available? My name is Sylvia—Sylvia Watson."

"Why do you want to meet me?"

"Because we are related. We are second cousins."

* * *

I was both intrigued and astounded, so I agreed to have her come over on Monday morning for coffee at ten o'clock. The children would be in school, and Ryan would be at work. It would be only Cally and me at home. But once I put the phone down, I picked it up again and called Bee. I needed to discuss this with her and ask her to be there, too. The whole thing sounded very odd, because I knew I didn't have any cousins or second cousins.

Bee agreed to come early on Monday, and true to her word, she walked up from the cottage soon after nine. Ryan had left for the office, so we sat out on the veranda together.

"Is something wrong, sweetheart?" she began.

"No, it's nothing like that. I just need you here when I have a visitor at ten."

"A visitor?"

"I don't mean to be mysterious, but it's all a bit strange. A woman called me on Friday and wants to meet me and see Providence. She says we are second cousins."

"What? Well, you don't have any cousins or second cousins on the Graham side. What's her name?"

"Sylvia Watson, and she had an Australian accent, which is what bothered me. Remember the story in Jane's journals about my grandmother Sarah's brother, Bertie, who married that awful Antoinette woman? Then she left him and ran off with an Australian chap with lots of money."

"Yes, I do."

"Well, she was pregnant when she left and told Bertie it was the Australian's baby, but could it be that it was really his baby?"

"Oh my goodness. Could she be claiming a right to own Providence?"

"That's what I was thinking, so I need you here to support me."

"Did you tell Ryan about this?"

"Goodness no. He'd have a fit. I want to find out more before I mention it to him."

Bee shook her head, as if she couldn't understand why I wouldn't share this with my husband. "Well, Vicki, she can't possibly have any claim to Jane's house or money. After all, Jane named *you* in her will. So, try not to worry. I will certainly stay with you. I'll go and put the coffee pot on, and we can sit out here with her and find out what she wants."

* * *

At exactly ten o'clock, a grey BMW rental car drove up the driveway and parked in front of the house. An attractive woman in her late forties or early fifties stepped out. She was dressed in an expensive beige pant suit and a peach silk blouse, and everything about her screamed wealth.

Thankfully, Cally was fast asleep in his buggy on the veranda, so I stood up to greet her.

"Hello, I'm Vicki Foster. You must be Sylvia Watson."

She came towards me and, ignoring my outstretched hand, put her arms around me and gave me a big hug. "It's lovely to meet you, Vicki, and to finally see Providence. The house is charming." Diamond and ruby rings adorned her fingers.

"I'm sorry, I'm confused. Who are you?"

Bee joined us on the veranda with a tray of coffee and biscuits. "Yes," she agreed. "We are intrigued. We don't think we have a relative called Sylvia Watson. By the way, I'm Beth, Vicki's aunt."

"Oh, Beth, it's lovely to meet you, too. I will explain everything. I apologize for being so mysterious, but I only found out about all this a year ago myself, just before my father died. Then, when my husband and I planned a trip to Canada this year, I decided I must visit Victoria and introduce myself."

I indicated a chair, and Bee poured us all a coffee. Sylvia Watson seemed pleasant enough, so I didn't feel threatened by her, but I also didn't want to be taken in by her gregarious charm.

"What did you find out?" I asked.

"Vicki, apparently your grandmother, Sarah McBride, and my grandfather, Albert McBride, were siblings."

"But Albert—or Bertie, as he was known—had no children, according to what I was told and what I read in Jane McBride's journals. So, how could you be a granddaughter?"

She laughed. "I suppose it was a bit scandalous back then. But you see, my grandfather Bertie was, as you probably know, married to *that awful Antoinette*—that's what we called her in our family. Unfortunately, she was my grandmother, I'm sorry to say, and she ran off with Cliff Sanders, the man I was told was my grandfather. Incidentally, Cliff was a lovely man and I adored him, but apparently Antoinette was already pregnant with my dad when she left Bertie in Canada."

"Yes, I heard that, but she told Bertie the baby was the Australian's, not his."

"Yes, that is what we all believed. Cliff Sanders was very wealthy—even richer than the McBrides, I'm told—and Antoinette was out for all she could get. Sadly, she let my dad believe that Cliff was his father, up until Cliff died. Then her conscience must have gotten the better of her, because before she died, she told my dad the truth—his biological father was Albert McBride."

"Really?" Bee intervened. "But how did you discover this?"

"Shortly before my dad died last year, he told me the story. He wanted me to know the truth about who his biological father was. He asked me to visit Canada one day and see the house Providence, so I would know my true roots. His mother had told him it was a lovely house, which she had wanted to own. She even admitted to him that she had treated Bertie and his family very badly. She said that Bertie was a good man."

"She certainly did treat him badly," I said. "So, what do you want now?"

Sylvia looked startled. "What do I want? Whatever do you mean?"

"Are you thinking that you should have been the one who inherited Providence?"

She burst out laughing. "Oh, goodness gracious! Is that what you thought? Vicki, I assure you, I have no intention of claiming Providence. I have more money and property in Australia than I know what to do with now, so I don't want to own more property in Canada unless we decide to buy something over here ourselves. My husband, Jim, has done very well as a sheep farmer too, so we don't need more money! Our children are both in university now, so we have an empty nest back home. This was just a friendly visit to get to know you and to see the house my real grandfather grew up in. You are the rightful owner of Providence."

I breathed a little easier, and even Bee was beginning to warm to her. After we finished our coffee, we gave her a tour of the house and grounds, and I happily regaled her with stories about the McBrides, with a special emphasis on all that I knew about the twin brothers—Albert and Edward. We planned a dinner date with her and her husband before they left on the rest of their Canadian tour.

* * *

When I told Ryan that night, he was understandably suspicious, just as Bee and I had been. But he did at least agree that we should go out to dinner with them.

We had a pleasant evening at a fancy new restaurant on the Inner Harbour and then we invited them back to Providence for a nightcap. We gave Jim Watson a tour of the house, and Ryan took him around the grounds. It appeared Jim loved heritage homes and asked Ryan if he would keep an eye out for a heritage house in Victoria for sale, suggesting that he would ask Ryan to restore it for them as a home whenever they visited Canada in future. He loved what Ryan had done at Providence. Money seemed to be no problem, and naturally Ryan was delighted at the prospect of receiving such a large commission.

I was simply amazed and relieved that Ryan had warmed to the Watsons, who were indeed a charming couple. I was sure it was the beginning of a lifetime friendship, with possible visits to Australia for us in the future.

The next morning, I told Kaitlyn about our visitors from Australia. a country she had been learning about at school.

"I hope we can go there one day, Mummy," she said.

"I hope so, too."

Cam interrupted: "But they play stupid *cricket* over there."

Kaitlyn, ever the peacemaker, said, "Well maybe you can learn cricket too, Cam, because you love all sports."

By then it was time for them to pick up their lunch boxes and head out for the walk to school, so the subject was dropped. And somehow the whole Australian episode got lost in the sands of time.

CHAPTER 26 (KAITLYN)

Of course, we never did go to Australia. Like everything my dad promised, it never happened. He didn't keep his promises to us about anything, and he often lied. I don't think he ever found a house for the Watsons, either, as he quickly lost interest in the whole thing. I know Mom continued to write to the Australian lady, but that was the extent of their friendship, even though Mom had seemed excited about it. I wondered how she put up with Dad. They were always arguing about something, but she always gave in.

As I grew older, I decided I would be a free spirit, a free thinker, and a rebel. I wouldn't be submissive to a man, like my mother was. No one seemed to care, anyway, so my path of intentional rebellion suited me perfectly. My dad paid little attention to what I was doing at school and was only concerned with Cam and how brilliant he was at all sports. Cam was also very smart academically and got good grades in every subject. I hated sports but I loved art, and it was the only subject I excelled at. I was pretty good, if I do say so myself. At least Mum occasionally praised my work. I decided that one day I would be a famous artist and live in an attic in Paris.

Cally was fascinated when I drew pictures for him, and by the time he was three years old, he was copying me. He seemed to have a natural talent for art, like me. When I was ten, I asked Mom and Dad if I could have art classes outside school. Mom agreed immediately, but Dad made fun of the idea.

"Kaitlyn, you'll never get anywhere in life being an artist, and you're teaching that little boy to be a sissy."

"Why? Just because he likes to draw?" I challenged.

"Boys should be interested in other activities. Sports, like Cam, for instance."

That infuriated me. "Of course, YOU would think that. Cam, Cam, Cam! All the time. Sports, sports, sports."

Mom intervened. "Kat don't talk to your father like that. He was just expressing an opinion."

Everyone called me Kat now, except Dad. Cally had started it when he first learned to talk. He couldn't say my name and would call me Kitty Kat at first. And then it just became Kat. I liked it and felt it suited my new personality. Right then, though, I wondered why Mom was defending Dad. She always said I was a good artist, and she loved it when I drew things for Cally.

Why didn't she stand up to Dad and say that art would *not* turn him into a sissy?

* * *

I didn't have any friends at school, other than Julie Barnes, who lived in a house on the "estate"—the houses built on land further along the Arm that had once belonged to the McBride family but had been sold off to developers by Mom and Dad.

It was a nice subdivision. I suppose, but the word "estate" made it sound too grand to me. Mom preferred to call it a subdivision because in England the word *estate* usually referred to a collection of similar lower-class houses. These houses were all different and were very nice, in my opinion. They were more in keeping with living in the 1970s and 1980s than Providence was. Providence reeked of old money from the last century, and it was so old-fashioned. I liked more modern houses.

One thing I couldn't figure out was how Julie's mom, a single mother with six children to support, could afford to live there!

"One of Mom's boyfriends bought the house for us," Julie told me one day. "Then he left her. I don't think they were ever married, but he is the dad of two of my siblings. My own dad left long before that, and I don't even know who he was. My other three little sisters all have different dads, too. Mom's boyfriends come and go, but the last one stayed way longer than most, and he helped Mom support us all."

"Good Lord," I replied. "I didn't know that. I wondered about your dad—or dads! I wish my dad would leave us. How did you make your dads go?"

"I didn't. They just went. There one day and gone the next. Sometimes Mom kicked them out."

"Wish mine would just go, too. Or Mom would kick him out." We were sitting in the gazebo in the garden, where Julie loved to come after school. Her mom never seemed to care where she went. Julie was even more of a free spirit than me.

"Hey, Kat, why don't you have any piercings?" Julie asked me suddenly.

"Mom said I can get my ears pierced when I turn thirteen, but that's two years away. I could never have any others, like you do."

"Good grief. I had my ears pierced when I was a toddler. Since then, I've had one in my belly button and one for the ring in my nose!"

I envied her. To me, getting piercings made her seem very exotic.

"Why wait until you're thirteen, Kat? I know a place in town where we could go and get you pierced easily. Why bother to ask your mom?"

"Well, she might agree about the ears, but nothing else, and Dad would kill me!"

"He couldn't do much to you once it was done. You say he never notices you anyway, so he probably wouldn't even see it."

"True," I said.

"Well. Let's go one day next week. And after that, we'll talk about some tats!"

God, I felt so adventurous. Piercings and tattoos! That would certainly annoy my dad—and maybe even make him take notice of me for a change.

* * *

"Oh Kaitlyn, you disobeyed me," Mom said. "I told you I would take you to have your ears pierced when you were thirteen, to a reputable place. Some of those shady places use infected needles."

"Good grief, Mom. I'll be twelve in two months, so it's not far off. All the girls at school have pierced ears. It's no big deal. Julie even has three. And she's never had an infection."

"And if Julie jumped off a cliff, would you do that, too?"

"Of course not. And she wouldn't do that, anyway. She's happy and would never try and kill herself by doing something stupid. She's just a free spirit."

"Yes, and that's what worries me. I've seen the tattoos on her arm."

"She has one on her back, too!"

"Really? Well, don't even think about it. Young people who get them never think about how their skin will look when they're older and their skin shrinks. The tattoos will look awful then."

"Never thought about that. Anyway, I only got my ears pierced."

"I guess it's okay, Kat, but please don't do anything else without our permission."

Dad didn't even notice my pierced ears. It was always the same. He hardly ever even looked at me. Cally loved it, though. He had turned five and was a sweet little boy, and he adored me and Julie. He loved being with us. Like me, he didn't seem to have made any friends at pre-school and he would be starting kindergarten at the elementary school in September. I'd only be there to look out for him for another year before Julie and I would head to the high school where Cam already was a student.

"Julie," I said, one day after school a few months later. "Where did you go to get your tattoos? I want to go, too."

"Hey, Kat! Good for you. Let's go next Monday after school. I can get you a good deal. Can you come up with about twenty dollars?"

"I guess."

"Now let's decide what you should get—and where."
"I want it to show, so my dad will notice it. How about on my arm? And I want something to do with art—perhaps a paintbrush?"

"Boooring! No, if you want to make a statement you have to choose something dramatic, like a phrase or a word that means something."

"Freedom! That's what I want, so that will be my tattoo word."

I took a $20 bill out of the box Mom kept in the kitchen for what she called "incidentals." I didn't think of it as stealing because, to my way of thinking, my tattoo was an essential incidental.

And maybe this time Dad would notice me, I thought.

CHAPTER 27 (KATLYN)

He noticed me all right. That night, the storm broke. And for once, I was the center of his rage. I had certainly got his attention.

"What the hell is that on your arm, Kaitlyn?" he said suddenly.

We were eating dinner when Dad spotted it. Mom looked at me in horror. She had only just seen it, too. Cam was laughing, and Cally looked terrified. He knew how Dad was when he had one of his violent tempers.

"It's a tattoo. I love it."

"Well, you can get it taken off immediately. Vicki, why did you let her do that?"

"I told her she was not allowed to get a tattoo. I warned her."

"Obviously your warning did not work on her. Kaitlyn, go to your room immediately. I will discuss this with you later. Cam and Cally, you can both leave too, once you've finished your dinner."

I knew what that meant. He would vent all his anger on Mom, and she would be blamed. I didn't want that to happen.

"Dad, Mom told me not to get a tattoo, but I disobeyed her. It's all my fault."

"It certainly is, Kaitlyn, and you should have listened to her. Vicki, you should have told me that Kaitlyn had asked you. Secrets are wrong. Now, go to your room, young lady."

I left, knowing he would still take it out on Mom. Whatever I said, I could never win. Mom just needed to stand up for herself.

* * *

I waited and waited for Dad to come up and reprimand me, but he never did. Once again, he had lost interest in my tattoo and in me.

I assume that instead he had vented all his anger on Mom, because I could hear his raised voice downstairs. Then there was just silence. How I wished she would kick him out or he would simply go and leave us all in peace.

The following September, Julie and I started high school, and we began to notice cute boys. I had just turned thirteen and was one of the last in my class to get my monthly period, which made me have weird feelings about the opposite sex. A lot of girls at school claimed they had kissed a boy, and some even boasted they had allowed a boy to touch their breasts. Mine were only just developing, so I couldn't figure out why a boy would want to touch them anyway.

The boys at school were attracted to both Julie and me because we loved to flirt. Julie just laughed it off and teased them all, except for my brother Cam, whom she really seemed to like. The only boy I liked was Billy Jenkins. He was in our class, even though he was a year older than us because he'd had to repeat a grade. He wasn't too smart, but I was attracted to him because he seemed more mature than his fifteen years. He obviously liked me too, so just before my fourteenth birthday I let him kiss me. It felt good. I had to stop him after that, as he obviously wanted more than just a kiss.

"Kat, watch that one. He's dangerous," Julie told me one day. "I've heard he's into drugs too."

"Geez, Jules, I thought you and I were free spirits. What's wrong with trying a little marijuana?"

"Cam told me it's the gateway drug to others like heroin and cocaine. It certainly was for my mom, so I vowed I would never start drugs."

"Oh yeah, my perfect brother would say that, wouldn't he? Jules, he's turned you into a miss prissy."

"Well, he's right, Kat. Since I've been going out with him, I understand that it's better to be healthy. Having watched my mom's downward spiral, I think I always believed it, deep down."

"Going *out* with him! What?"

"Well, we went to the movies one night, and he always wants me to come and watch his games."

Suddenly I felt hurt. I always thought she came home with me because she liked me, and I was her best friend. But now I see that Cam was the big attraction. It made me want to spend even more time with dangerous Billy.

* * *

By the end of Grade 10, Billy and I were an item. I knew deep inside I was going down a dangerous path when he encouraged me to smoke and then got me to try what he called "pleasant, easy" drugs that would make me feel better about my life.

He was right, and I did feel better. I didn't care about anything anymore—my dad, my mom, my home, Julie, or even little Cally. I believed everything Billy told me. I was mesmerized by him. We frequently had sex, and even that was better when I was high.

Sometimes I stayed out all night with him. Twice my mom phoned the police and they tracked me down in a park where I was hanging out with Billy and his friends. The police took me home, screaming and swearing all the way.

The only thing I felt good about was my art. Mum tried her best to get me to focus on that, but I was so hooked on Billy that nothing she said made sense to me anymore.

"Are you on the pill?" she asked me one day.

"Of course, Mom, I'm not stupid."

"Well, I wish you had come to me, and we could have talked about it first."

"Why? You weren't so smart about the pill, obviously, because you had two more children after Cam that Dad didn't want."

"How dare you say that, Kat! I might have at least advised you to wait until you met someone worthy of you."

I laughed. "*Worthy* of me? What makes you think I'm worthy of anyone? Dad hates me. You go along with him all the time and never have an opinion of your own. Cam is obsessed with sports and now with Julie, so I don't even have a girlfriend anymore. Only Cally loves me, but he probably doesn't like me very much right now. I'm just a total loser."

I started to feel tears forming, so I walked away and went outside. I sat in the gazebo on my own for a long time because I didn't want to be vulnerable and let her see me crying.

* * *

At the end of Grade 11, Billy told me he was leaving school and wouldn't bother graduating. He asked me to leave too and move in with him.

"Where would we move?" I asked.

"I'd find us a place, babe. I have connections."

That sounded thrilling to me.

My grades were so bad that I was sure I wouldn't graduate anyway, so I thought it might be a good plan to leave school also. I wouldn't turn seventeen until the end of August, so when Mom heard that I wanted to leave, she arranged an appointment with the school counsellor before school broke for the summer. Dad didn't seem to care what I did.

"Kaitlyn, you really should complete Grade 12," Mrs. Barlow, the school guidance counsellor, told me, as I knew she would. "Graduating would help you win a scholarship to art school."

"I don't need a scholarship. My parents could afford to send me."

"Well, why don't you want to do that? Why do you want to leave school now?"

"Because school sucks! I hate it."

"You may feel that way now, but you will regret it later. You need to graduate."

"I'll think about it." I could see that both my mom and Mrs. Barlow were happy I'd said that, but I had no intention of thinking about it. I'd already made up my mind.

That night, I packed my knapsack with all my art supplies, a pad and a few other essentials and left Providence.

Billy was waiting for me, as we had planned.

CHAPTER 28 (KAITLYN)

Billy had found us a dingy one-bedroom apartment on Johnson Street, but within a week he said we should move to Vancouver, where he had "connections" for a job.

We skipped town without telling the landlord or paying the first month's rent and went on the first available ferry as walk-ons. I was a bit nervous, but Billy seemed so confident that everything would be fine. I made a quick call home before we boarded and left a message on the machine because no one was home. I said we were heading to Vancouver, and I would let them know where we were after we got settled.

"Why bother telling them?" Billy said.

"Because my mom will worry herself sick. I'm trying to be mature, Billy."

He laughed. "Mature, you! Remember, babe, you're just a free spirit, like me. We go where the wind blows us."

The wind was now blowing us across the Strait, and we ended up in East Vancouver, which is bordered to the north by Burrard Inlet, to the south by the Fraser River and to the east by the city of Burnaby. I don't know why I remembered all that, but three years ago Aunt Bee had brought Cam and me to Vancouver for Expo, and she told us a lot about Vancouver then. She also told us about Mom's great-grandfather, who had been a captain on the Fraser River and had owned ships. He'd also made money in the Fraser and Cariboo gold rushes—which sounded exciting to me.

I also knew that East Vancouver was not a particularly nice area to live, especially around East Hastings, which was known for drugs, poverty, and crime. From the looks of some of the people on this street where we arrived, there was also a lot of prostitution. Even this early in the day, women in very short skirts stood on every corner. In fact, the streets were full of people just sitting on the sidewalks. Some were strumming guitars; others were painting canvases on easels.

"If we had come ten years ago, we would have gone to Kits, where all the hippies were hanging out. That must have been a great time to live back then. Freedom personified." I think he was referring to the Kitsilano area, which I had read about.

I looked down at my tattoo. *Yes, freedom,* I thought. *I have it now. I can do whatever I want. Once I get established as an artist, I won't even need Billy.*

Billy led me up some steps of a rundown building where his "connections" apparently lived, and we were greeted by a bearded older man.

"Billy, my boy. Nice to see you made it. And this lovely young thing is your main squeeze, I assume."

"Yeah, this is Kat."

The man leered at me. "I hear you are quite the artist, Kat, and very qualified in many areas."

I smiled. "Thank you, but I'm not qualified in much—just art."

"We'll get your man here busy on a job I have in mind for him, and then I'll find something for you." He ran his hand up and down my arm, which really freaked me out.

"Yes, I think you'll be perfect for what I have in mind."

* * *

The bearded man, whose name was Charlie, owned the house, and we were all his tenants, but I never saw any exchange of rent money. Instead, all his tenants appeared to work for Charlie in one capacity or another. Every night we all sat around singing and smoking pot in the basement or outside on the steps.

I felt relaxed, and while Billy was gone during the day, I spent my time drawing or painting. Charlie kept buying me art supplies, which seemed odd. Why was everyone working to earn their keep except me?

That night I asked Billy about it. "I really want to earn some money, Billy. You work, and everyone else does. Why not me?"

"I think Charlie has something in mind for you too, but he doesn't think you're ready yet."

"What does he have in mind?"

"Kat, you're so thick! What do you think we all do here? The guys sell drugs for Charlie, and the girls do what you all do best."

"Art?" I said innocently.

He laughed so loud I thought he would split a gut. "Whoring, babe. The oldest profession in the world. I told him you were a good lay."

He walked out of the room laughing, slamming the door behind him. I couldn't believe what he had just said. I thought he loved me. How could he have agreed to turn me into a prostitute?

* * *

That night, I got high with the others, as usual.

I was in this mess, and now I just wanted to obliterate it. Being high made me forget everything. But during the daytime, when my head was clearer, I realized how blind I had been. It was so obvious what this house was. It was full of drug dealers who made deals during the day for Charlie, and girls who walked the streets or brought guys home at night. Charlie was their pimp. How could I have been so stupid?

I wondered how much longer it would be before he used me as one of his girls. He had left me alone for two months now and had even bought me all those art supplies. Why? Was he saving me for something else? I had to do something quickly, though. This was just the lull before the storm. Somehow, I had to get away from this place—and soon.

One of the girls, who looked about my age, was called Cindy. She was always friendly to me, and I assumed she was the girlfriend of Brian, another of the guys who lived here. One day we were sitting outside on the steps, and I was drawing a picture of her.

"Kat, you're so talented. That drawing is incredible. Why are you here?"

"I don't know. I thought I was in love with Billy, and he brought me here from Victoria. I didn't know what would happen."

"Once these guys get hooked in by Charlie, all they can see is the big money to be made. The thing is, most of the money goes to Charlie. We're just his pawns."

"Does Brian sell drugs for Charlie, like Billy? And do you ...?"

"Yeah, of course he does and, yeah, I give the guys Charlie sends me to whatever they're paying for ... It's not too bad, once you get used to it. And at least Charlie keeps us all fed and provides a place to sleep. I'd be sleeping on the street otherwise. I left home because my dad was fucking me. Came to my bedroom every night, and my mother was too hooked on drugs to care. I ran away to Vancouver and met Brian, and he introduced me to Charlie, and we came to live here."

"Wow, that's awful."

"But you seem like you came from a good family, and you have this incredible talent. So, how come you're here?"

My own story seemed tame compared to hers. How could I tell her I lived in a mansion and had decided not to graduate from school because I wanted to be with Billy? How could I explain my dad was a man who verbally abused my mom and little brother and ignored me most of the time? It all sounded so tame compared to a young girl being sexually abused by her father. So, I shrugged and said nothing.

But secretly I began to plan.

* * *

When Billy was out the next day, I started to put things in my knapsack, which I hid in the corner behind a box in our room. I also rolled up some of my artwork in a tube and put that in the knapsack, along with some art supplies and my pad. When the time was right, I would be ready to go with only the clothes on my back. But where would I go? I hadn't decided yet.

That night, things got bad. Charlie came to our room and told me to go downstairs with him. He took my arm, and Billy didn't stop him.

"Why?" I asked.

"I have someone I want you to meet, curious little Kitty Kat—to help with your career. He's an important client of mine."

Was he joking? My career! Was he really going to introduce me to someone who might be interested in my artwork? I thought about Cally, the first one to call me Kitty Kat. Oh, Cally, I wish I could see you now.

Charlie took me down to the basement, which was dimly lit and smelt of marijuana and sweat. When my eyes adjusted to the darkness, I saw a man sitting on the bed in the corner. This didn't look like a place to interview me about my work. The man had rings on all his fingers—diamonds and rubies, and there were gold chains around his neck. He smiled at me and nodded at Charlie.

Charlie offered me a drink. I drank it quickly but immediately realized my mistake. It was no ordinary drink. The room began to spin, and Charlie's voice sounded strange.

"Just to relax you, Kat. I want you to be good and please Mr. Smith here. He particularly likes first-timers. Pity ... you're ... not a ... virgin." His voice began to drift off, and I felt myself being lifted onto the bed.

Suddenly everything went dark. *Hells bells, this drug is good* was my last thought before oblivion took over.

* * *

When I woke up many hours later, I was back in my bed in the room I shared with Billy. He was lying beside me.

"Hi babe. You're awake," he said.

"What happened? Where am I?"

"Charlie said you did well. His client was pleased and paid a lot for you."

"I don't remember ... I want a shower. Help me up."

As soon as I raised my head, the room began to spin. I leaned over the edge of the bed and threw up.

"Holy shit, babe, couldn't you wait until you got to the bathroom?"

I closed my eyes again. I wanted to die.

Next time I woke up must have been hours later. Billy was gone, but at least he'd cleaned up my mess on the floor. I sat up slowly this time. What had I been given that night? Had I been raped by both Charlie and his client? I didn't remember any of it, but I knew I was very sore, and I felt violated. My head was still not clear, and I couldn't think straight. If this was "freedom," I didn't want it. I just wanted to be clean again. To be *me* again—whatever me was. When did I become this drug-addled woman with purple-streaked hair and a ring in her nose?

I staggered to the bathroom and ran a shower. The water was only lukewarm, but I scrubbed myself from head to toe. It made me feel better, but the exertion of doing it was so tiring that, once back in our room, I fell on the bed and closed my eyes.

I woke again a few hours later, and it was two o'clock in the morning. Everyone was either sleeping or passed out from smoking pot. Even Billy was snoring beside me. I slipped out of bed quietly, pulled on my torn jeans and a t-shirt and grabbed my knapsack. Only then did I think about money. Luckily, Billy had left some change and a few notes on the table in the corner. There were a few twenty-dollar bills that I supposed he would be giving to Charlie. Without a second thought, I picked them up and stuffed them in my pocket. I decided it wasn't stealing. I'd earned every penny of it.

I crept down the stairs stealthily, trying to avoid any stair that creaked. I couldn't face anyone tonight in this flop house, and especially not Charlie. That made me smile. *Flop house? Yeah, where everyone flops into oblivion every day and every night,* I thought.

Once out the front door, I ran and ran until I was out of breath. I needed to leave Vancouver, or else they would find me. I hailed a taxi and hoped I would have enough money to pay for a ride to the ferries. I'd wait there until the first ferry in the morning.

I just wanted to go home.

* * *

By cab, ferry, bus, and a whole lot of walking, I was finally back in Victoria, but I wasn't ready yet to face Mom and Dad at Providence. I was totally exhausted, and it was pouring with rain by then, which made things feel worse.

I thought about going to Aunt Bee. I knew she would help me, but she lived too close to the house, so instead I thought of Uncle Joe Caldwell, Dad's partner. I headed towards their office in town, thinking that I would first need to make sure Dad wasn't there.

I loved Uncle Joe. When Cam and I were still little, he came to the house often, and he was lots of fun. But as the years went by, Dad made it obvious he didn't want him there. I heard him telling Uncle Joe once that he wanted to separate his business life from his home life. I couldn't figure out why. How could he work with his friend but not want him near our house? And how were they ever friends in the first place? They were so different.

But now I thought about him, and I needed to talk to him. By the time I reached downtown, it was late in the afternoon. I was drenched and I only had about two dollars left in my pocket. Rain was coming down in torrents, and I could hear cracks of thunder in the distance. Dad's car wasn't in the parking lot, but Uncle Joe's was still there—a good sign. I sat down on the curb beside his car and pushed my knapsack under it in a futile attempt to keep it dry. I hoped my artwork inside hadn't already been ruined.

Eventually I saw him coming towards the car, holding his briefcase over his head. I stood up and saw the shock on his face. I must have looked awful.

"Kat, sweetheart. What are you doing out here in this rain?" He gave me a big hug even though I was soaking wet. "It's wonderful to see you, but let's jump in the car and stay out of this weather." I didn't argue. My teeth were chattering with the cold.

Once inside, he asked if I was waiting for my dad. "No! I was waiting for you, Uncle Joe. I don't want to see Dad right now."

He raised an eyebrow. "Well, I can certainly drive you home. Your dad is meeting a client right now."

"I don't want to go home. I want to stay with you."

"Kat, your mom is worried sick about you. You must let her know you're home."

"I'm not sure I'm going home, Uncle Joe. I don't know what to do. Can we go back to your place and talk?"

"Of course, we can. And it looks like you could use a warm bath and a hot drink. Do you still like hot chocolate?" He took off his jacket and placed it around me.

He started the engine and turned on the heat, which made me feel better, but his kind words and the mention of hot chocolate made me feel like a little girl again. I felt safe for the first time in many months.

I nodded, and we drove off.

* * *

He didn't bombard me with questions about where I had been or why I was now back. He just waited patiently for me to have a bath while he made the hot chocolate. He had offered me a big, white, fluffy robe and taken all my wet clothes and put them through the dryer.

When I emerged from the bathroom of his condo, he was sitting on the couch.

"Kat, would you let me telephone your mom now to put her mind at rest that you are safe here with me?"

"Not yet. First—first I need to tell you everything. Uncle Joe, I am so ashamed of myself. After you hear it all, my mom and dad probably won't ever want to see me again."

"I doubt that very much. We all love you, Kat."

So, I began. I told him everything—my rebellion, the piercings, the tattoos, the drugs, and how I had fallen in love with Billy, who turned out to be a drug dealer for a pimp who offered him big money. And then I told him about what they intended for me and what had happened on that last night that I couldn't remember. I told Joe I thought I'd been raped. He didn't interrupt but just nodded his head and occasionally squeezed my hand.

"Kat, I am proud of you. You got out of a very bad situation, which could have been even worse. And you got away in time. But it's likely you're addicted to certain drugs now. That's why you're still shaking, and your eyes are bloodshot. You might need to go to a rehab facility and see a doctor to make sure you're okay. Do you understand, sweetheart?"

I nodded. "How could I have been so stupid? Billy was willing to turn me into a hooker just to make money. I hope to God he sees the light and gets away from that monster."

"You can stay here tonight and get a good night's sleep, but I need to let your mom know that I'm bringing you home tomorrow. She will have to make these decisions for you, Kat, but I will support her and you, to make sure you get healthy again, I promise."

The hot chocolate felt so good and his hug even better. Never once had he judged me. He just wanted to help. I wished in that moment that he was my dad.

Next morning, I woke up with a blinding headache, but I got dressed in my dry clothes, had some breakfast—which made me feel a bit nauseous—and agreed to go home. He told me he had phoned my mom last night and she was happy and relieved that I was safe. She asked us to come after Dad had left for the office. She wanted to be the first to see me. She had told Cally I was back, and he had asked if he could stay home from school.

Mom and Cally were waiting on the front porch as we drove up. Mom ran down the steps and hugged me so tightly I could hardly breathe. She mouthed the words *thank you* to Uncle Joe. Then Cally flung himself at me.

"Oh, Kat, I'm so glad you're home."

Their hugs and the expressions of joy on their faces were all I needed. Being loved was freedom. The rest of my problems would take care of themselves.

CHAPTER 29 (CALEB)

I was so glad to see my sister home. She looked bedraggled, and I had no idea where she had been or with whom, other than what Mom told me a few months ago—that she had moved to Vancouver. I was only ten, so nobody told me anything. I just knew that, since she'd been gone, I'd felt very lonely.

I never had a best friend at school, right from kindergarten. Most of the boys called me a sissy because I didn't play rough games with them at recess. I preferred to sit with some of the girls or on my own, reading a book. I also liked to draw with Kat, and she taught me a lot.

At home, Julie came over all the time, but mostly to see Kat and then later to be with Cam. I caught Cam and Julie kissing once in the gazebo, my special place, so I didn't go there for a while.

I loved Providence, though. The gardens were so peaceful, full of birds and flowers, and there was no traffic noise. On the other side of the Gorge Arm, there was a lot of industry, like boat and machinery shops, but luckily, we couldn't hear any of the noise from that on our side. Our garden was like an oasis.

Once I'd learned to swim, Mom let me take the boat out on the water. I took to boating straight away, but I wasn't allowed to go far on my own. Naturally, I obeyed because I was terrified of Dad. He was always shouting or making fun of Kat and me, so I wasn't surprised when Kat left home to get away from him. Sometimes I wished she had taken me with her.

She hadn't been back long when suddenly she had to go away again. She told me she had to go into a sort of hospital for a while, but she would be back soon, once she was better.

"Are you sick, Kat?"

"Kind of. I have what they call an addiction, so I need help."

"An addiction? What's that?"

"Something I hope you never get, little bro. When you're older, I'll tell you all about it and help you steer clear of false gods."

"What are false gods, Kat?"

"You ask too many questions, Cally. I promise I'll be okay, and we'll get back to our art again soon."

That was enough for me. I couldn't wait.

* * *

The next disaster happened when Cam and Julie announced they were getting married.

Dad hit the roof. Mom said nothing, but her face went white.

"You've just graduated. You're seventeen. How the hell can you afford to get married?"

"Julie's pregnant, and I intend to marry her. I won't let her down. I still want to go to university, and I will study hard to get my degree. Julie plans on working from home once the baby comes."

"Home! And where exactly will that be? Good God, boy, haven't you ever heard of condoms?"

I hadn't, so I hoped he would explain.

"I was hoping you would let us stay in the suite for a while. It's been empty since Aunt Bee moved to the cottage," Cam said.

I looked at Mom, who was now visibly shaking. She was probably thinking how the whole family was falling apart and it was all her fault. One kid leaving home and now in hospital being cured of something called "addiction," and her eldest getting married to a girl who was pregnant. I guess that would make her a grandmother.

This news was so shocking and so surprising that no one seemed to care that I was still in the room, listening to it all.

About three months later, Kat came home again, and she looked much better. She didn't wear all that yucky stuff on her face anymore, and she'd taken the ring out of her nose. Her hair was its original color again, and she told me she was going back to school to take Grade 12 and graduate. She was so brave.

After that, Mom paid for her to go to the Emily Carr Art Institute. I knew about Emily Carr, who was once a famous artist in Victoria. She was a bit eccentric, like Kat, so I thought that was very appropriate.

And so, the years went by and life at Providence went back to normal again, except we now had Cam and Julie living in the suite. Their baby girl, Wren, was born first, followed by Sage, and by the time I was thirteen in 1992, their third baby girl, Willow, arrived. Three girls in only four years. Dad was incensed. He thought his "golden boy" was destroying himself by tying himself down with a wife and kids. He even made fun of the names they had chosen for their girls.

But Mum was proud of Cam, working so hard to get his first degree, and Julie insisted on paying rent for the suite from the meagre earnings she made from selling her homemade jewelry and paintings. Like Kat, she was very talented. And of course, Mom was only too happy to help by babysitting the girls.

But, by then I had another problem, one that had been bothering me since I'd turned twelve. The only person I felt comfortable talking about it with was Kat.

* * *

One day after we both got home, me from school and her from college, I asked her to come down to the gazebo with me. I told her I really needed to talk to her.

"What's wrong, Cally? Are you in trouble?" she asked gently as we sat side by side on the bench inside the gazebo.

"Not really *trouble*. I'm just confused."

"Okay. What's up?"

"When did you first become interested in boys, Kat?"

"Oh, gosh, that's a million-dollar question. When I was about your age, I guess. Why?"

"So, shouldn't I be interested in girls by now?"

"Not necessarily. Some kids develop later. It's no big deal."

"Well, it really is, because ... I think I'm more interested in boys than girls."

"Yeah, girls go through that, too. We sometimes get a big crush on another girl, so I suppose boys get crushes on other boys."

"It's more than that, Kat."

"How do you mean?"

"I have a friend, Jamie, at school that I really like and ..."

"And?"

"We held hands one day, and he kissed me. It felt good."

"Okay, little bro. Don't worry about it."

"But I think I'm gay—and I'm not sure I want to be."

"Cally, even if you are gay, there's nothing wrong with that. We will still love you."

"Maybe you and Mom will, and even Cam and Julie, but think about Dad—he'll go berserk."

"He goes berserk about everything, so no big deal. Just don't worry about it, Cally. When you are sure about your feelings, just let Mom and Dad know, and they will have to accept it."

It took another two years before I told them, and then only because they caught me crying one day while I was sitting on the couch in the living room and they both came in and asked what was wrong.

My dad looked at me in horror, as though I had some disease. I will never forget that expression on his face.

CHAPTER 30 (KAITLYN)

It felt so good to be normal again. I could finally breathe when I returned to Providence after being in rehab. The first few weeks there were awful because I was in withdrawal. I felt so confined, and I was sure I would never feel better again. Prior to going there, Mom had taken me to a doctor who examined me very thoroughly and proclaimed I wasn't pregnant and didn't have any sexually transmitted diseases. I was so relieved, I promised myself I'd never have sex again as long as I lived!

Back at Providence, I felt grounded again, despite all the drama with Cam and Julie and the surprise baby. As usual, Dad had done a lot of shouting, calling Cam an idiot and Julie a slut. Apparently, that last remark provoked Cam to hit Dad, and Mom intervened to stop it going any further. When Cally told me about it, we both laughed and agreed that Cam had done the right thing. I liked the idea of Julie being my sister-in-law, and we soon resumed our friendship.

I enrolled in art school and found I really enjoyed it. I even made friends—perhaps because of my better attitude after getting clean and seeing life more positively. I did worry about my little brother, who seemed so confused and worried about his sexuality.

That he was quite obviously gay didn't bother me at all, but I told him repeatedly that he should tell Mom and Dad and they would just have to accept it if he went ahead and told them. He waited until he was thirteen, and it only made things worse for him. Mom of course accepted it, but again went along with Dad's obvious horror at being the father of a gay son. It all seemed ridiculous to me, so I did my best to support Cam and boost his morale.

I was twenty by then and had graduated with honors. Trying to figure out what should come next, I would often go downtown and gaze in the windows of the Wilson Art Gallery on Fort Street. Oh, how

I would love to have my paintings in a show at a gallery like this one. I read that there were Wilson galleries in Vancouver and Toronto, too.

One day, lost in thought, I noticed a man getting out of a car and heading for the gallery entrance. He was staring at me with a puzzled expression.

"Are you going in?" he asked as he held open the door.

"Actually, I was just daydreaming."

"You seem familiar. Were you a student at Emily Carr?"

"Yes, I was."

"Ah, then I'm right. You must be Kat Foster. I was trying to place you."

How on earth did he know me? I was astounded. "Yes, I am, but—"

"Forgive me for being so forward. I'm Troy Wilson, the owner of the gallery. The institute often sends me portfolios of their promising students, and I'd seen your photo, plus your artwork. You are very talented."

I blushed. Was he simply coming on to me? I hadn't dated anyone since Billy, so I was suspicious of all men.

He seemed a lot older than me, though, and was obviously very successful. He was well dressed, very tall, with black, wavy hair, and he was extremely handsome.

"Please come inside, Kat. I kept your portfolio in my office and was intending to contact you. I might be able to help you sell some of your work."

Yeah, I thought. *I bet. But what's the catch?* I wouldn't be taken in by a man again.

Nonetheless, I followed him inside as he was greeted by the staff and led me to his office surrounded by glass. He ordered coffee for us both and asked me to sit while he located my portfolio.

We spent the next hour discussing art and his suggestions to help me sell my work. One landscape piece I was proud of was a view from our lawn looking down onto the Gorge Arm, and he said he wanted to display it in his gallery. He was very professional and there were no hints of sexual innuendo, so I finally let myself relax. He was all about business. He gave me his card and asked for my contact number.

I think I skipped all the way home.

* * *

When I told Mom, she was delighted.

Dad's reaction was surprising. "I've heard of that guy, Kat. He's a good businessman." He turned to Mom. "Maybe we should invite him out to dinner one night and make sure he's on the up and up with Kat."

I could see Mom was both surprised and pleased. She didn't often get the opportunity to entertain, and immediately she began planning for all the family to be there.

"Don't overdo it, Vicki," Dad interrupted.

I tended to agree. "I don't want to overwhelm him, Mom, but I can help you prepare a small dinner. Nothing fancy, but I will ask him sometime."

I didn't have to wait long, because two days later, he phoned me to say that someone had purchased my painting. "He offered full price, Kat—three hundred dollars."

I was astounded. "My goodness, that's amazing."

"Kat, I'd love to come out one day and see the gardens of Providence, where you do all these amazing pieces."

"Yes, of course. You're welcome, and we'd love to have you stay for dinner, too. My dad and Joe Caldwell are partners at Foster & Associates; you might know them."

"I've met Joe on a few occasions, but I don't know your dad. That would be wonderful—if you're sure."

"Mom loves having company." At least I knew that was true. I didn't want him to think I was coming on to him by inviting him to meet my quirky family. If he was going to help my career, I wanted it to be all business, and so far, it had been, so I added: "You can bring your wife, too."

"I'm not married," he said with a laugh, "but I will bring your cheque."

We planned a dinner date for a Saturday one week later.

Troy arrived early and I showed him around the gardens. He was very impressed. "I can see why you get inspired here, Kat. It's so beautiful, and very peaceful."

The dinner went well. Troy was very charming to my parents and loved chatting with Cally, who showed him some of his art, too.

"What a talented family you all are," Troy said. He turned to Mum. "And I've read some of your articles, Mrs. Foster. Always so interesting."

Mom blushed, and I was glad that Dad had even allowed us to invite Uncle Joe, because having him there gave me and Mom support. He heartily agreed about Mom's writing talent, and he and Troy got on like a house on fire, which appeared to annoy Dad. I was reminded that he always liked to be the center of attention, which meant he had long ignored Mom's talent, just as he had with Cally and me.

Towards the end of the evening, Troy drew me aside and handed me a cheque—my first commission. "This is just the beginning, Kat. I want to put more of your work on display in the coming days."

"Really?"

He laughed. "Don't look so surprised. The next one I'd like to show is the one you call *Hope: The girl with the dogwood flower.*

"You think it would sell?'

"Absolutely. I love it. Who was the model?"

"She was a very sad girl I met in Vancouver called Cindy. I sketched her in black and white, and later I painted her in watercolours. And I love the dogwood, British Columbia's tree, which I felt would give her hope to get out of a bad situation."

He raised an eyebrow and smiled down at me. "How kind you are."

He then said goodnight to everyone and profusely thanked my mom for dinner again.

I stood on the porch for a long time watching him drive off, clutching the cheque to my chest.

I was finally a real artist.

* * *

Next morning, Mom cornered me in the kitchen. "What a lovely evening that was, Kat."

"Yes, it was." I nodded.

"Troy is such a nice young man. He's so polite and intelligent."

"Mom, you don't have to sell him to me. He's not a boyfriend. We're just in business together—and guess what, he wants to show another of my paintings."

"That's wonderful, Kat, but I also saw the way he looked at you."

"What do you mean?"

"I think he likes you more than just as a potential client."

"Mom, he's a lot older than me. He's not interested in me in that way."

"He's only thirty."

"How do you know that?"

"Joe told me."

"Well, I'm not twenty-one yet, and I don't intend to date anyone right now. I'm concentrating on my career."

I left the kitchen quickly, but I heard her laughter behind me.

CHAPTER 31 (KAITLYN)

Troy displayed *Hope: Girl with the dogwood flower* with a price of one thousand dollars on it. I thought it couldn't possibly sell at that outrageous price, but one week later, he phoned me to say it had sold!

"The client is keen to see more of your work, Kat," he said. "Maybe we should meet soon and discuss what other paintings you would like to display."

I was in shock, trying to wrap my head around anyone paying a thousand dollars for my work.

"Yes, yes, of course," I managed to mutter.

"How about dinner tonight?"

Before I knew what happened, I had agreed, and he picked me up at seven that evening and took me to a high-end restaurant in town. We talked for a while about my art, and we decided on which paintings I should next display.

"You had better get busy on more, Kat. I'm thinking about having a show for you. Maybe in Vancouver, if you agree."

The thought of Vancouver still gave me shivers. "No, not Vancouver," I replied quickly. "I'm grateful to you, but I don't think I'm ready for the big city."

"Kat, you are more than ready, believe me."

"Would it mean having to go to Vancouver?"

"Not necessarily, but when we have the opening, people generally like to meet the artist."

"I'll think about it."

"You are quite the recluse, aren't you? I promise, I will be there with you. I'll take you over and bring you home safely."

"I have ... bad memories of my time in Vancouver."

"If you'd like to talk about it, I'd be willing to listen."

"You'd probably think less of me if I told you everything."

He laughed. "I very much doubt that."

I hesitated.

"Look, I understand, Kat. If you want to talk, this is not the place. We've had a lovely dinner talking business, but if you need somewhere more private, let's go back to my apartment for coffee."

He must have seen my expression of fear and suspicion. "No strings attached, I promise," he added.

I couldn't decide if I was happy or disappointed, but I agreed, and we left the restaurant together and headed to his apartment overlooking the harbour. The building was two blocks from where Uncle Joe lived, and for some reason that made me feel safe.

* * *

Troy's apartment was beautiful, with wide, expansive views of the water and the mountains. He told me to sit on the couch and make myself comfortable while he made the coffee.

"Unless you would prefer some wine, Kat?"

"No, coffee is fine." I wanted to keep a clear head. I felt sure that Troy didn't have an ulterior motive for inviting me here, but I still felt suspicious of every man who showed interest in me. Troy was no exception.

He handed me a cup and sat down beside me.

"Now," he said kindly, "why do you hate Vancouver?"

"It's just that ... well, I ran away from home to Vancouver with a boyfriend when I was not quite seventeen, and I got myself into a really bad situation."

"Want to talk about it? No pressure and no judgment."

"It all seems so stupid now, but it still gives me nightmares thinking about what might have happened if I hadn't got out of there."

I paused, and then suddenly I wanted to tell him everything. "I was a rebel, Troy," I began. "I hated myself and I particularly hated my dad. He was so cruel to me and my mom—and still is. But he is especially hard on my little brother, who is gay and struggling with it."

And then the rest of my story poured out, and Troy let me go on without interruption. It felt good to unload everything, and when I finished, he took my hand in his and moved closer to me.

"So, your prize client was a drug addict! Pretty shameful, eh?" I said sheepishly.

He pulled me to him and put his arms around me as he gave me what could only be described as a brotherly hug. "We all do stupid things when we're young, Kat. You were smart enough to get out of that life and the path you were heading down." He then drew away and placed his hand on my cheek. "I'm very proud of you, Kat."

"Really? I thought you would hate me."

"Why would I hate you? I would never do that." He looked at me intensely and I was sure he wanted to kiss me. I wanted it also, but instead he only brushed his lips against my cheek and drew back.

"I won't force you to go to Vancouver until you're ready, Kat. But I have a feeling you are going to be a big name in the local art world soon, so people will want to meet you at shows. Maybe we could do one in Toronto first—but again, it's up to you."

I nodded.

"And I will be with you, I promise."

He took me home an hour later and gave me another friendly hug on the porch at Providence. As I watched him drive away, I knew in my heart that he was a good man. He respected me, and his kindness overwhelmed me.

Over the next few weeks, I worked hard on more paintings. I was suddenly inspired with a wealth of ideas for landscapes, still-lifes, and human subjects.

True to his word, Troy organized a showing for them, first in Victoria, where many more sold. I opened a business account at the bank and deposited all my sales there. I compared my expenses for supplies against the sales, and I was still making a large profit.

The next show was two months later in Vancouver, and Troy took me over, arranged accommodation for me at a hotel two blocks away from his gallery, and drove me back to Victoria the next day. The opening was a big success, and I made many contacts in the art world.

Troy had made no advances towards me. It was all strictly business with him, but I sensed he was attracted to me, and this made him even more attractive to me. The situation rapidly changed one night a week after we returned from Vancouver, when he took me out to dinner and invited me back to his apartment afterwards.

I had turned twenty-one in August of that year. Now it was almost Christmas, and we had been celebrating all my sales and the upcoming season.

And that's when I finally knew how he really felt about me.

* * *

I was still refusing to drink very much, but that night I decided one glass of wine wouldn't hurt.

Troy put on some music and went into his kitchen for the wine. We settled back on the couch, and he raised his glass. "Here's to us, Kat. We are a great team."

I sipped the wine and laughed. "We are, Troy! I can't believe what has happened in my life over the past months. But it's all thanks to you."

"No, Kat, it's because of your extraordinary talent." He put his glass down on the coffee table and moved closer to me. "Kat, may I kiss you?"

"I thought you'd never ask."

We kissed. Then he drew away. "Kat, I don't just want a fling with you. I'm serious about you. In case you didn't know by now, I've fallen in love with you. I think I've been in love since the moment I first saw you gazing in the gallery window that day."

"I think I might be in love with you too, Troy," I replied.

"I want more, Kat. I want to marry you."

"Oh, Troy, I'm not ready for marriage!" I was stunned.

"Why not? If we're in love, isn't that the next obvious step? I've never felt this way about anyone before. I love you, and I want you to be my wife."

"Despite everything I told you about my past?"

"Of course. I love you. I don't care about any of that. Let's get married. I really want to live with you."

"Troy, I will willingly move in with you, but I'm not ready for more yet."

"Yet? But when?"

I laughed. "I'll make a deal with you, Troy. I will move in with you right now if you want me to if you promise not to keep mentioning marriage. Is that a deal?"

He smiled that irresistible smile of his and took my hand. "If you're sure about moving in, I can't promise I won't keep mentioning the marriage word, because I probably will. So, do we still have a deal?"

"Yes," I replied. "But I can't promise I won't keep saying no for a while."

He kissed my hand. "Then we need to seal the deal with a kiss."

This time we kissed for a long while. When we finally broke apart, I held on to his hand and we both stood up.

"What are we waiting for?" I asked as we walked towards his bedroom.

CHAPTER 32 (CALEB)

Life became even more unbearable for me after my sister moved into Troy's apartment at Christmas that year. I missed her so much.

They invited me to the apartment sometimes, and those were the best times, but life back home was intolerable. I was lonely, and without any friends at school I was totally miserable. Kat and Troy later moved to Vancouver, so I saw even less of them. He wanted to marry her, but she was content the way it was. Personally, I hoped they would get married and move back to Victoria, but I understood their decision, because most of Troy's work was now in Vancouver and Toronto.

Dad constantly made fun of me, calling me queer and a lot of other horrible names. He frequently told me that if I had some gumption, I could become straight. He made it his mission for the next few years to de-gay me. At least I grew taller and was no longer "little Cally." Dad was about six feet and Cam six-one, but I outgrew them both at six feet, three inches. My height made me look older and gave me confidence.

Despite my height, I was still bullied at school, and by the time I was sixteen and graduation was looming the following year, my life was hell. I couldn't talk to anyone about it, not even Mom. Kids at school would go drinking downtown, but of course I was never invited. I wondered if there might be a gay bar somewhere where I could go, but those places were careful to stay under the radar. I eventually found one on Johnson Street called The Purple Rainbow, and one Friday night I went. I told Mom I was going to the library to study and, as it was not a school night, she didn't question it. Dad wouldn't have cared either way.

My eyes adjusted slowly to the dimly lit interior of the club as I descended the stairs. It was mostly men, sitting around at tables, listening to music, drinking, or dancing together, but there were also a few girls there dancing together. As I walked over to a corner table, people smiled at me, and somebody said "Welcome!" The atmosphere felt warm.

A waiter dressed in purple pants and a sparkly purple waistcoat, approached me.

"What is your pleasure tonight, sir?" he said.

I was dazed enough at being addressed as "sir" without the added pressure of trying to think of a suitable drink to order. I had never had any alcohol before. I knew Dad drank beer or whisky, but other than that, I didn't have a clue. Mom never drank.

"Beer, please."

"On tap, or something else?"

Oh, God, this was getting worse. But before I replied, I noticed a very handsome man coming my way. "Bring the young man a martini, Chris, on my tab."

He sat down beside me and smiled. "Hope you don't mind me interfering, but it looks like this is your first visit here, am I right?"

I nodded.

"It's a bit overwhelming, isn't it?" He had a very aristocratic English accent.

I nodded.

"My name is Giles Finkel." He put out his hand, which I shook.

"Finkel, that's a strange name."

"We only go by first names here," he said, laughing. "We simply make up silly surnames!"

"Really? I'm Cal ..." I wanted to think up an equally silly surname, but all I could think of was Kat's tattoo, so I added her word. "Freedom. Cal Freedom."

"Nice to meet you, Cal Freedom. Tell me about yourself. How old are you?"

"Are you the owner?"

"Oh, God no! Don't worry, I'm not about to turn you out for being underage. You *are* underage, aren't you?"

"I'm sixteen. Seventeen next May."

"Well, I won't tell if you won't." He chuckled to himself.

I became a little bolder after sipping the martini that arrived soon after. "How old are you, Giles?"

"As old as my tongue and a little older than my teeth." He laughed.

That made me giggle because it was an expression my mom often used.

"But seriously, I'm twenty-four, Cal, which probably sounds ancient to you."

"Well, my brother is twenty-four, and he already has four kids! Can you believe it! And my sister, Kat, is twenty-three, and she lives in Vancouver with her boyfriend. She still seems very young to me."

"And then there is little Cal." He touched my hand. "I'm glad I don't seem too old for you." Did he say *for* you, instead of *to* you?

After a second drink, I understood exactly what he had said, especially when he suggested we go back to his place.

Giles had a charming little apartment in Esquimalt, and we sat talking in his living room for a long while. He didn't pressure me for anything else, so I felt comfortable with him, and I found myself telling him everything about my life. It was good to unburden myself of all the loneliness and hate inside me, especially as his story was very similar to mine; not being accepted by his family in London, who were quite wealthy; being bullied at university; hating himself, and eventually moving to Western Canada. He had stayed for a while in Edmonton, where homosexuality was more accepted, but when he broke up with a boyfriend, he moved to Victoria.

"I know what you mean, Giles. I know that I'm gay, but at the same time I want to be like everyone else. To be normal."

"Ah, and there's the rub, dear fellow. You must realize you *are* normal. You must accept the way you are because it's okay."

"Is it? But where do I fit in? I'm told I need to find a date for the grad dance next year, for instance. How would it be if I said I wanted to bring a guy as my date?"

"Don't worry about that, Cal. I can fix it for you. I'll find you a girl who is also gay and having the same problem as you, and you can go together."

"But that's deceiving, isn't it?'

"It's only for one night, so who cares? It just smooths things for you and the girl. After that, you can be your true self, and to hell with everyone."

I liked that. *To hell with everyone.* I was who I was.

"Cal, dear chap, I want you to know I am not promiscuous, but I do want to make love to you. I care about you very much. You fascinate me. So, are you willing?"

We moved our conversation to his bedroom, and what he did to me there made me sure once and for all that I was certainly gay and very willing.

CHAPTER 33 (CALEB)

It was an hour past my curfew when Giles dropped me off at Providence. My mother was still up. I had tried to slip in through the back door unseen and was tiptoeing upstairs when she appeared from the library, dressed in her robe.

"You're late, Cally."

"Yes, sorry, Mom. I met a friend at the library, and we got talking and went for a coffee," I lied.

"Okay. I just couldn't sleep until you were home safely."

She walked to me and gave me a hug. I felt ashamed that I'd lied to her. She simply seemed happy that I had found a friend. But what would she have thought if she knew where I'd really been and what I had done tonight?

All I knew was that I had found someone who really cared about me as an equal. Someone who understood me. I was over the moon because I had a boyfriend—even if our relationship had to be a secret right now. Once I left school and was considered an adult, I would shout it to the world, regardless of the consequences.

Giles and I met secretly for the next few months, and each meeting was wonderful. Life at home, however, was still miserable. Mom spent more and more time with her granddaughters, helping Cam and Julie whenever she could. Dad continued to bully and belittle me at every opportunity, and at school it was even worse. Why were people so cruel because you were a little different?

Giles arranged a private meeting for me and a lesbian girl called Jodie, who came to the club sometimes. She agreed to go to my grad if I would go with her to hers, because she went to a different school. We would pretend to be a couple. I liked her and agreed to the bargain. I felt an enormous amount of relief and was grateful to Giles for setting it up.

As Christmas approached, Dad was becoming more and more unpleasant. I had heard him raging at Mom about the fact that Uncle Joe had broken up the partnership and opened his own business in Oak Bay. I wasn't a bit surprised. It must have been hard for Uncle Joe to work with a man like my dad, who could be charming one day and a total prick the next.

"He said I've changed, Vicki. He said he can't work with me anymore," I heard him screeching. "He's crazy. I always thought we were friends."

I heard Mom sympathizing with him, though she must secretly have agreed with Uncle Joe. Of course, she never expressed her own opinion about anything. She always agreed with Dad just to keep the peace.

Christmas came and went, and June graduation loomed. I'd told Kat about Giles when she and Troy came over for the Christmas holiday, and she was happy for me. "Just remember, Cally, you have to be careful. Make sure you and Giles keep it monogamous. There's a lot of this disease, AIDS, going around."

"Well neither of us is promiscuous, Kat. And we do take precautions."

"Good boy," she said as she gave me a hug. I really loved my sister. She was a good person. Apart from Giles, she was the only bright light in my life.

* * *

"What are your plans after graduation?" Dad asked me one day out of the blue. He had never shown any interest in my future before.

"I've enrolled in Visual Arts at Camosun, Dad. I start in September. Didn't Mom tell you?" I immediately regretted saying that, as he would no doubt accuse her of keeping things from him.

"No. she didn't! Why Visual Arts? Where will that get you in life?"

"I have a talent for art—like Kat. And look what's happened to her. I love art, Dad, so I'm hoping it will give me a chance to get into a lot of fields."

"I doubt it!" he sneered. "But I suppose you'll fit right in with all the other arty farts." I was relieved when he left the room because I was on the point of tears. I wanted his love and respect, but all I ever received from him was contempt.

In early May, Giles called one day to ask me to meet him downtown in a coffee shop. It was not our usual day, so I was surprised but happily agreed.

And with that, my world fell apart. He told me he had met someone else and fallen in love. I couldn't believe how callous and matter-of fact he was about it.

"But I thought you loved me, Giles," I sobbed.

"Oh, Cally, you are such a dear boy, and our time together has been wonderful, but I've moved on. You must respect that."

"I don't understand. I love you." I knew I sounded pathetic. People were looking at us.

"I'm honored to have been your first love, dear boy, but there will be others."

"I don't want others," I pleaded. "I want you."

"Believe me, you will soon find someone else. Now, be a good chap, chin up and all that, and then I'll drive you back home."

I let him lead me outside to where he'd parked his car, but I felt my life was over.

That night, I cried myself to sleep. I had fallen deeply in love with a man, so I knew I was gay, but deep down I hated myself for being this way. My father despised me for it, and I had wanted his love for so many years. Being gay felt like a curse. It must be! I longed to be like everyone else.

The thought of being *like everyone else* reminded me about graduation in two weeks. I no longer wanted to graduate, and I certainly didn't want to go to a stupid dance with a girl, just so everyone would think I was their idea of normal.

The next day, Mom gave me five hundred dollars to buy a pair of dress shoes for the dance. She had already rented my tux. It was far too much money for one pair of shoes, and I knew it would be a waste because I didn't intend to go to the dance anyway.

Nonetheless, like a robotic fool, I went downtown to the most expensive shoe store on Government Street and purchased a pair of black leather shoes for three hundred dollars. As I was leaving, I spotted a pair of hot pink runners. I had more than enough money left over, so I went back to the assistant and asked if they had them in size 12. Once I'd tried them on, I knew I wanted them, so I added them to my bag.

* * *

I had one more exam left to take, the next morning in the school hall. It was my least favorite subject—biology.

It all seemed a waste of time. I'd already made up my mind that I didn't want to graduate. What happened at breakfast had only convinced me more that I was making the right decision.

"What the hell are those things on your feet, Cal?" Dad said as I came into the kitchen.

"They're my new runners, Dad. I bought them yesterday."

"I thought your mother had given you money for a pair of dress shoes." I could see his temper about to erupt.

"I did buy some nice dress shoes, too, but these caught my eye, and with the money left over, I bought them."

Mom said nothing, but Dad's face was turning red. "Well, you're not leaving the house wearing those fancy things *that caught your eye,* you faggot."

"Oh, Ryan, leave him be," Mom pleaded quietly, but he ignored her.

"You heard me, take the fucking things off."

"NO!" I screamed at him. "I won't. I'm wearing them to school. Sorry, Mom, I don't want any breakfast."

With that, I ran out of the house. I couldn't take it anymore.

I headed for school and sat through three hours of hell in the hall, staring at the questions on the test and writing ridiculous nonsensical answers to them all. My mind was somewhere else, making decisions, deciding what I should do.

I told Mom that night that I had already eaten dinner and went outside for a long walk, hardly able to breathe. I walked down to the Arm and threw rocks in the water, trying to release years of pent-up anger.

When I returned to my room, my pink shoes had disappeared.

"Have you seen my new runners, Mom?" I called down.

"No dear. They're not down here. Aren't they in your closet?"

They weren't. I went back outside and wandered aimlessly around the grounds before I noticed the garbage bins our new Portuguese gardener, Adriano, had rolled down the driveway for tomorrow's pick-up. Something drew me to them.

Returning to my room, I took out a sheet of paper and began methodically writing a long note. Later, when everyone was asleep, I slipped quietly downstairs, leaving my note in a drawer of the desk Mom sometimes used in the library. She would find it there eventually, I thought, as I crept down the stairs. I couldn't leave it in her office up in the turret, as that would have required going through their bedroom.

By the time she found the letter, I would be out of the house, leaving all my pain behind.

PART THREE

Moving On

(1996-2024)
(VICKI, JANE)

CHAPTER 34 (VICKI)

"Ryan, have you seen Cally this morning?"

He looked up from his paper. "No."

"Well, I don't think he slept here. I looked in his room and his bed hadn't been slept in," I said.

"Perhaps he got lucky last night and stayed with some other gay blade."

"Oh, Ryan, that is so cruel. I'm really worried about him. He was so upset yesterday about those runners—and then later when he couldn't find them, he looked so forlorn. I hope he's all right."

"Good God, Vicki. You have to stop babying him. He's seventeen years old and has this stupid notion that he's gay. Hopefully he'll grow out of it."

"Ryan, homosexuality is not something you grow out of!" I was angry with him for saying what he had, and I didn't care if his usual fury boiled up like it always did whenever I disagreed with him. But all he said in reply was "Whatever," like a disgruntled teenager.

"I'm going to call around to see if anyone has seen him." I knew those words were futile, because Cal didn't have any friends that I knew of, so who would I call? Instead, once Ryan had left for work, I called Kat in Vancouver.

She sounded bright and cheery at the other end of the phone.

"Hi, Mom, what's up?"

"It's Cally. I'm really worried about him. He was so upset yesterday, and now I don't know where he is. He didn't sleep here last night. Do you have any idea where he might be? Did he call you?"

"Oh God, was it something Dad said or did to him again?"

"Yes. It was an argument about some pink runners, but ..."

"Try Uncle Joe. He might have stayed there. Oh ... and he also had a boyfriend, Giles, but I think their relationship was over. I believe I still have Giles's number, so I'll try him. Don't worry, Mom, we'll find him. Troy will help me."

I was shocked to hear about a boyfriend. "I didn't know about Giles, Kat."

"Well, I'm sure he wouldn't have wanted to tell you and Dad."

"I would have listened, Kat. It's just Dad—"

"Yeah, it's always *just Dad!*" she replied bitterly.

I hung up and immediately called Joe at home, hoping he hadn't left for his office.

He picked up the phone immediately. "Victoria, what's wrong?"

"Joe, did Cally stay with you last night?"

"No."

"Oh God, I don't know where he is. He didn't sleep here last night. He isn't with Kat, and I don't know where else to look."

"Don't worry, we'll find him. I'm sure he's all right. Probably just needed some time out."

"Yeah, from Ryan ..." I felt so disloyal to Ryan for saying that, but Joe's words felt so comforting. He was truly concerned about my son, whereas my husband seemed not to care. "I'll come over. I'll be there in ten minutes," he said.

After hanging up, I left the house. I needed some fresh air. I wandered aimlessly round the garden and then headed down towards the water. I wondered if he'd taken the boat out, but it was still tied up at the dock. I noticed Adriano had arrived and was unloading his truck by the garage. He had brought some more plants.

As I passed the boathouse, something pink caught my eye through the window. Was it Cally's missing runners?

I walked quickly to the window and saw that what had caught my eye was indeed the runners, but they were hanging in the air and—

I ran around to the door and yanked it open, making the runners sway in the draft. They were on Cally's feet. And Cally was hanging from a high beam.

My beautiful son had hanged himself.

I rushed to him and clutched his legs, my first insane thought being that I was glad he had found his pink runners.

And then I heard a terrible sound, a howl like an animal's, ringing in my ears. A second after I realized the agonized wail was coming from my own throat, I sank to the ground and was enfolded gratefully in darkness.

CHAPTER 35 (VICKI)

Suddenly there was noise everywhere. I heard sirens. And people! So many people everywhere! Where did they all come from? I was sitting on the lawn, and Bee had her arms wrapped tightly around me. Mary was there too, and so was Joe. Adriano was pacing up and down, and police and paramedics surrounded us.

"Take Cally down. Bee, ask them to take him down. He might still be alive," I cried.

"The paramedics are in there now, luv. They had to wait for the police."

"Who called them? And how did I get here? I want to see Cally. He was in such pain yesterday. Bee, I saw how anguished he looked, and I didn't help him. Why didn't I help him?"

"Vicki, it's not your fault. It's not your fault, luv." She kept patting my back. "Adriano heard you screaming, and he saw you had fainted. He carried you out here and ran up to get me. Then Joe came, and he took care of the rest."

"Is Ryan here?"

"He will be, in a few minutes. Mary called him."

"Why Bee, why? Why did he do it?"

She shook her head. "Let's go up to the veranda and sit there. I'm sure the police will want to talk to us."

I reluctantly let her help me up as I saw Ryan's car barreling up the driveway. He got out and ran towards me. "Vicki, what happened?"

"He hanged himself, Ryan. Our beautiful son hanged himself in the boathouse."

"What? No, surely there's a mistake."

"No mistake, Ryan," Bee said as she continued to walk with me towards the veranda.

"Why are the police here?"

"Why do you think, Ryan? Our boy killed himself. They will be talking to us soon."

"I'm going down there." He ran down the lawn and confronted Joe, who was walking back up. "What the hell are you doing here?" I heard Ryan confront his ex-partner.

"Victoria called me to see if Cally had stayed the night at my place. She sounded very worried, so I came over to help look for him."

"Oh, of course she would phone YOU! ... Cally wasn't missing!"

Joe ignored him and walked away as Ryan ran down to the boathouse, where he was stopped by a police officer who was placing yellow tape around the area.

"I want to see him. I'm his father, for God's sake." We heard his screams from the veranda, where Joe had joined us. "Victoria, I can see my presence here is annoying Ryan, so maybe I should go."

I shook my head. "Please stay, Joe. I can't bear this. It all seems unreal."

He hugged me. "I know, I know. I'll stay if you need me."

His words comforted me as we waited for the police and a barrage of questioning.

* * *

"I'm so sorry for your loss, Mr. and Mrs. Foster," a police officer said. "Do you feel up to answering a few questions now?"

I nodded. Ryan had finally joined us but said nothing. I gripped Bee's hand as Joe walked a short distance away.

"Please, sir, I need to know who you all are," he said as he waved Joe back. "I've already talked to your gardener, who found you collapsed in the boathouse, Mrs. Foster. I'm so sorry you were the one who found your son ..."

I could feel the tears welling up. "What do you need to know? My son was depressed. I know that now. I wish I had seen his pain earlier. It was so obvious."

"Why was he depressed?"

I looked at Ryan, who said nothing. "He was gay, officer, and my husband couldn't accept that."

Ryan glared at me.

"But was there something else that might have triggered this happening?"

"He'd had another argument with his dad yesterday." I knew I was betraying my husband. I was placing the blame squarely on him. I didn't really know what I was saying. But everything had suddenly become crystal clear.

"Did he leave a note for you, Mrs. Foster? We have searched the boathouse, but there was nothing there."

"No."

"We need permission to search his room."

Bee spoke. "Of course. I can take someone up there."

"Don't leave me, Bee."

Ryan finally said something. He looked pale and in shock. "I'll do it. You stay with Vicki, Bee."

I then saw the ambulance pulling away. "Wait!" I screamed. "I want to see my boy before you take him away."

I rushed over to the ambulance, and the driver stopped. I remember someone advising me to come back, but I didn't listen. I insisted they open the door, and I stepped warily inside. All I remember was that my beautiful son's face was purple and void of expression.

I don't remember much else about that day, except that I was glad that Cam and Julie were there, too. No one could believe what had happened. I felt like I was in a trance. The police finished their questioning, getting stories from us all.

Finally, everyone left, but the yellow tape remained around the boathouse. Bee insisted on staying with me. She made tea and something for us to eat, ignoring Ryan's protests. I was glad. Eventually Ryan went upstairs.

"I phoned Kat and Troy, luv," she told me. "They will be here first thing in the morning. I will stay with you until they arrive."

"Kat will be so sad, Bee. She loved her little brother. Bee, you can go home. I'm going up to bed soon, I'll be fine. And Cam and Julie are here in the suite."

"I can sleep in one of the bedrooms ..."

"No, please go. You've been wonderful, but I need to be with Ryan."

She raised her eyebrows but agreed to leave after giving me another long hug. "We will get through this, Vicki."

After she'd gone, I walked into the library—our den, where Cally and I had spent many happy hours together. I sat at my desk at the window, staring into space. I don't know why, but something made me open the drawer on the right, and that's when I saw it.

An envelope addressed to "Mom" in Cally's calligraphic handwriting.

* * *

My hand trembled as I ripped open the envelope. What would I find inside?

Dear Mom:

By the time you read this, you will know the terrible thing I've done. I am so sorry to hurt you, but I'm feeling so much pain and I just can't face another day on this earth. Please tell Kat I am sorry too. You're the only ones who truly love me.

Things have just become too much for me. It's all overwhelming. Dad will no doubt say I was a coward to end my life, and maybe I am. The last months have been unbearable.

YES, I am gay and always will be—but I don't really want to be. I tried to fight it. It was no good. There was a man I didn't tell you about, Giles. I love him, but he's moved on. I've been bullied constantly at school, and at home I'm persecuted by Dad every day. He looks at me with disgust. He's probably thinking, "How could the great Ryan Foster have produced a fag son?" I honestly believe he thinks of all his children as disappointments, even Cam, who let him down by getting Julie pregnant at such a young age. But look at him now, Dad. Have you ever once said you were proud of the way he has supported his family and NOT neglected his education? And Kat, who ran away from home at sixteen and got mixed up in drugs—but again, look at her now, Dad. A famous artist in a relationship with a good man. Have you ever once congratulated her?

And then there's me—I've been the worst disappointment of all, right? After Dad sneered at me about the runners and then I couldn't find them anywhere in my room, I went looking for them outside. You know where I found them? In the garbage bin! Dad just threw them away. That really broke my heart. Seems like a silly thing, I know, but it broke this camel's back.

So, I fished them out and put them on. And now I'm in my room, writing this to you before I leave you. I love you Mom, and I always will. I pray you find the strength to tell Dad to leave. He's a sick and troubled man.

Please forgive me for what I have to do now.

Your beloved Cally always.

p.s. Please tell Kat to marry Troy. Troy loves me too, and he will help Kat get through this.

By the time I reached the end, I was sobbing violently. *Oh, my poor baby. Darling Cally. What have we done to you?*

My immediate reaction was to storm upstairs and confront Ryan. He had killed our son. I wanted him to feel so much pain that it would be unbearable, just as my pain was now, but once I stood outside our bedroom door, I could hear him snoring. How could he possibly sleep? I hesitated, clutching the tear-stained letter to my heart, and I walked away.

That night I slept fitfully in a guest room on my own, with the letter clutched in my hand. I would not show it to the police yet, so they could see how despicably ruthless Ryan had been to his youngest son.

I needed to think about this first and await the right time.

CHAPTER 36 (VICKI)

Kat and Troy arrived in the early morning. They hadn't waited for the first ferry; instead, Troy had hired a helicopter.

Kat was sobbing as she flung herself into my arms. "Mom, I can't believe this. Why? Why? If I had known that Cally was that desperate, I would have come over and talked to him."

I accepted their hugs with a calmness I had somehow found during that long night. I hadn't seen Ryan that morning, so I hadn't confronted him yet about Cally's letter. I had decided to save it for now. I would simply show Kat.

"Kat, I want you and Cam to make the funeral arrangements, please. It is just too much for me to think about. Bee will help you both."

"Of course, Mom. Troy and I will help with everything. What about Dad?"

"It will be too much for him, too. And I want to go back to Vancouver with you for a few days after the funeral, if that's all right?"

"Of course, Mom. I will need you, too. You can stay with us for as long as you like." Troy nodded his agreement. He was so supportive and kind. I agreed with Cally: Kat should marry him.

I don't remember much about the next few days. I walked around in a trance. The doctor had prescribed me a strong antidepressant that at least helped me to sleep at night, but during the waking hours, I felt like a robot. I was convinced this nightmare could not be happening to our family.

I remember little of the funeral, but as we all stood in the church, I was thinking of the past rather than the future. The McBride family had endured so many heartbreaks. Poor little Jane Hopkins and her tragic life before she married Gideon McBride. And the babies she lost, and their firstborn son who only lived two short years. Then she lost her husband, and later her daughter and son-in-law at sea on the *Princess Sophia*. So many tragedies. How did she survive them? Were all the McBrides cursed?

I noticed the police officer in the church, the one who had questioned us on the day Cally died. I walked over to him.

"Thank you for coming, Officer. I would like to talk to you back at the house if possible. I found a letter my son had left me. I want to keep it, but I will show it to you. It will explain everything."

As we walked back down the hill afterwards, Ryan took my arm. "What was that about? I saw you talking to the detective."

"Yes, Ryan. I found a letter that Cally had left me. It was in my desk drawer in the library. I need to show it to the police."

"What? Why didn't you tell me? What did it say?"

"I didn't show you because you've hardly talked to me since that day. And because the letter doesn't show you in a very good light. But the police need to close the file and know why Cally hanged himself."

He took my arm in a tight grip. "What did it say, Vicki? Tell me."

I pulled away from him and started to walk ahead. "Don't touch me! You will know after I've talked to the detective," I called behind me.

I could tell he was furious with me, but I didn't care anymore. I couldn't wait to show the detective what a complete and utter bastard my husband had been to our son.

* * *

"I'm so very sorry for you," the detective said after reading Cally's note to me. "It must be hard to know how unhappy your son was. I would like to take a copy of the note so that we can close the file as a suicide."

"Of course it was suicide," Ryan said. "How could you think otherwise? He hanged himself, for God's sake." Ryan was incensed after learning the contents of the letter and was finding it hard to accept the fact that his son was virtually blaming him.

"I know that now, Mr. Foster, but we had to explore all possible avenues."

"Like what?"

"Foul play, to see if he had any enemies. A staged scene, to make it look like he had killed himself ..."

"Well, by reading this, you might still think I killed my son."

"There was additional evidence that proved it was suicide, sir."

"I loved my son," Ryan said lamely. "I just didn't understand him."

You hypocrite, I thought. *You never showed him any love or tried to understand him.*

After the detective left, I told Ryan I would be going over to Vancouver with Kat and Troy in the morning. "I need to get away for a few days, Ryan. I feel too angry to stay here right now."

He scowled at me. "Do whatever you want. I can see you blame me for Cally killing himself. You always sided with all the kids against me—"

"I did not! I always supported you. That was the problem!" I shouted.

But he walked away, and soon after, I heard his car driving off. For once in his life, he knew he was wrong, but he couldn't accept it.

I slept in the guest room again that night and didn't speak to Ryan before heading out to the ferry early the next morning. I had shown Cally's note to Kat and Troy before we all left. Maybe it was wrong to do that, because Kat was so angry at her father that she also refused to say goodbye to him.

I carried that guilt with me all the way to Vancouver.

CHAPTER 37 (VICKI)

After a few days with Kat and Troy, I began to feel smothered by their kindness. So one morning I asked them to drive me to the ferry. I needed to go home and work things out with my husband. After looking at it from his perspective, I realized I might have been too harsh in blaming him entirely for Cally's death.

Kat raised her eyebrows when I told her that, but they agreed to drive me. The ferry ride over was pleasant, and I hired a taxi from Swartz Bay into town. As the cab drove up the driveway, I saw Ryan's car parked at a strange angle and not in his usual spot. I hadn't expected him to be home at this time of day.

After I paid the fare and entered the house, I heard noises upstairs. Strange noises. Was it from the television? Had Ryan left it on in our bedroom?

The noises grew louder as I slowly climbed the stairs. There were discarded items of clothing on each stair. More were down the hallway leading to our bedroom—a shirt, a silk blouse, a pair of pants, two shoes and ... a bra! Whose were they?

Our bedroom door was wide open. Ryan was in bed and there was someone with him. I gasped and then I screamed. They both jumped, and the woman tried to disappear under the duvet—but not before I had seen who she was. Ruth, Todd's wife—Ryan's sister-in-law!

"My God, Vicki. What are you doing here? I thought you were still in Vancouver," Ryan said.

"Obviously you thought that. This is my home, Ryan, so that's why I'm here. And what exactly do you think *you* are doing here?"

"It's not what you think, Vicki."

"Oh really? So, what exactly is it? And you!" I shouted at Ruth. "You can get the hell out of my bed and my house—NOW! Pick up all your clothes and leave!" Ruth wrapped a sheet around herself and began hastily picking up discarded clothing in the bedroom as she headed into our bathroom.

Ryan stared at me, clutching the duvet around his own nakedness as though I had never seen him unclothed before. I tried to remain calm as I looked at the man I had loved for so long. I was so angry inside, but at the same time I felt a sense of freedom rush over me. Freedom from an obsession that had imprisoned me for the past twenty-seven years. Finally, I was seeing him for what he truly was. A narcissistic liar who had made my life hell for far too long. And now this!

"How could you do this, Ryan, and with *her*? Your own brother's wife? In *our* bed. You disgust me."

"Vicki, you know how she always comes on to me. It means nothing to me. I love you, but you left me and went to Vancouver, and I couldn't bear all the guilt I felt about Cally. You shouldn't have gone away."

"Don't you dare put the blame on me! I came home early to try and work this out with you—like I always have."

"Darling, we still can work this out. Please believe me. This meant nothing."

"*Really! Nothing?* So, within a couple of days of my being gone, because *you* felt so bad, you took another woman into our bed. I wonder how many times that has happened in the past when you felt you didn't get your own way or felt bad about something."

At that moment, Ruth appeared again, clothed but looking dishevelled and embarrassed. She still dared to say, "He loves me, Vicki. He's always wanted me instead of you."

"Well, you can have him, Ruth, with my blessing. I just hope you realize what you've done to Todd and your children. You have no morals, just like my husband. You make a good pair. But rest assured, Ryan won't stay faithful to you or anyone else for long. Life will be hell living with him."

She sneered at me. "Well, he only looks elsewhere because you're not enough for him. He's always wanted me."

"GET OUT! NOW! And never come back into my house!" I was screaming.

She ran down the corridor, calling behind her, "I'll wait in the car for you, Ryan."

"Better not keep your whore waiting!" I screamed at him.

"Vicki, let me get dressed and then we'll talk. Please, I still love only you."

"You have a damn funny way of showing it."

He pulled on his pants and a t-shirt and walked towards me.

"Get away from me, Ryan. It's over! Get out of the house and don't ever come back. I'll pack up your things and leave them on the porch in the next few days. Just get out of my sight. I can't bear to look at you right now."

I was calmer now as he ran down the corridor and flew down the stairs. I had turned into a wild banshee, scaring even myself. He flew out the front door, leaving it ajar, and then I heard the car leaving.

That's when I sank to the floor on the top stair, my head leaning against the banister rail. I'd thought I had no more tears left inside me after Cally's death, but now I began to sob unrelentingly, as my heart broke into a million more pieces.

* * *

There was a soft tapping on the open door and a voice. "Anyone home?" I didn't look up until I heard footsteps running up the stairs.

"Victoria, sweetheart. What's wrong?" Only one person called me by my full name. It was Joe.

I looked up at his worried face. "I ... I can't ... oh, Joe ... it's so awful." I couldn't even find the words to explain how I was feeling or what had just happened.

"Victoria, it's okay. Take your time."

He sat down on the stair beside me and put his arm around my shoulder. "I came over to see Ryan about an outstanding file we still have after we dissolved our partnership. He wasn't at the office, and they told me he'd gone home, but when I turned off by the bridge, I saw him flying off in the opposite direction. Kat called me this morning and said you'd left their place, and she was worried about you, so I knew you'd be home by now. Then I saw the front door was partly open."

"Oh, Joe ..."

"Tell me what happened, when you're ready."

Between sobs, I told him everything. "How could he do this to me, Joe? And with her? His own brother's wife? After Cally—it's just too much to bear."

Joe patted my shoulder and placed his left hand on my cheek, drawing my face towards his shoulder. I could feel his breath against my hair and hear both of our hearts beating. It was a peaceful feeling of being safe, but then his lips brushed my cheek and moved to my lips, and it was suddenly so much more. The passion between us was intense. Our bodies seemed to fit together as we kissed, at first gently and then passionately until eventually we broke apart with the realization of what we had just done.

Joe spoke first. "Victoria, forgive me. I took advantage of you—but I've wanted to kiss you for so long. I should not have done that now, though, when you are so vulnerable. I don't know what I was thinking ..."

"I'm sorry, too. I was just as much to blame. I just needed—"

He didn't let me finish before adding, "I don't regret it, though, because I've wanted to kiss you since I first met you all those years ago, on that awful double date we had."

I managed to smile through fresh tears. "Yes. I remember it was at the Century Inn. What happened to that girl you had with you, anyway?"

"Don't even remember her name, or any other woman I've ever been with. I've always been in love with you. Only you."

"What? I had no idea. Why did you never say anything?"

"Because I knew you loved Ryan, and he was my best friend."

"Yes, I really did love him, Joe. How could I not have seen him for what he was? Through the years, he crushed my spirit, you know. He crushed all of me, but I was too foolish to see what was happening. But when I saw him in bed with her, I was so angry that I felt the old me returning."

"I fell in love with that 'old you' all those years ago, Victoria. I've always hated everything he was doing to you and the kids."

"I feel now that I failed them all. I didn't stand up for them when I should have, especially Cally."

"Don't think that way, please, Vicki. Ryan changed. He always did have some kind of chip on his shoulder, but over the years he became someone completely different. He let all his past grievances get the better of him. I told him many times to find help for his irrational behaviour, but he ignored me. He even became impossible to work with, as you know. Being married to him must have been unbearable for you. You're not to blame, Vicki. I'm sure you were just trying to make your marriage work."

"I did try, Joe. I really did, but he was a different person sometimes. He became so angry, and when I suggested he should get some help with anger management, he just got violent."

Joe became alarmed. "My God, did he hit you?"

"No, thank God, nor the kids. But he was abusive in every other way—emotionally and verbally—to the kids as well as me. I wonder if I'll ever be strong again."

Joe put his arms around me tightly again. "You will, Victoria, and I will help you. Since I first saw you that night so long ago, I knew I was looking into the eyes of the most beautiful soul I would ever know, and that is still true. When you're ready to move on, I'll be waiting. I love you so much, but I'm not going to pressure you."

"Oh Joe, I have a lot of work to do to find myself again. I can't even think straight right now, so please be patient with me."

"Always and forever. Now, can I do anything for you right now? Can I make you some tea or coffee? Get you something to eat?"

I let him pull me to my feet. "No thank you, Joe, but can you arrange to have someone come out and change all the locks? I don't ever want him back in this house."

"Consider it done."

"And one more thing. Please stop by the cottage and see if Bee is home. If she is, will you send her up?"

"I was planning to do that on my way out anyway, sweetheart."

How did this man always know exactly what I needed? And why had I never seen that before?

CHAPTER 38 (VICKI)

Bee was there minutes later. She hugged me tightly and took me into the library, where we sat together on the comfortable sofa.

"Joe said you needed me, luv. What happened? I didn't know you were back home yet."

I slowly told her everything, leaving out nothing. "I have been so stupid, Bee. You all warned me about Ryan. You and Sam and even Judy. He cut me off from all my friends. He wanted me to be obsessed with only him, and that's why he even resented our children. I see it all now. He is a very sick man, Bee, and he needs help."

"Yes, he is, Vicki, and I'm relieved for you that this has allowed you to see him for what he truly is."

"Perhaps you're right, Bee. But I have so much to get through now before I can move on, and I need your help. First, I need someone to remove the mattress and all the bed linen from the master bedroom. I want it burnt. Then I'm going to close that room. I will never sleep there again. I'll use one of the guest rooms as mine. But before that, I will take all Ryan's clothes out and pack them in boxes and leave them on the front veranda. He is not coming back into the house again—ever. Joe is arranging to get the locks changed for me. I also intend to turn the library into my office, so I need to go up to the turret and move my stuff downstairs. Once I feel better, I want to write that book about Jane and Gideon that I have put off for far too long. It will help me get through my grief about Cally.

"Later, I might travel, and I hope you will feel able to come with me. I want to go back to England and visit Judy and her family, and then to France to find my Uncle Stephen's grave—my father's brother, who died in World War I. I wish I could find a grave for my father somewhere in France, but I know that's not possible."

"My goodness, girl. You have big plans. And I would love to travel with you, while I'm still young enough to do it."

"Good! But first, I'm going to ask the Caldwell firm for their best divorce lawyer. I'm divorcing him, Bee."

She smiled and nodded.

"I'm not feeling very strong, Bee, even though I may sound like it at the moment. But I am finally resolved to do these things for myself before anything else."

"You will, Vicki, one day at a time. But for now, come back to my place, and Mary and I will cook dinner. Get out of the house, and I'll arrange all the other stuff for you."

"There is one more important thing I need your help with."

"Anything. Just name it."

"I'm setting fire to the boathouse."

"What?"

"I can't bear to look at it anymore. I need you to help me."

"But—I understand, but why not just have it dismantled and taken away? And are you sure, Vicki, because it is part of the heritage of Providence."

"I know, Bee. I'm sorry about it because of all the hard work that went into building it by Foo and his Chinese friends who lived in it while they were building Providence. They will never be forgotten, just as Cally will always be part of Providence. But, no, I want to burn it down. Tomorrow!"

* * *

Early the following morning, before anyone was up and before Adriano arrived, I took a can of oil from the garage. Bee and I dragged two garden hoses across the lawn and down towards the boathouse. I wanted the boathouse gone but didn't want the flames to spread to the adjacent trees.

I spread the can of oil over everything and threw a match towards the building, hoping the fire would take hold before anyone spotted it and called the fire brigade. The fire did indeed quickly ignite, and the flames spread upward, destroying everything in their path. I became mesmerized by the twist and swirl of complete destruction. The woman I had become while married to Ryan went with them, but at the same time I regretted losing part of the history of this place I loved.

I'm so sorry, Jane and Gideon. I'm so sorry, dear Foo, but it must go now. I must let go of the past and rise from the ashes, like the phoenix. Please say you understand and forgive me ...

Bee was looking at me strangely as she took my hand and squeezed it tightly, and we watched the fire together. "I'm glad you're letting go of Ryan, sweetheart, but always remember the love you had for Caleb."

"I will never forget my son, Bee. I will put a memorial here for him once the site is clear. Maybe we'll plant something. I'll ask Kat. She will know what to do."

"That's a good idea, luv. We will do it together. But grief can be so overwhelming. Often, it comes over you in waves of pain, so please don't ever close your heart to love. I hope you find it again eventually."

I thought about Joe's kiss and everything he had said to me yesterday. I knew I was nowhere near ready for a loving relationship with another man yet, but inwardly I smiled.

"Maybe, Bee. Maybe one day."

Bee nodded, and then we heard voices. It was Cam and Julie running from the back of the house, with my four granddaughters in hot pursuit.

"Mom, what's happening? I'll call the fire department."

"No, Cam. The fire is under control. I have a hose right here in case it should spread further. I set the fire."

"What?"

Bee took Cam and Julie aside, and I heard them whispering together. Cam walked back to me and put his arm around my shoulder as Julie stood on the other side, linking her arm through mine. The girls were jumping up and down, chanting, "Is it Halloween already, Daddy? We have a bonfire."

Eventually the boathouse was gone, and the fire was out. We doused the ashes and any of the hot spots nearby with water. Cam and I stayed there together, making sure it was safe. The others all went back inside, Bee and Julie saying they would cook breakfast for everyone in the large Providence kitchen. Cam and I spent a silent moment remembering Cally as the young man he was and all that he could have become.

Then Julie called us back to the house and we all sat around the large kitchen table honouring Cally with our memories. I refrained from telling anyone that when I had first come through the front door and looked up at Jane McBride's portrait, I'd seen her smiling down at me.

CHAPTER 39 (VICKI)

The Caldwell firm found me the best divorce lawyer in town, and before the week was over, everything was in place and the papers were filed.

I had agreed to give Ryan back the thirty-five thousand dollars he had initially put into Providence when he moved in, but nothing more. His lawyer demanded that with inflation that figure should now be at least one hundred and thirty thousand, but I remained resolute.

There were also a few pieces of furniture that were his to dispose of. He had already stopped by to pick up his belongings, which Bee had helped me pack in boxes, from the front verandah. When Ryan arrived, Cam handled it for me and made sure he did not try to enter the house—though Joe had already sent out a locksmith to change all the locks anyway. Ryan begged Cam to allow him inside to talk to me, but I refused. I was glad for Cam's support, or I might still have weakened.

A few days later, Ryan's mother, Dorothy, stopped by, looking very distressed. "Vicki, what happened?" she said. "Ryan came home for a couple of days and said you were separating, and then he left town. Nobody knows where he went."

"We are divorcing, Dorothy. It's over. I have no idea where he went either, but I assume my lawyer found him before he left, as he has been served with divorce papers."

"But why, Vicki? I thought you two were happy."

"I guess *he* was happy, Dorothy, but I certainly was not. He treated me and our children appallingly. I refuse to talk badly about him to you, as you have always been so kind to me and I know you love your son, but he has hurt me so much, and I can't live that way again. If you want to know anything more, you'd better ask Todd."

"Todd? Why Todd? He's gone back to Toronto now, but before he left, I sensed there was also something going on between him and Ruth. They were arguing, and I don't think they left together."

"Really? Well, I hope Todd gets rid of her. Oh, Dorothy, I'm sorry. I've never liked her, but right now I really hate her, and I don't want to talk about it."

"What did she do?"

"Go and talk to Bee. She'll tell you the whole sordid story. But it wasn't only that. I should have left Ryan years ago because of what he did to our children, especially Cally."

"He was never cut out to be a father, Vicki. Ken and I could see that, and we felt bad for you. I'm so sorry for what my son did to you and the kids. I could not understand him."

"I think he has a mental sickness, and he needs help. I'm sorry too, because I should have helped him, but he always insisted he was fine and wouldn't agree to seek help from a professional."

I know I had shocked her, and I was glad when she left to make her way down to the cottage to talk to Bee. How could I possibly tell her that my husband had slept with her other son's wife?

* * *

Joe visited Providence often over the coming months to check on me.

I told him all my plans, and he nodded his approval. He was a great friend to me and supported me in everything, but he never pressured me for anything more, which I appreciated. He knew more than anyone that I wasn't ready for another relationship yet. He was especially pleased when I told him that I finally intended to write a novel about Jane and Gideon McBride and me being the missing part in the family mosaic.

"I knew you would do it one day, Victoria. I'm sure it will be a best-seller." How I had longed for Ryan to say something like that about my work through the years.

My lawyer told me that Ryan had reluctantly agreed to the terms of our divorce, although he thought he deserved much more. He had even asked for half the value of Providence in the current market. My lawyer told his lawyer that when he initially did all the restoration work, he was paid adequately at that time. He would get nothing more.

* * *

Within a year, the divorce was final, and I was finally free of him by the middle of 1997. On the same day, Kat and Troy came for a visit with some big news.

"I've finally said yes to Troy's many proposals, Mom. We want to get married on New Year's Eve, and we'd like to have the wedding and the reception here at Providence, if that's okay."

"Oh Kat, that's wonderful news. Congratulations." I hugged them both with genuine joy as I admired the large diamond ring on Kat's finger.

"Cally was right about this man, Mom. He was so intuitive. I hope he's looking down on us now."

I felt a tear escaping down my cheek as I replied: "I have no doubt he is, Kat, and probably saying, 'It's about time you said yes.'"

We then began to plan the wedding that would take place in the grand hall at Providence, with just a few selected guests. Kat did not want a big wedding, so it was mostly going to be family and close friends.

"I haven't heard from Dad, and I have no idea where he is, so I won't be inviting him, Mom. Don't worry."

"The last I heard was that he had moved to California. I'm sure his mother has an address if you decide you want to contact him." I thought it was only fair that she should let her father know, but her reply was adamant.

"He is not coming to my wedding, and that's final. He never took an interest in me, so I'm sure he wouldn't care about whether I married Troy or not."

How sad, I thought. Ryan had missed out on so much. And then she surprised me completely.

"I would like Uncle Joe to give me away. He has been more of a father to me through the years. Are you okay with that if I ask him?"

I realized I was more than just okay with it.

* * *

After a wonderful Christmas day with our families gathered around the enormous tree in the grand foyer, we had even more to celebrate on New Year's at Kat and Troy's wedding. It was a perfect end to 1997 and the beginning of a new year.

I felt something stir in the pit of my stomach as I watched Joe escort Kat down the grand staircase in her elegant but simple satin wedding gown. It seemed so perfect and so right, but still I felt a moment of pity for the man who should have been doing this today. I had invited Dorothy and Ken to the wedding, for after all, they were Kat's grandparents, but I felt sad for them, too. They still loved their son and all their grandchildren, but they decided to leave right after the ceremony and not stay for the dinner.

Only family and close friends were seated in the dining room for a spectacular catered four-course meal of asparagus or mushroom soup, Beef Wellington or turkey, a variety of salads and smoked salmon, followed by three different desserts and then the cutting of the wedding cake.

Joe delivered a speech, first congratulating the couple. He added:

"I am honoured to be here today to stand by Kaitlyn, who I have loved as my own daughter since she was a baby. We have been through a lot together through the years, but we always got through it, just as I knew we would. We all miss Cally on this special day, but we know he is here with us in spirit and delighted you finally said yes to Troy.

"I could tell some funny stories about this young lady, but I decided I wouldn't, because this is her wedding day, and we are celebrating with pride what an incredible woman she has become—not only a famous artist, with her work displayed across Canada and around the world, but also a beautiful person, inside and out.

"I wish you, my Kitty Kat—as your little brother first called you—and your very lucky husband a wonderful life together. Here's to the happy couple, and"—he paused and looked straight at me for an embarrassing long minute— "to new beginnings."

We all raised our glasses and clapped as Troy responded with an equally emotional speech that had everyone on the verge of tears.

At the table, it was just Joe and me, Kat and Troy, Bee, Cam and Julie, Sam, Jack, and Bella, and my four granddaughters, Wren, Sage, Willow, and Sorel. It was only afterwards that I realized there were fourteen of us.

*   *   *

The hall was cleared, and the happy couple took to the floor for their first dance.

As the evening progressed, I found myself constantly looking up the stairs at Jane's portrait and inwardly asking her if I had been right to divorce my children's husband, but she gave no sign.

As midnight neared, Joe claimed me for a dance, and when the old faithful grandfather clock struck twelve, we all joined in a countdown into the new year. Joe continued to hold me tightly, and then he kissed me with a gentle passion, after which we all blew whistles and sang "Auld Lang Syne."

"Happy New Year, Victoria. Here's to new beginnings."

"New beginnings, Joe." I knew I would soon be ready to commit my heart again. Day by day, my old self was slowly returning. I didn't care if anyone noticed the powerful chemistry between us. It had been there all along, but I was just too foolish to see it.

And that night, when I climbed the stairs to head for bed, Jane was smiling. I swear I heard her voice say: *You see, it should have been fourteen on that Christmas Eve long ago—just like tonight.*

How different would my life have been?

CHAPTER 40 (VICKI)

That spring of 1998, I spent hours with Joe discussing my novel. He helped me by reading pages and commenting on them. He made some valid suggestions.

After numerous rewrites, by early April, I thought it was finally ready to send the manuscript to a publisher. My old firm in London, Parker & Parker, had agreed to look at it. They had already published some of my other books.

"It certainly is ready, Victoria. It's a wonderful story," Joe agreed.

"I intend to mail it off to my old publishers before Bee and I go on our trip to Europe."

"Ah yes ... the trip! I'm going to miss you so much, my love. Please don't stay away too long."

"I won't, Joe, but I need to do these things for myself to become completely whole again. I'm slowly getting there. And we'll only be gone a couple of months."

He smiled gently as he brushed a stray lock of hair back from my eyes. "It will seem like forever."

I mailed off the completed manuscript to the publisher in late April, telling them I would be in England soon if they wanted to discuss it. Electronic mailing with attachments online made everything so much easier these days. The age of technology had arrived in a big way as we headed into a new century.

Then, in the middle of May, Bee and I flew by Air Canada from Vancouver to Heathrow. We stayed two nights in London at the Mount Royal Hotel before taking the train from Liverpool Street to Grange Park, where we were met by a very excited Judy and her eldest daughter, Penny.

Judy insisted we stayed with them at their Elizabethan-style house, which had more than enough bedrooms. Her husband, Tony, was a lawyer, and they were obviously doing well.

"Not quite as posh as Providence, Vicky," she said as she showed us to our rooms. But the house was a delightful combination of old and new, and it made me sad to think I had allowed so many years to pass without visiting my best friend again.

Meeting all of Judy's family and being squired around our old familiar haunts was a delight. Bee also enjoyed visiting some of her old friends, and one night I asked her about her late husband.

"You've never talked about him, Bee, and you have never been seriously romantically involved with anyone else, but obviously you had a lot of friends and could easily have married again. Was there ever anyone else?"

"We were very young when we married, but we were madly in love. I was only nineteen and he was twenty-two—far too young to make such a commitment, but it was wartime, and you never knew from one day to another what might happen. We thought our love would last forever. He was on leave during the blitz of 1940 and killed by a bomb in London, the night before I was going to join him."

"How awful! I'm so sorry, Bee."

She smiled. "Yes, it was awful, but ... life goes on. A year later, your mum met Harry Blake, and he fell like a ton of bricks for your mum. I felt so sorry for Harry because I knew right from the start that she didn't feel the same way, whereas ... "

"Whereas?"

"Sweetheart, after your dad, Cal Hamilton, died, I decided to help your mum and Harry raise you, and then she died too, so ... "

"You moved in permanently to help take care of me?"

"Yes, and my compassion for Harry turned into much more."

I stared at her. "You mean you and Dad ...?

She shook her head. "I fell in love with him, but it never went anywhere. He was still grieving your mum, and he did until the day he died."

"Oh Bee, that is so sad."

Her revelation gave me so much to think about. My wonderful aunt had lost a husband to war and then had devoted her life to her sister's child. She deserved so much more. She deserved to have had her own love affair and her own children. Life was sometimes very unfair.

* * *

After six weeks in England, we made a trip from London to Paris by train through the Chunnel, which had opened in 1994 and was an incredibly quick way to travel between the two cities.

We spent a few days in Paris, in a charming boutique hotel, sampling sumptuous food and good wine and doing all the usual touristy things. We then hired a car and I drove north towards the Courcelette Canadian Memorial, where my father's older brother, Stephen, was buried.

On a hot, sunny morning, we took the AI motorway towards Lille and continued for approximately 135 kilometres before taking exit 14 for Bapaume. From there, the directions were easy to follow towards the turnoff for Courcelette. We were there in an hour and a half.

I had read about the battle of Courcelette, when three divisions of the Canadian Corps had launched a valiant attack on German lines to capture the ruined remains of the small village of Courcelette, and I knew from reading Jane McBride's journals and all the letters she had kept what a horrendous experience it must have been for her grandson, Stephen. When we finally found Stephen Ernest Hamilton's tablet, marking his last resting place in one of the main cemeteries, I felt overwhelmed.

I knelt on the ground in front of his grave, where a solitary rose wound its way around, as though embracing him. As I read the inscription my thoughts immediately travelled back to Providence. I thought about my great-grandmother, Jane, and all the losses she had experienced in her life. I thought about my grandmother, Sarah, and the tragedy of her love affair and losing Stephen, her firstborn son. I was grateful she had never had to experience the loss of her second son, my father. I thought about my mother, who had loved Cal Hamilton and borne him a daughter—me.

But most of all, this place reminded me of my own son, Cally, who had surrendered his life so tragically. So much unnecessary loss. In the McBride family, it seemed that the more things changed, the more they stayed the same.

And then the intense grief of losing Cally came over me in waves, until I couldn't bear to think any more. I felt Bee's comforting hand on my shoulder as I sobbed and sobbed, until there were no more tears left.

* * *

My eyes were still misty as we drove southwest towards Sainte-Quentin in Picardy, a charming town with museums, parks, and incredible architecture. I thought how much Joe would love it here. We stayed there for two nights. But there was one more thing I needed to do before heading back to England. I wanted to see the Normandy beaches and look out across the English Channel and visualize where my biological father had lost his life at the end of World War II. Although I knew all this travel was taking a toll on my seventy-nine-year-old aunt, she readily agreed, and the next morning we travelled south towards Normandy.

We found a hotel in the area and booked a tour of the beaches known in wartime as Utah, Omaha, and Juno. Again, I felt overwhelmed with emotion, especially at Juno Beach, where 144,000 Canadians and 6,400 British troops landed on D-Day. The museum there was entirely devoted to commemorating Canada's unique contribution. My father would have been airborne through those years, giving up his own life in that way.

At Omaha Beach, we stood on the high bluff overlooking the wide expanse of beautiful sand glistening in the sun and found it hard to imagine why it was once referred to as "bloody Omaha"—the courage of the men who landed there and who became living targets for landmines and guns was inconceivable.

Oh, Dad, if only you had lived to witness that all this bloodshed did bring victory in the end, and a peaceful Europe.

"I think it's time to go home, Bee," I said, and she nodded.

The next day we returned to England and spent another week with Judy. I had an email from my publishers, who wanted to meet with me about my manuscript before I left England. I took a day trip to London with trepidation, awaiting their verdict on the book. I could hardly believe it when they offered me a contract to publish it the following year, in their spring collection of 1999.

That night I took Bee, Judy, and her entire family out for dinner to celebrate, and two days later Bee and I were on a flight back to Vancouver. We had been away for nine weeks, and I couldn't wait to get home.

My heart wanted to see Providence again, but more than anything, I wanted to see Joe.

CHAPTER 41 (VICKI)

We were both exhausted after the long flight from Heathrow to Vancouver and then the short hop over to Victoria. We hadn't told anyone of our exact arrival time and had planned to take a taxi home from the airport to Providence,

But as we came through Arrivals and were about to walk to the carousel to claim our luggage, I saw him. His face lit up when he spotted me, and I didn't hesitate. I simply ran into his arms.

"Joe, Joe, how did you know when we'd get here?" We kissed for a long time, and I didn't care who saw us.

"I had a little help with that," he finally said, and then winked at Bee, who had caught up with me.

"Bee, you didn't tell me. You agreed we would look for a taxi!"

"Guilty as charged." She grinned. "Joe had asked me for the time of our flight arrival, and I knew how badly you two would want to see one another, so I let him know. I thought it would be a nice surprise for you, Vicki."

"It is," I replied.

"And I certainly couldn't wait a moment longer to see you, Victoria. You've got that right, Bee. Thank you. Now, let me help you ladies to retrieve your luggage. My car is very near the exit."

"And you can drop me off at the cottage while you take this young lady home to Providence. I'm looking forward to a quiet evening and my own bed tonight."

It was all done efficiently with Joe's help, and before I knew it, we were driving down the highway towards Victoria. I could not believe how good it felt to see Joe again.

When we drove through the gates at Providence, Joe pulled over and helped Bee into her cottage with her luggage. Mary greeted her friend and smiled at me.

"Talk to you tomorrow, Vicki," Bee called as Joe got back in the car and drove up towards the front porch of Providence. He parked and then carried my luggage inside.

"Do Cam and Julie know the time of our arrival?"

"I think Bee only told me." Joe smiled.

"That's good."

Suddenly we both felt shy.

"Shall I take your luggage upstairs now? Or ...?"

"Yes, please."

"I badly want to kiss you, but if you're not ready ..."

"I think—no, I know. I'm ready."

We left the luggage in the hall and, hand in hand, climbed the stairs and headed for the guest room at the back of the house that I had turned into my bedroom. And there we made love for the first time.

And my life was finally right.

* * *

After we showered and went back downstairs, Joe made us something to eat with what he found in the fridge, while I put the coffee on.

"Victoria, I want to marry you, if you'll have me. Are you ready for that?"

"Yes, I think I am, Joe."

"But would you live with me in my condo—or we can buy a house somewhere if you'd prefer. I love this house, but it doesn't feel right for me to live here when it was yours and Ryan's home. I know you don't want to sell Providence, so perhaps we can work something out."

"I'd be happy to live with you in your condo, Joe, but you're right, I can't bear to sell Providence. Cam and Julie and the girls are still here and probably will stay for a while. The girls love the grounds, and it's been a great place for them to grow up."

"I agree. You know, you could still use the rest of the house for any big family gatherings."

"Yes, that would certainly work. And Bee and Mary are nearby to keep an eye on the place."

"I love you, Victoria."

"And I love you, Joe. But I don't want the shadow of my marriage to Ryan between us anymore. So, before we go any further, I want to be honest with you about everything. My marriage to Ryan was a mistake, and I realize that now, but I really thought I was in love with him, I really did. Thinking back now, I was probably too young, and I rushed into the relationship without thinking. He was so charming, and I desperately wanted it to be right. You see, after my dad died I was quite rebellious for a long time and I know I was sometimes awful to Bee. Then when I was nineteen, I met this man who swept me off my feet, and I left home and moved in with him. That was not a thing proper English girls did in the '60s, as you know. Bee had warned me about him, and within a year I knew she was right. He was a womanizer and had absolutely no intention of settling down or ever marrying me. Finally, I walked out and went back home.

"Then, when I was twenty-three, I came to Canada and was faced with this enormous inheritance. I was overwhelmed having to decide whether to move here. Everything here was so new and different, but it was also exciting. Within a few months, I'd met Ryan, and this time I wanted to believe it was all meant to be. He was the man for me. I wanted a happy marriage and a family—but he changed so much after we were married, Joe. I soon realized I had made another mistake, but I refused to believe it. The thought of failing again was too much and I couldn't face divorce, so I allowed him to manipulate me. It took me years to understand that he had some kind of mental health issue, but by then it was too late. Then we lost Cally and I just lost myself, and—well, that's why I've taken my time deciding about us."

"My darling, you don't have to explain it all to me. I understand. I'm just relieved that you can love again, and that I'm the lucky man. I promise I will never let you down. This time it will be right."

After we had eaten and talked some more, we went back upstairs. That night, with Joe beside me, I slept better than I had in years.

* * *

While we were having breakfast the next morning, Cam knocked on the back door. He and Julie, followed by their four very excited little girls, came in and all gave me hugs with cries of "Welcome home!" from everyone.

"We missed you, Nana!"

"Oh, and I missed you all," I said. It felt so good to be home. No one seemed the least bit surprised that Joe and I were eating breakfast together.

"We thought you must be home yesterday, Mom, but we knew you were probably tired, so we left you in peace." Cam smiled at me, and I saw him wink at Joe.

"But Uncle Joe was here," said Wren who was now eleven and knew far too much for her own good. "He was with you, but we weren't allowed to come over to see you until this morning."

"No, we weren't," echoed ten-year-old Sage, seven-year-old Willow, and little six-year-old Sorel. Oh, how I loved my four granddaughters.

Julie intervened. "Girls, Uncle Joe had picked up Nana and Aunt Bee at the airport and that is why he was here."

"But—"

"I had a very important question to ask your Nan last night, girls," Joe said. He looked at me, and I nodded.

"I asked her to marry me, and guess what? She said YES!"

Everyone let out a whoop of joy. Cam and Julie didn't seem the least bit surprised.

"Oh, can we be bridesmaids? I love weddings. When will it be ...?" And on and on, the four little princesses chanted.

Cam shook Joe's hand, and he and Julie hugged me tightly. "It's about time you were happy, Mom," he whispered. "We are delighted for you both."

"I have to phone Kat and let her know before we set a date," I said as the girls climbed all over me.

Julie laughed. "I think she already suspects!"

"Good grief, did you all know this would happen before I did?"

"YES!" they all said in unison.

Later, when I talked to both Kat and Cam on their own, I asked them how they really felt about me marrying again, after my disastrous marriage to their father. Both assured me they could not be happier for us both. Kat also told me that she and Troy were expecting a baby in the middle of January 1999, and they had found out it was a boy. My first grandson! My marriage to Joe, another grandchild, and my novel being published! What a year. Suddenly, my happiness was beyond belief.

Joe and I planned a quiet wedding at Thanksgiving with just the family. The minister from St. Luke's-on-the-Hill performed the ceremony in the garden gazebo at Providence, and the weather co-operated with an Indian summer that continued for the remainder of October. We had a family dinner together at a small reception in the house. Joe then surprised me with tickets to Italy for our honeymoon, and we spent three glorious weeks in Rome and Venice, two of my favorite cities.

I moved to Joe's condo downtown but visited Providence often. We had a big celebration for Christmas and planned another for New Year's Eve, but that one was interrupted by Kat going into early labour. She was rushed to the Victoria General Hospital, where she gave birth to my first grandson just after midnight, the first baby born in Victoria in 1999. She named him Matthew Caleb Troy Wilson. Kat and Troy stayed at Providence after she was discharged from the hospital, and Julie took wonderful care of her.

Of course, I spent a lot of time there as a doting grandma, and sometimes I took the four girls out on trips, or we had sleepovers with them at the condo. It felt so good to lead a normal life and be happy, without having to be on guard all the time. Joe also enjoyed being a granddad when the girls changed his name from Uncle Joe to Papa Joe.

We arranged for a small dogwood tree to be planted on the site of the old boathouse. It was Kat's choice, because she said the dogwood flower signifies rebirth and is a symbol of purity, faithfulness, and hope. She wanted love and hope for anyone who has considered committing suicide, in memory of her little brother Cally.

* * *

My book was released in May and was an immediate success. I was astounded to find I was suddenly famous, and I felt a little overwhelmed by all the book signings, tours, and celebrations the publishers arranged. I was fifty-five that year, but suddenly, with Joe beside me in support, I felt more like twenty-five again.

One day that summer, Cam and Julie came to the condo for dinner and Cam made an announcement.

"Mom, we have purchased a two-acre lot and are having a house built near Elk Lake. It should be finished by next year or in the early spring of 2001, so we'll be vacating the suite at Providence then. I wanted to give you lots of notice."

"I really appreciate that, Cam. I know we'll have to make some decisions about the house soon. I'm so proud of the way you two have worked so hard and saved your money to do this."

"Thanks, Mom, and if it helps, Kat told me that she and Troy want to have a place as a base over here in Victoria, so they might want to move into the suite. I have a feeling they'll try for another baby soon. She loves being a mother."

I laughed. "Wow, I never thought I would hear that."

Julie added, "Our girls have loved growing up at Providence and being able to play on the grounds, so it will be ideal for little Matthew and any future children Kat and Troy have. They may never go back to Vancouver, other than for business."

Cam's words came true in May 2000, when, just five months into the new millennium, Kat gave birth to a daughter and named her Jane Victoria, my name in reverse. We finally had another Jane in the family, and I was thrilled beyond words.

Life suddenly seemed to be passing by far too quickly. Early in 2001, Bee's friend Mary passed away and their antiques business was finally closed. Bee kept herself busy with various projects and seemed happy, but I was sure she must be lonely living alone. She loved spending time in the Providence garden, and we would often find her there on her hands and knees, helping the gardeners pull weeds.

One September morning, Joe and I went over to visit her, and this time found her glued to the television.

"Oh my God, have you heard?" she cried as she opened the door to us.

"Yes, we just heard on the car radio. Is it true? Did a plane really fly into one of the twin towers in New York?"

Joe was studying the footage appearing on the television, and none of us spoke for a while. We could not believe what we were seeing.

Finally, I said, "I have to phone Kat. I know she and Troy have many friends and business acquaintances in New York. I hope they're all safe. This is awful."

We spent the rest of the morning watching the television as more terrible events evolved. It seemed the world had gone mad.

It took a few more days to piece everything together. Kat had contacted her friends in New York and, thank goodness, they were all safe, but the loss of life and devastation of this dreadful attack was totally beyond comprehension.

Cam and Julie moved into their house the following year, and the girls seemed happy to still have acreage to run around in and explore. Wren, now thirteen, going on eighteen, felt very important and responsible when asked to babysit her little cousins, Matthew and Jane, on occasion after they moved into the suite with their parents.

That same year, I decided to put the house and property into joint ownership with my son and daughter, and the three of us formed the McBride Foundation as joint owners.

Matthew and Jane would now grow up at Providence, and life for our family was evolving just as it was meant to.

CHAPTER 42 (JANE)

I was born in Vancouver, but we moved to a big house in Victoria just before I was two. My earliest memories are of Providence and playing with my big brother, Matthew, in our large garden. We were always told to stay in a certain area and not to go down to the water without an adult.

Uncle Cam and Aunt Julie had lived upstairs in the suite before us, but they had now moved into another house, a short drive away from town. Before them, I think Great Aunt Bee and her friend, Mary, had lived there in the suite and my Nan had lived in the rest of the house with the man who was my real grandad and my mother's father. His name was Ryan Foster, but I never met him, and Mummy never talked about him, only to say that he had moved far away, and Papa Joe was now my grandad.

I loved Papa Joe and Nan so much. They lived in a tall building by the harbour, but they visited the house often, and so did my aunt and uncle with my four cousins, Wren, Sage, Willow, and Sorel. We had a lot of fun together when everyone was there. Mummy's friend was my aunt Bella, who also had two children, and Bella's mom was Aunty Sam, who was my Nan's best friend. It was all rather complicated, as Aunty Sam was also Papa Joe's cousin, and they were Caldwells. They always said that the McBrides and Caldwells had been friends forever.

One day when I was about five and Matthew was six, we were playing in the garden when we heard the shrill sound of an ambulance siren coming nearer and nearer to the house. It drove in through our gates and stopped by Great Aunt Bee's cottage. I saw that Nan and Papa Joe's car was also down there, so we ran down the driveway to see what was happening.

Papa Joe came towards us and held up his arms to stop us in our tracks. "Go back inside to your mummy, children," he said.

"What happened, Papa Joe?" I asked.

"It's Great Aunt Bee. She is sick, but the paramedics are taking care of her."

By then, Mummy had run down the driveway and joined us, and I heard Papa Joe whispering to her something about a "heart attack." I wondered who had attacked Great Aunt Bee's heart!

Eventually the siren stopped, and the lights weren't flashing anymore, so I thought Great Aunt Bee's heart must be all right now. But after talking to Papa Joe again, Mummy took us away, and she was crying. Then I saw Nan come out of the cottage and watch the ambulance drive away. She was also sobbing, and Papa Joe's arms were around her. Everyone was sad because apparently Great Aunt Bee had died. I wanted to hug Nan, because I hated to see her so sad, but Mummy took us back to the house and explained that older people died. She said it was very sad because we would miss them, but we should always hold happy memories in our hearts.

Next time I saw Nan and Papa Joe, I told them that, but it just made Nan cry again.

* * *

As I grew older, Matthew and I sometimes went into the other part of the house when no one was around. I thought it was rather spooky, especially the top landing, where there were pictures of all the family. Some were old oil paintings of our ancestors, but there were also more modern paintings of the family I knew. The whole thing reminded me of a royal palace, where they hang portraits in the halls like that. Nan said that the lady in the middle, dressed in a yellow dress, had the same name as me, and she and her husband Gideon, whose portrait was in the downstairs library, were the people who first built the house, long ago.

The whole place was full of history, and I enjoyed hearing all the stories from the past. I felt honoured to come from such a prestigious pioneer family.

One day when I was about eight, I remember Mom looking at her phone and then rushing out the door leading to the landing in the big house. She looked concerned, so I called out to her, but she obviously didn't hear me and kept running. In her hurry, she hadn't quite closed the door behind her, so I sneaked out to see what was happening.

Nan was downstairs in the grand hall, and she and mom were hugging as they whispered softly. Why hadn't Nan come up to see us first, the way she usually did? Why did she just text Mom to go down there to meet her? I tried to listen to what they were saying, but I could only catch the occasional word.

"Todd phoned me to tell me," I heard Nan say.

"Where was Dad?"

"Still living in California."

"I'm not sad, Mom. I hardly remember him now."

Who was Todd, and who were they talking about?

Eventually Nan left and Mom began to slowly ascend the stairs. I crept back to our suite and waited for her.

"What happened, Mom?" I asked. "Was Nan down there?"

"Oh, Jane. Did you hear?"

"Sort of. Who is Todd? And why are you crying?"

"I'm not really crying, just a bit sad. Todd is my real father's brother, my uncle, although I haven't seen him for years. He phoned Nan to give her news about my dad, and Nan came over to tell me. She promised to come back later to see you and Matthew, but we are both a bit ..."

"Sad?"

She nodded.

"Was it something about Nan's first husband, Mom? Your real dad."

"Oh Janykins," she bent down and hugged me, using the old name she and Dad called me when I was a baby. "My real dad died."

I hugged her back. "Was he Ryan? And why did he never come to see us?"

"That, my darling girl, is something I will never understand. When you are much older, I will tell you about him, but for now, just be glad that you have a wonderful dad who loves you so much. You and Matt are very lucky."

It was many years later when she told me that her dad, Ryan Foster, had died of a heart attack after years of alcoholism and drug abuse. When I understood the full story of Nan's marriage to him and the way he had treated her and their children, I was indeed so grateful for my own wonderful dad.

* * *

By the time I was eleven, I had read my Nan's book about the McBride family. She was a famous author, and Papa Joe was a heritage architect, but he had retired by then.

My dad was an art dealer and Mom a very famous artist known across Canada. There was so much talent in our family, so I felt obligated to do something spectacular in the world—especially as I had been given the same name as the first lady who lived in Providence. Nan told me she had started life as an orphan in a home for unwanted children in England but had risen to become the great chatelaine of this house. She and her husband, Gideon, were hard-working pioneers who had come to the New World in the nineteenth century and contributed so much to Canada. Nan also said she thought that the first Jane haunted the house—but in a good way. It still freaked me out, though.

A year after Great Aunt Bee died, her antiques shop was converted into a gift shop where they also sold my mom's artwork and Nan's books. I loved going in there, as Great Aunt Bee's antiques were still there and they intrigued me.

I think it was about that time that I first became interested in the early history of colonialism, and in September 2013, when I was thirteen, we held a big celebration at the house for the 150th anniversary of Providence. The house had been designated a national heritage building that year.

It was a very grand affair, and many dignitaries were invited. The four mayors of Victoria, Saanich, Esquimalt, and Oak Bay came to the event, as well as history professors and archives people. I eavesdropped on some of their conversations as I wandered around the lawn and through the big house. It was fascinating. Celebrating the 150th birthday of a house in Victoria was certainly special, although Nan told me there were much older houses and buildings in Europe. Mom and Dad had taken Matthew and me to England once, so I knew that was true.

My school graduation party in 2017 was also held at Providence, and I was allowed to invite all my friends and even have a dance in the grand hall with a hired band and a deejay. At the end of the evening, we had a fireworks display over the water, which was spectacular. My prom date was my boyfriend, Chris Sullivan, and he and I danced the night away. We were excited about the fact that we were both heading to the University of Victoria in September.

The following morning, I slept late but was delighted to find that Nan and Papa Joe had come over to visit. Papa Joe was talking to Dad in the garden, but Nan was sitting on the front veranda.

"Ah, there she is," Nan said. "So, how does it feel to be graduated and on your way to a new life, Jane?"

"Exciting."

I poured myself a coffee and sat down beside Nan on the swing. "I've been doing a lot of thinking about the Indigenous people who once lived on this land, and I've decided I wanted to take Indigenous

Studies, archival studies and psychology at UVic, Nan. What do you think?"

"Well, it sounds like an excellent idea, if that is what interests you."

"It does, Nan. I've recently been reading the Indian Act and a lot about the Department of Indian Affairs, which was created when it was first passed in 1876, to administer policies regarding First Nations. Did you know that the Indian Act defined who was considered a "status Indian" but people who qualified were made *wards* of the government? The Act treated them as if they were children and wards of the court, in need of care. It was despicable! Before 1951, which isn't really that long ago, "Status Indians" weren't even deemed to be "people" under the laws of Canada, and they were denied many rights other Canadians enjoyed. Status Indians could only become "persons" by voluntary enfranchisement—which meant relinquishing their Indian status. Only if they did that would they be allowed to vote, or own property, and have the rights of other Canadian citizens. It makes my blood boil, Nan, and don't get me started on the children who were taken away and put in residential schools to take the "Indian" out of them. A lot of them died of disease and abuse—they suspect the bodies of thousands of them were buried near the schools. They're finding some in various places, and I'm sure there will be more."

"Well, it was terrible. And I can certainly see how passionate you are about this."

"That's why I made that decision about my future studies. I want to make a difference, and I also have an idea how Providence can play a part."

"Really?"

"Would it be possible to turn the house into a museum one day? I could manage it from the suite once I get my degree. Mom and Dad are thinking of buying a condo in your building downtown. Mom said she wants to be near you and Papa Joe as you get older, so she can keep an eye on you both!"

Nan laughed. "Does she indeed?"

"But perhaps I could still live in the apartment, and the rest of the house could be open to the public. We could display the whole history of this area, including the Indigenous people who lived and worked on this land before our ancestors got here."

"It does sound like a good idea, Jane. I hope you would include both sides of colonialism—including the hard-working pioneers and settlers like Jane and Gideon McBride, who carved out a better life for themselves here."

"Yes, I agree. It's so important to see both sides of the coin. To face the bad things that also happened, but to learn from them."

So, it was arranged. Mom and Dad moved to a condo downtown, and I was allowed to stay in the suite at Providence while attending university. I took great care of the rest of the house, as I considered it my legacy, but at the same time, I began planning how it could one day become a museum, an historical site to honor the past, with me as curator once I got my degree in four years.

CHAPTER 43 – JANE

Late on Friday, March 13, 2020, the large, extended members of the Caldwell and McBride families were beginning to arrive for a family celebration at Providence for Papa Joe's 80th birthday. Nan was seventy-five that year, but they were both active and young at heart, and to me they seemed more like sixty.

We opened all the bedrooms in the house and in the cottage by the gate so that during the three-day celebration we could all stay together, and no one would have to drive home until Monday morning. It was wonderful to see so many members of our family in one place, which was very rare.

But something else was lurking in the back of everyone's mind as we ate dinner on that first night. A strange and often fatal virus had been discovered in China and was slowly spreading around the world. Governments everywhere were announcing lockdowns, and we were bewildered about what this might mean for us.

Everyone seemed to be checking their phones frequently for updates. Nan usually insisted on people leaving their phones at the door when we had a large family gathering. But this time, even she was checking her phone.

To me, it all seemed so far away, like the SARS outbreak a few years earlier. At first, I was annoyed that all this worried talk was putting a damper on the big party we had planned for the next day. But two days earlier the World Health Organization had declared the coronavirus to be a pandemic, which I knew was far more serious than an epidemic. So I listened more intently to everyone's opinions.

I heard Papa Joe's brother, Paul, say that more than 88,000 people had already been infected globally, and apparently the virus had been named COVID-19: the 19 referred to the fact it had originated in China towards the end of the previous year.

Paul and Papa Joe had reconciled in recent years, after a long period when Papa Joe had been estranged from his family because they disapproved of his career choice. He hadn't pursued law, like all the other Caldwells. After seeing how happy and successful he had become as an architect and then married to Nan, he was back in the Caldwell fold again—which to me seemed only right. Everyone should be allowed to pursue their own dream.

"Well, I certainly hope our medical system can cope here in B.C." someone added.

"Dr. Bonnie Henry is excellent as the chief medical officer, a fine leader," someone else said.

Papa Joe weighed in. "I don't think this virus will be eradicated until a vaccine is created, and that might take a while."

Once dinner was over, Nan stood up and addressed everyone. "Let's all stop talking about this for now. We'll see what happens next week. Meanwhile, let's celebrate my wonderful husband, whose birthday is tomorrow."

"Yes indeed," Paul added. "Let the celebrations begin!"

* * *

Chris Sullivan and I had become especially close over the past two years. We had considered ourselves to be boyfriend and girlfriend since Grade 12, and our love grew during our first years at university. We had a similar outlook on the world and what we wanted to do with our lives. He had taken economics and business management, and I had concentrated on Indigenous studies and archival research.

Chris had been invited for the weekend, along with other husbands, wives, and significant others of our family and friends. Mom told me Nan would have been scandalized to know that she had allowed Chris to share my room. I'd always thought Mom was far more liberated than Nan, but then I discovered that Nan and her first husband, Ryan, my blood grandfather, had moved in together at Providence before they married, and that was back in the '60s! So, I didn't think Nan would object. This was now 2020, after all. I challenged Mom about it, and she reluctantly agreed that maybe Nan wouldn't mind. The times were changing.

Celebrations for Papa Joe's birthday began in earnest the next day. The weather was mild for March, so we spent a lot of time outside in the morning. We played croquet on the lawn, while others challenged each other on the tennis court. A buffet lunch was served at noon, after which some of us played board games set up on tables in the grand hall. Others sat around in the living room or the library, telling stories and getting to know more about one another. I really felt the strong power of family love that day, and, during a quiet moment, I told Nan about my feelings.

"This is all so special, Nan. I'm glad you thought about getting everyone together for Papa's birthday. It was a wonderful idea," I said.

"I agree. You never know what will happen in the future. There has been so much hurt and anger in the world lately, and with this epidemic coming ..."

"Oh Nan, I hope it doesn't get worse."

"Me too. So, let's all enjoy the moment and the fact that we are all together as a family. One day at a time." She smiled and gave me a hug. "Maybe the next big celebration will be a wedding?"

"Who knows?" I said, somewhat cryptically.

* * *

The party that night was fabulous. A formal dinner on two dining tables extending from the dining room into the living room allowed sixty members of family and friends to sit down and enjoy a catered meal of roast beef, ham, turkey and various pastas, with vegetables and scalloped and roasted potatoes. All of that was followed by scrumptious crème brulé, fruit, a cheese platter and of course a very large birthday cake, served amid a riotous chorus of "Happy Birthday."

The grand hall was then cleared, and the three-piece band arrived promptly at nine for the dancing to begin. We all danced the night away, including Nan and Papa Joe, who were enjoying every moment and didn't seem a bit tired.

At midnight, we all headed outside to watch the fireworks display set up by Uncle Cam, with spectacular displays shooting over the water. I realized in that moment how fortunate we all were. This one celebration must have cost our family today a fortune. I mused that we should never forget our ancestors, who worked so hard to enable this to happen generations later.

That was the night, as we watched the fireworks together, that Chris officially asked me to marry him. Of course, I said yes. There was simply no other answer.

But when the party broke up on Monday morning, after another joyful day together on Sunday, we were all forced to face reality. The pandemic was looming, and life as we once knew it was changing, maybe forever. Everyone departed realizing we might never be able to have a large gathering like that again.

By March 17, schools were suspended indefinitely, all gatherings were banned across the province, non-essential workers were told to stay home, dentists were suspending non-essential work, and even church services were not allowed. In many places, bars and restaurants were closing down, too. The province declared a public health emergency.

On March 18, the Canada-U.S. border was closed to non-essential traffic in both directions, by the leaders of both countries. By the end of March, we were living in a silent world, forced to limit ourselves to small family "bubbles" of fewer than six people.

Chris had returned to his family, while Mom and Dad stayed with me in the suite and Nan and Papa Joe decided to stay in the main house, so that at least they could go outside and enjoy the fresh air of Providence. If any of us left, which we did only for essential reasons, masks were mandatory. Aunt Julie, my mom and all the girl cousins were using their sewing skills to make colourful masks to sell in the gift shop or online, but only medical masks were allowed in most health areas.

People began working from home, and all school and university courses moved online. We all quickly learned to use FaceTime and Zoom if we wanted to see anyone else. Things gradually grew worse over the summer and fall of 2021, and I frequently recalled Papa Joe's words that weekend in March—that things wouldn't get better until a vaccine was developed. Covid-19 cases continued to rise at an alarming rate throughout Canada and around the world, and people were dying by the thousands. With a lot of unemployment and businesses going broke, there was also a big concern about other health issues, like depression.

At Providence, it taught us all to be grateful every day for remaining healthy, while waiting for the next shoe to drop.

I was thankful that vaccines were finally available and being widely distributed in 2021, and once we all received our "shots," life slowly began to look a little more normal. But it was still a long way to reach the light at the end of that dark tunnel.

CHAPTER 44 (JANE)

Not only had our world dealt with the most horrendous pandemic since the Spanish flu of 1919, but by 2023 we were also becoming very aware of climate change effects: floods, fires, and unprecedented high temperatures. In Victoria, the summer of 2022 had included a ferocious "heat dome," with temperatures reaching the 40s, and we all virtually melted. Nan decided to have air conditioning installed at Providence that year.

But it was not all doom and gloom. In the summer of 2023, we had much to celebrate. Chris and I had graduated from university and planned our wedding for July at St. Luke's-on-the-Hill, where so many of my family had married before me.

The evening before our wedding day, I left the house on my own and walked down towards the water. It was a beautiful evening, and I enjoyed watching the sun sink and spread its orange glow over the water. A thick mist began to descend over the water. To my surprise, I still noticed an eagle sitting in its nest on one of the two tall trees across the water. The buildings on the other side of the Arm disappeared in the mist, and all I could see was that eagle. It was strange, as I couldn't recall seeing the nest before, though I'd often looked out from this spot. Down below in the mist, I caught a glimpse of figures in canoes on the water. Just then, the eagle majestically rose, flapped its wings, and flew away, disappearing from sight.

I felt a shiver down my spine as I turned to walk back to the house. As I'd been watching the sun set, the lawn and house had also become shrouded in that white mist. Instead of seeing Providence, I saw trees and wildflowers, and a young woman running towards me through the mist, followed by a man.

I distinctly heard her voice. *That's it, Gideon.*

What's it?
The name of our house. Providence!

He lifted her in his arms, and they laughed as he swung her round and round.

I blinked.

The mist cleared and, like the eagle, the young couple were also gone.

What had just happened? Had I seen an apparition? Two ghosts? A glimpse into a distant past? Nan had told me she often experienced Jane McBride's presence in the house, and that her portrait on the landing sometimes changed expressions. I'd always felt that was nonsense, just an old lady's superstition. I really didn't believe in the supernatural and ghosts.

But this strange vision gave me pause. Before I walked up the lawn, I glanced backwards. Everything was the same as before. Had I really been shown something? A glimpse into the past, to show me what I must do now?

* * *

After a beautiful wedding reception and a honeymoon gift from our parents of a week at Harrison Hot Springs on the mainland, we returned to Providence renewed and refreshed for our life together.

The last large family gathering occurred in September that year, when we celebrated the 160th anniversary of Providence. It was not as large as the gatherings we'd held before, when we were blissfully unaware of how a pandemic could change everything.

The state of the world was depressing. There was war in Ukraine and in Israel, and Palestine, causing unbearable suffering to so many. Chris and I tried to be optimistic about our future. We wanted to start a family, but we also worried about bringing children into a world that had gone so very wrong.

We obviously couldn't solve all the problems of the world, but at least we could try to sustain our own lives and help others in some small way.

I now knew for certain that we must preserve the legacy of Providence, so that it would survive into a distant tomorrow.

EPILOGUE:

THE FUTURE
2045

Providence still stands on Primrose Lane today, and at first glance much appears to be the same—until you look a little deeper.

In keeping with Jane McBride's original 1945 will and codicil, the house was never sold and is still held in trust by the McBride Foundation, created and managed by the McBride and Caldwell families as a charity to provide for those in need. With Providence officially becoming a heritage site in 2013 and a museum in 2025, the visitors who come to the mansion along the Gorge Waterway today are mostly tourists.

Only one McBride descendant still lives there. Victoria Caldwell's granddaughter, Jane, moved into the north wing suite as a child and remained there while attending university. She continued to live there with her husband and their twin boys, Edward and Simon, who were born in 2027. Jane and her children stayed on after her husband died in 2030, and Jane has continued to take care of Providence and oversee the operation of the heritage museum and the McBride Foundation.

Jane Sullivan has always been a strong advocate and ally for First Nations, and, apart from her private suite, the remainder of the house has continued as a heritage museum that is open to the public.

One Saturday in the summer of 2045, a group of tourists were greeted by a volunteer guide—Chelsea, a third-year university student—who met the group in the main hall.

"Welcome to Providence, everyone. My name is Chelsea, and I will be your guide today," she began, following that with a brief introduction to the story of the McBride family and how they came to Victoria.

"I hope you will enjoy travelling back in time on this delightful heritage site," she said, her gestures inviting the visitors to gaze around the space. "We begin here in the Grand Hall, with its black and white marble floor. The marble was imported from Italy by Gideon McBride, who supervised the building of the house and was the first owner."

The visitors all admired the floor and the expanse of the grand entrance.

Chelsea continued, "This Grand Hall was once the scene of many balls and parties but is now a display center containing both Indigenous and Colonial memorabilia. The exhibits to your left detail the origins of the land on which the house stands as the unceded Coast Salish territory of the Lekwungen First Nation people. The displays tell the story of those first people who walked the land and made their living there from fishing and hunting. As you wander around, please feel free to touch the screens and enjoy the moving exhibits before you. Some of these stories are brutal and raw, and that same brutality and disrespect for the Indigenous people continued well into the 21st century. Other displays describe the Residential Schools, where native children were taken from their parents to "de-Indian" them by obliterating their knowledge of their own heritage and language. These children were abused by the actions of both government and church, and many died, their remains placed in unmarked graves throughout the province."

The two children in the group looked at Chelsea in horror.

"Taken from their parents!" said one. "Why?"

Chelsea touched the tablet she was holding, and immediately one of the photographs in a display came to life in holographic 3D. It showed children being herded into vehicles as they were driven away from their homes. Other moving photographs showed the children sitting at desks in the schools, wearing uniforms.

Chelsea nodded to the boys. "Yes, it was a very sad time in our history and one that should never be forgotten," she remarked. "But the displays to your right tell the other side of colonialism. Here we learn of pioneers, like the McBrides, who settled in Victoria in the 1840s, 1850s and 1860s. Again, please touch the screens and you will see images come to life of the herring industry in Scotland, where Gideon McBride grew up, and stories and images of workhouses and homes for abandoned children, like the one where Jane Hopkins McBride was left. These displays reveal the strength and determination of those early pioneers, who simply wanted to escape to find a better life for themselves in the new world. The McBride family and their descendants feel it is important to tell both sides of the story, and not obliterate any part of the past."

Chelsea paused in her speech to allow the group to enjoy all the displays.

She continued after a while. "As you know from your history classes, in 2008, the prime minister of Canada apologized to the Indigenous people for the Residential Schools, and in July 2022 Pope Francis visited Canada to also apologize for the atrocities of the past. And that was only the beginning of the Truth and Reconciliation process. As you know, five years ago, in 2040, we Canadians elected our first Indigenous prime minister."

Chelsea then led the group through the rest of the house, describing artifacts of the McBride family's once grand lifestyle.

"This old grandfather clock, with regular maintenance, still strikes the hour just outside the wood-paneled library. The large living room and dining area to the right boasts elegant Victorian and Edwardian furniture and sparkling chandeliers. The table is set for thirty people, displaying the family's very best china and silverware—please respect the card that says: PLEASE DO NOT TOUCH.

"You are now welcome to climb the grand redwood staircase. The wood to build it was brought here from California. And please admire the newel posts inlaid with mother-of-pearl at the bottom. Bedrooms in the south wing still contain Victorian furniture, though the bathrooms have been modernized. Balconies lead off most of the rooms. The master bedroom includes a spiral staircase leading to a turret. Those who climb those stairs will be enchanted by the small turret room above, which offers a 360-degree view of the elegant gardens from all the windows, as well as a distant view of the snowcapped Olympic Mountains in the United States."

One of the young boys, apparently a little bored by all these facts, spoke up. "Are there ghosts in the house, Miss?"

Chelsea laughed. "Oh yes, indeed. Would you like to hear some ghost stories?"

"YES," the boys responded in unison.

Chelsea loved telling these stories, though she had never personally sighted a ghost herself.

"Well, at night, when all the visitors have left for the day and the house is very quiet, a caretaker claims to have often seen a small child lying prone on the landing over there, gazing down at the hall below. The first time he saw the child, he rushed up the stairs, thinking someone had been left behind on the tour, but when he reached the top, the vision had disappeared and there was no one there.

"Others claim to have heard a piano playing, but when they investigate, there is no one playing either of the two pianos. Sometimes when the grandfather clock stops chiming on the hour, a loud gong can be heard coming from the dining room. This usually occurs at seven o'clock at night, which was the time when Ah Foo, the house boy, would summon the family for dinner.

"On another occasion, a cleaning lady saw smoke coming from under the library door. She rushed over, thinking something was on fire, but when she opened the door, the smoke had disappeared. However, she could distinctly smell the aroma of a pipe, and there was ash in the vintage ashtray, which she had already cleaned. Did a visitor smoke in there earlier? Not likely, because no one smokes these days."

The boys were open-mouthed in astonishment, waiting for Chelsea to continue with the next story.

"All these sightings are accepted as part of a heritage house where the walls often talk in the silence of the night, and we are privileged to see and hear these apparitions. All the sightings in Providence appear to be harmless and happy, so no one is concerned. They are just part of the charm of an old heritage house that has been home to one family for generations."

The rest of the group had gathered around, listening with interest. "I heard there is also something ghostly about one of the portraits," one of the adults said. "Is that true?"

Chelsea smiled. "Yes, indeed. By far the most frequent resident from the past is Jane McBride herself, the woman whose portrait hangs in the center of the upstairs landing. Alongside her portrait are other family portraits of children, grandchildren, and great-grandchildren. She occasionally appears late at night, dressed in an elegant gown of pale primrose yellow satin, like the one in the portrait. She seems content with the way things have turned out and is always smiling—perhaps because she likes the fact her descendants loved Providence as much as she did. So, who knows? Her expression in the portrait changes sometimes."

Everyone gazed at the portrait for a moment, all hoping to see it change. "I would now encourage you to wander the grounds, admire the rose garden, and enjoy the dogwood, arbutus, and ancient oak trees. Don't miss the elegant gazebo, which is draped in sweet-smelling wisteria. Where the rolling grass lawn ends and meets the water of the Gorge Arm, there is a special dogwood tree planted in the 1990s, which in springtime blooms more fiercely than all the other trees. Please notice the plaque at its foot, which reads:

On this site a boathouse once stood where Ah Foo and his other Chinese friends lived while building Providence. The boathouse was burned to the ground in 1996, following the untimely death here of Caleb Blake Foster, aged 17. Forever loved and missed.

"There are also converted horse stables and a tennis court to see, and many fountains throughout the grounds, all of which are meticulously maintained by an army of gardeners."

Chelsea paused before adding: "And please be sure to stop by the Lodge at the entrance on the way out. It's now a gift shop where you can buy mementoes of your visit and perhaps a copy of a book written by Victoria Hamilton Caldwell, titled *House of Tomorrow.* The book tells the story of her great-grandparents, Jane and Gideon McBride, and how she became the missing piece in the McBride family mosaic when she inherited the house. The first part of the story is based on Jane McBride's diaries, which are now digitized and housed at the city archives. The author is said to have destroyed a few of the more personal entries and letters, their contents known only to her and the first matriarch of Providence.

"A short stroll up the incline leads to St. Luke's-on-the-Hill Church, built on land donated by Jane and Gideon McBride in the 1860s. There is a large McBride plot housing all the graves of the family, the first being Caleb Gideon McBride, aged two, infant son of Jane and Gideon McBride, and the two most recent being Victoria and Joe Caldwell, who died within six months of each other in 2035."

When the group had dispersed—some to the gardens, others to the church or the gift shop—one stranger lingered behind. He was very tall and remarkably handsome. He leisurely walked over to Chelsea.

"I wonder if it would be possible for me to speak with the family member who now lives in the house," he said.

"Yes, of course, Mrs. Sullivan always likes to talk with visitors. I'll let her know. You can wait on the front porch."

Chelsea went upstairs to Jane Sullivan's suite and knocked on the door. "There's a gentleman downstairs who would like to talk to you, Jane," she said. Jane agreed to come down. She found the man still waiting on the porch.

"I'm pleased to meet you, Mrs. Sullivan." He shook her hand before adding, "I wanted to congratulate you on this wonderful museum, and especially the display of the First Nations history on this land."

"Thank you. I must admit I am very proud of it."

"And rightly so. I'm also a descendant of people who once lived on this land. My ancestors were here even before the McBrides built this beautiful house."

"Really? How interesting," she said. "I'd love to hear more. May I ask your name?"

"Baron," he replied.

"Your name sounds familiar for some reason. I think I've heard it somewhere ... perhaps in the book my grandmother wrote?"

"You might well have. I'd be happy to take you and your husband for lunch or dinner one day, and I can tell you the whole story of how I came by it."

"That would be so kind, but my husband passed away some years ago. It's just me and my twin boys who live here now, and they will be off to university this September."

"I'm so sorry about your husband, Mrs. Sullivan. Forgive my blunder. But the invitation still stands."

Jane looked up at him. He was very handsome, and something about his charm touched her heart.

"I would be happy to accept and hear more, Mr. Baron."

"Please call me Gideon. That's my first name."

"Gideon? The only Gideon I've heard of before was the man who built this house, Gideon McBride."

"Yes, my ancestor knew him well."

"Really?"

"The story of how they met has been in my family for generations, and my own parents decided to name me for this great man."

"My goodness. Who was this ancestor of yours?"

"He was also mentioned in your grandmother's book, and he attended Craigflower school with Sarah McBride, the daughter of Jane and Gideon McBride. Captain McBride later helped him by sponsoring him through law school. He changed his name to William Baron, and that was the beginning of a much better life for all our family, for generations."

"I remember hearing that story from my own grandmother."

Jane's heart was beating fast. She loved history, and to meet this Indigenous man was indeed amazing, so many generations later. She was also intrigued by him, and, she had to admit to herself, a little attracted to him. After Chris had died prematurely from a heart attack when their boys were only three, she'd had no interest in another man. But she found herself wanting to learn more about this one.

"Would you like some coffee?" she suggested. "You're welcome to come inside, and we can talk more."

Gideon smiled, appearing equally charmed by her.

"I would be happy to," he replied. "As you might know, William Baron's original name was Willow Running Bear. Does that name mean anything to you?"

A shiver ran down her spine. "Oh yes, it does indeed. Funny, one of my older cousins is called Willow," Jane responded.

And so, after almost two hundred years, a different Jane and Gideon entered Providence together. Pausing in the Grand Hall for a moment, Jane looked up at her namesake's portrait on the landing and, for the first time, she saw Jane McBride's expression change. She was smiling.

Could a new McBride story be just beginning?

THE END

ACKNOWLEDGMENTS

The story of the fictional McBride family has been a part of me for many years, and I thank them all for living in my head and heart for so long. Although they are real to me, I want to emphasize that every character is completely fictional and merely a figment of my overactive imagination.

Their "voices" have directed me throughout. In fact, I hate to say goodbye to them, and I hope you, dear reader, feel the same way. For that reason, I have allowed their story to continue into an imaginary future that might well be true— or completely different from the one I have depicted in my story. You can decide.

I want to especially thank my own real-life family, who've enabled me to work on these books and given me the freedom to explore other places and other centuries—especially my husband, David. I'm sure that being married to a writer is not easy!

I also want to thank Myles Lamont for taking a chance on The McBride Chronicles and Doreen Martens and everyone at Hancock House for their diligence in the editing, design, and production of all four books.

In addition, I thank numerous archival sources that have helped me write about the more recent history of Victoria from the 1970s until the present day. A hundred years from now, these decades will also be looked upon as "history," and that is why I stepped briefly into the future in my Epilogue, imagining how things might evolve for Providence and the McBride family. As you will see, I simply could not let them go!

Last, but by no means least, I want to thank every reader who has kindly purchased the books in this series. These books were my debut into fiction after writing many non-fiction and true-crime books. It was

a big step in my writing career in my senior years, but I am delighted
to hear that many of you have so far enjoyed the transition.

   Valerie Green, 2024

ABOUT THE AUTHOR

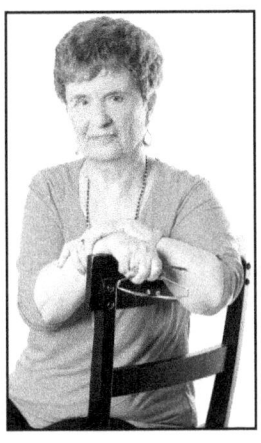

Valerie Green was born in England and studied journalism, short story writing and English literature at the Regent Institute of Journalism in London. She aspired to being a writer since she was a child and has always been passionate about history. Before immigrating to Canada in 1968, Valerie's employment included a short stint at the War Office for MI5, as well as legal secretarial work and freelance writing. Her writing career is extensive and includes writing a weekly history column for the *Saanich News* for nineteen years, a monthly column for the *Seaside Times* in Sidney, British Columbia, for ten years, articles for the *Victoria Times Colonist*, as well as more than twenty books on local and regional history, mysteries, and social issues. She has enjoyed her transition into historical fiction.

Now semi-retired, Valerie writes book reviews for British Columbia Reviews and intends on continuing to write for as long as possible. She lives with her husband in Saanich, BC, on Vancouver Island.

Visit her website at www.valeriegreenauthor.com

Valerie loves to hear from her readers, so feel free to contact her at hello@valeriegreenauthor.com

"a definitive history of British Columbia"

The McBride Chronicles is a four-book series through six generations of two families, from the 1840s to present day. It offers a picture of both sides of colonialism in British Columbia, Canada, from early settlement to today's truth and reconciliation. Strong women characters who overcome incredible odds are included in each of the four books.

Hancock House Publishers Ltd.
19313 0 Ave, Surrey, BC V3Z 9R9
www.hancockhouse.com · sales@hancockhouse.com
1-800-938-1114